Praise for **Dragon • Pri**ncess

"A dark madcap quest filled with educational (and often bloody) identity crises. The tragicomedy is never deep, but it's plenty of fun." —*Publishers Weekly*

"Swann piles on some inventive mishaps with a lavish hand. . . . Add a nicely unconventional 'happy' ending, and it's a fun romp for fans of funny fantasy." —*Locus*

"An amusing lighthearted quest fantasy . . . uses the concept of movies like *Freaky Friday* to tell a fun tale, through the filter of a mediocre thief."
—Genre Go Round

"A plot twist that you really don't see coming. . . . You can connect with the characters and ultimately understand the decisions they make. *Dragon Princess* is a good story for those who like an adventurous fantasy to enjoy."
—Fresh Fiction

"Fun without being fluffy, and entertaining without being inane. It straddles the line between humorous fantasy and some of the darker stuff and does so with style. *Dragon Princess* has wit, action, and hilarity in equal measures and should prove an enjoyable read for those looking for something fast-paced and fun. I hope the author does more in this vein, because I enjoyed the writing style and would love to see Frank and Lucille's further adventures." —Owlcat Mountain

"*Dragon Princess* is full of witty banter, comical situations, irre_____ ted irony."
_____ Talking About

Dragon · Thief

S. Andrew Swann

DAW BOOKS, INC.

DONALD A. WOLLHEIM, FOUNDER

375 Hudson Street, New York, NY 10014

ELIZABETH R. WOLLHEIM

SHEILA E. GILBERT

PUBLISHERS

www.dawbooks.com

This one is for Joe, who's jealous of the princess getting all the attention.

CHAPTER 1

My name is Frank Blackthorne, and I'm going to tell you a story.

Bear in mind that I'm making the radical assumption that you, my audience, have been paying attention. For those of you who are late to my story, here is what you need to know:

I began as a semi-accomplished thief. An unscrupulous wizard allegedly working for the Royal Court of Lendowyn conned me into attempting to rescue the king's daughter from a dragon.

Any sane individual could tell from that premise that all was not as it seemed, and they would be correct. The "rescue" was an intricate plot by said wizard to grab hold of a peerage by winning the princess's hand in marriage.

Any sane individual could tell you that such plans are likely to go awry, and, again, they would be correct. It went wrong in a spectacular fashion, resulting in a cascade of mishaps both magical and mundane.

Those mishaps left me in the body of Princess Lucille, said princess in the dragon's body as my prince and husband, the aforesaid dragon in the wizard's body in an elfland jail for outstanding gambling debts, and the aptly named wizard, Elhared the Unwise, in my body and quite dead, leaving us no way to untangle the mess.

The story at hand begins midwinter, five months after I had been princessified, inside a tavern about five miles from the capital of the Duchy of Dermonica, in a small town just on the right side of the border with the Kingdom of Grünwald.

I huddled alone at a table in a shadowed corner of the common room. I warmed myself with a hot tankard of spiced cider, keeping watch on the other patrons and the door, a black cloak draped over my elven leather armor, looking as little like a princess as I could without being obvious about it.

As to why I was in Dermonica: Now that the princess was no longer available for marriage, her main substantive role that did not seem to involve painfully elaborate dresses and painfully tedious royal festivities was diplomacy.

In theory it should have been the one part of the job that exercised my own aptitudes to any degree—specifically aptitudes in duplicity and concocting elaborate straight-faced lies. Generally I would have preferred sneaking around and lifting people's purses, but I like to think of myself as adaptable.

The diplomatic mission from Lendowyn was officially here in Dermonica to open talks of trade with the duke. No small task, since for half a century all that had crossed the border between Dermonica and Lendowyn had been the occasional insult.

When I had agreed to join the mission with the

prince—the Dragon Lucille—I think I had a more optimistic view of my role. I wasn't here to negotiate anything. That's what the ministers and the prince were for. I was here to give an additional royal imprimatur to the proceedings, nod my head, and approve of the negotiations conducted around me.

Basically I was a prop, and it was even more boring than holding court at Lendowyn.

The bright side was that, after months sealed within the royal cocoon in Lendowyn, I could at least see new people—and once I used my professional skills to slip away unseen from the diplomatic mission—those people weren't the so-called aristocracy or their minions.

That was the reason I sat in this tavern five miles away from where I was supposed to be, and a mile from somewhere I should never go again unless I wanted to start a war. I needed a break from my new life.

The Dragon Lucille, from all appearances, had taken the transition from princess to scary fire-breathing lizard rather well. Despite some tears at the start, she now seemed to revel enthusiastically in her draconic glory. At times I felt maybe a little *too* enthusiastically—which might have been the one point of agreement on anything between me and her father, King Alfred the Strident.

By contrast, becoming Princess Frank, despite undergoing what would objectively seem a much less radical transformation, left me feeling as if I was having a much tougher go of it. After the initial chaos of our transformation—facing down Queen Fiona of

Grünwald and the Dark Lord Nâtlac himself—the lack of dire threats to me or the people around me left me too much time to ponder my own discomfort.

Discomfort that, five times now, had a habit of becoming distressingly physical.

My first experience with cyclic feminine distress had been a few days after the wedding. I had initially panicked and thought I had been suffering from delayed internal injuries caused during the battle with the late Queen Fiona's minions. Or perhaps I had fallen prey to some evil disease brought on by contact with the Dark Lord Nâtlac, and the illness was finally rotting away my insides.

Political marriage of convenience or not, I didn't think my husband's laughter was an appropriate reaction to my screams of horror. It certainly didn't make me feel any better.

That incident, and the four repetitions since, had given me an appreciation for every woman I had ever run across who had appeared happy, calm, or relatively sane. It was also a literal gut-level reminder of what I had lost.

One thing I had lost, in particular.

Whatever my outward appearance or internal symptoms; I was still me, and there are some itches I needed to scratch, at least occasionally, or I started to get cranky. I couldn't turn to Lucille, my husband and one friend in the royal court, because— even had my transformation brought with it a preference for male companionship—her being a dragon made anything of the sort physically impossible. And creepy.

And, while I could probably find any number of

retainers and hangers-on in the Lendowyn court who would willingly help the princess out with such an issue, *that* itself was part of the problem. Everyone involved in the aristocracy at any level spent every waking moment engaged in endless game-playing and constant jockeying for power. The constant conspiratorial atmosphere made the environment around Lendowyn Castle stifling. For me, at least, it killed the mood.

But things had gotten to the point that it forced me to engage in the same kind of elaborate plotting that I found so unappealing in noble circles. In defense of that particular hypocrisy, my goals were a bit more modest than was typical for such royal shenanigans.

So here I was, on my own personal covert mission.

I stared into my half-empty tankard and sighed. I glanced around the tavern at the few retainers who stood silent guard at opposite corners of the common room. They were part of a cadre that was fiercely loyal to the princess—at least to the role she had taken after I had defeated the late Queen Fiona of Grünwald. I found it depressing that I wasn't even able to conduct my own skulduggery on my own.

But I wasn't crazy. Even if I didn't look the role of the princess at the moment, I still *was* the princess, with all the baggage that entailed. In this world it was risky enough just being female and attractive without an escort. Add in the possibility of royal intrigue and ...

I felt nostalgic for the days when all I had to worry about was the local Thieves' Guild threatening to break my fingers.

At least I could afford better booze now.

Out the windows the evening had gone full black, and I couldn't see a thing beyond the lamplight in the common room. Conversation swirled around me; the room was packed with travelers, mostly tradesmen and merchants. Out of habit I found myself sizing up the patrons, judging the weight of their pouches and the state of their inebriation.

If I wanted, I could probably paste on a smile, lower the hood of my cloak, and slip up to the table with the trio of Delmarkian tradesmen who were busy committing drunken crimes against the folk songs of their homeland. You couldn't ask for better targets for a pickpocket's skill, and given my current status as a member of the fair sex, I suspected I could slip my hands inside a belt or two without any objection.

I stared at the fat drunken northerners and came up with a few objections of my own and quickly returned to my cider, shuddering a little internally.

It wasn't that I hadn't been trying to adapt to my current gender, but the fact was my entire life up to a few months ago trumped any arguments nature and this body could come up with. It didn't help that, so far, every male whom I'd run into who happened to be on the same side of that argument as nature and my body hadn't been that concerned about my consent. The last person who had tried to consummate that sort of impulse had ended up with a lethal rearrangement of his neck bones.

It had been unintentional on my part, but over time I'd found my guilt fading over the incident.

I looked at the singing tradesmen again.

It was getting harder and harder to imagine picking up the pieces of my old life, and dealing with my new one hadn't become any easier. If I was honest with myself—and there's a first time for everything—my little covert activity away from the diplomatic mission stank of desperation. This was the fifth day in a row I had slipped away. I only had a couple of days more.

In the end, royal conspiracies may just have been more than I was cut out for. It was sort of a shame. Given my position in the royal household—even one as impoverished as that of Lendowyn—a proper thieving mindset should be able to leverage *that* into ill-gotten riches beyond the wildest imaginings of pre-princess Frank Blackthorne. In my darkest moments, I had begun suspecting that I had lost more than the obvious in the transition.

I drained the cold dregs of cider, dropped the tankard on the table, and got up to leave.

"I guess it's not going to happen," I whispered, resigned to another night alone.

I was about to vacate the table and the suddenly depressing venue, when the door opened letting in a swirl of snow and a fur-draped mountain carved into the vague likeness of a barbarian warrior decked out in the unmistakable spiked black armor of Grünwald.

Actually, referring to him as a warrior was being too generous. I hadn't known Brock to show competence at any martial skill aside from enthusiasm. Fortunately for him, his skill was rarely tested since, being an intimidating mass with a girth almost equal to his considerable height, potential foes mostly found reason to advance directly away from him. Despite all that, he'd taken a dagger in his substantial gut for Lucille, so his heart was in the right place.

I had already convinced myself that my covert mission had been a failure, and for a moment, seeing Brock returned, standing alone in the doorway, confirmed my fears. Then a smaller figure stepped out from behind him. The new person wore a fur-lined cloak and lowered the hood as she stepped into the tavern. As she shook the snow off herself, I couldn't stop myself from grinning.

She had come.

The woman underneath the cloak had the same blonde hair and blue eyes as the Princess Lucille had bequeathed to me. Beyond that, she had slightly more generous height and more than slightly more generous curves than I had at the moment. Her face was a bit more angelic than I remembered, though that was discounting the rather worldly half-smile that crossed her lips as she caught my eye.

Her name was Evelyn, and she was a tavern wench from an inn named The Three-Legged Boar located in the city of Brightwood, the capital of Grünwald. The last time I had seen her I had been in need of a tavern wench's outfit—long story—so Brock and I had stripped her, tied her up, and had shoved her in an empty beer barrel. It was consensual, and an exchange of money was involved, but I had still been worried that the experience might have soured her on further contact with me.

On the off chance it hadn't, I had sent Brock to invite her for a second meeting. Brock, specifically because he was known to Evelyn, could credibly say he was running an errand for me, and could cross the border into Grünwald without risking a war.

Evelyn walked over to my empty table and sat down across from me. "It is you," she said. "I thought you had forgotten about me."

Brock watched her come over, shook his head, and walked off to another table.

"I haven't forgotten," I told her, "though I do have an admission."

"Yes?"

"I didn't send Brock across the border so I could return your clothes."

She had an honest laugh. She touched the back of my hand and said, "I know."

If I had needed any confirmation that inhabiting the body of a virginal princess hadn't changed my preference for intimate company, her touch confirmed it. Different places got warm now, but they meant the same thing.

She leaned forward and whispered, "So you're a princess?"

I sighed and nodded.

"Why me?" she asked.

"Pardon?"

"Why bring me here? I'm sure that there are plenty of people, men and women, would be happy to. . . do your bidding?" She didn't look into my eyes as she talked, and she traced lazy circles across the back of my hand with her finger.

I thought of politics, court intrigue, and the fact that at Lendowyn Castle my every move was watched. "Because you were honestly interested in me."

She raised her head just enough so that she was looking me in the eye.

I shrugged. "We may not have met under the best circumstances, but everyone else lately has been more interested in me as a princess or as a potential victim."

"I'm sure some of that is because you're a very attractive young woman."

"Potential victim," I repeated.

"That isn't always a bad thing," she said. "Seems to have worked out for me."

"Not the same thing. You were more accomplice than victim."

"You still tied me up." I would have expected a bit more anger from a woman saying that. Instead I got that half-smile and her face half turned from mine. Suddenly I began feeling like an awkward teenager who had never tried to pick up a woman in a bar before.

"I'm sorry about—"

"Shh—" She leaned over and kissed my cheek. She whispered in my ear, *"Accomplice, right?"* I felt heat on my face and blamed Lucille's body. Evelyn squeezed my hand as she sat back down and I felt an uncharacteristic surge of honesty.

"Before we go on," I said, "there are a few more things I should tell you—"

"Like why you call yourself Frank?"

I opened my mouth. Closed it. Opened it again.

"I'm okay with it," she said.

"Brock?" I asked, trying to regroup.

"He didn't say anything." She leaned over and quietly said, "But it's not really a secret. Royal weddings are general topics of rumor and conversation even when they aren't as strange as yours. You're famous and . . ." Her eyes dropped and she began tracing patterns on my hand again.

After a moment I realized she was blushing herself. "And?" I prompted.

She sucked in a breath. "What's it like to be the Dark Queen?"

CHAPTER 2

I shouldn't have been surprised. It wouldn't be hard to connect my last two trips to Grünwald. Like she said, it was no secret.

However, I would have expected my checkered past to be at least a little bit off-putting.

"Yeah, that . . ." I said, not quite sure what she wanted. "Queen Fiona didn't leave me much choice."

"I heard stories about how she crumbled before you."

Torn apart by an angry Lord of Darkness was more like it.

"Did you make her beg?" she asked.

"Did I . . ." I trailed off as a few details about Evelyn began to sink in. First, she hadn't actually shown any attraction to me until after I had threatened her. Sure she'd taken my bribe, but I had still ordered her to strip, help me dress, and then I had tied her up and left her in an empty beer barrel. For most people I knew, that would have been an ordeal.

I began to realize that, for Evelyn, it had been foreplay.

I watched her expression as she talked of my overcoming the prior monarch of Grünwald, the Dark Queen of Nâtlac—especially the way she bit her lip.

The good news was, Evelyn found my exploits versus the last Dark Queen of Nâtlac exciting in the same, somewhat disturbing, manner as she had been excited by our last meeting when I'd basically kidnapped her, stripped her, and tied her up....

I guess that also counted as the bad news.

"Can we talk about something else?" I asked quietly.

"Of course, mistress," she said, confirming my growing suspicions.

I felt even more the awkward teenager.

Not that I begrudged Evelyn's idea of fun. But the idea of playing mistress to fulfill whatever fantasy role she had for the Dark Queen came a little too close to the reasons I was trying to avoid an assignation with someone from within the Lendowyn court.

I think, when it comes to romantic encounters, I'm more egalitarian.

But, after the effort I had put into bringing her here, and the faith she'd shown by following Brock here, I decided that I owed it to both of us to give it a try.

I took Evelyn up to the private room I'd been renting with my meager royal stipend for the past five days. I felt even more like some teenager on the cusp of losing his virginity. Even if it was, given my new body, the literal truth, it wasn't how I'd expected to feel.

In retrospect, it made sense for a number of reasons. I was still uncomfortable in my new skin, even after a few months with it. I also hadn't been intimate with anyone for longer than that. And, while I had plenty of experience with women, none was *as* a woman, meaning my *relevant* prior sexual experience was absolutely nil.

So there were reasons to be nervous, even with a willing, enthusiastic partner.

But there's also this running theme with my life: Whenever I am afraid things will go wrong, they never do so in exactly the way I expect them to.

However, for a brief shiny moment I did forget my apprehension. Once I closed the door and we faced each other in private, she asked, with her head bowed and hands behind her back, "May I kiss my mistress?"

"Well that *was* the idea behind bringing you here."

That, at least, was something that hadn't changed with my new body. Even if our embrace had a few more curves involved than I was used to. I held on to her with all the desperation of the past few months.

It went downhill from there.

Somehow I had come to a point in my life where I had a woman ready, willing, and able to join me in activities that I had only been able to imagine for the past six months. I had her on her knees in front of me, calling me mistress. She looked up at me with a gaze that was equal parts lust, submission, and worship and asked, "What does my mistress want?"

And I drew a blank.

I had no idea what to tell her. It wasn't just my inexperience with any sort of female-only relationship. I had spent years as a guy. Such things had crossed my mind.

But the impact of this woman asking me to command her like a slave had managed, somehow, to completely wipe away any thoughts of an erotic nature from my mind.

"Mistress?"

I stood there, motionless. Inside I began to panic, and I didn't even know why.

"Is there something wrong?" To my relief, her voice lost its servile character and took on a note of actual concern. My panic started fading.

"Frank?"

I sighed. I guess I wasn't going to do this. "Evelyn," I said, "I don't think—"

Fortunately for my budding reputation as a dominatrix, I was interrupted by a scream coming from outside.

While screams of terror were never a good sign, I ran to the window with the naïve belief that, whatever the emergency was, it had to be less awkward than my standoff with Evelyn. I opened the shutters to look out at what was terrorizing the townsfolk outside.

"Oh crap."

It *never* goes wrong in quite the way I expect.

"What's going on?" Evelyn called after me.

I turned around and ran for the door. "I have to go out there before things get out of hand."

As I went out the door, I heard her call after me, "Before *what* gets out of hand?"

I ran through the tavern, past a crowd of people who had pushed their way in from outside. My own personal guards, including Brock, were already outside to meet the threat. I had a brief impulse to find a rear door to the place, slip away from the royal guard, and the court, and what waited outside.

The impulse was brief enough that I didn't even slow down.

Outside, waiting for me, was the worst-case scenario for any woman attempting to engage in any extramarital dalliance.

My husband.

It didn't help matters that my spouse was a fifty-foot-long fire-breathing lizard. Apparently my efforts at stealth didn't matter all that much once someone realized that I had gone missing.

"Frank!" the dragon greeted me as I ran out the door. Lucille filled the crossroads in front of the tavern, and a circle of people, mostly my escort, Brock, and elements of the city watch, had formed a perimeter around her at about forty paces. Her wings spread out to block most of the sky.

"Lucille," I answered. It was hard to keep the resignation out of my voice. It had sunk in that there wasn't any way out of the box I found myself in.

I stopped advancing, because something felt wrong. I could see it in my own retainers, who knew her as well as I did, and they seemed as frightened as the city watch.

"Lucille?" I repeated, really looking at her now. I had become somewhat accustomed to her as a dragon, enough so that I really didn't think of the implications of it anymore. However, I was good at reading her expressions by now, despite the lack of mobility in her reptilian face.

This expression I hadn't seen before.

I thought I had seen her angry. I was wrong. She stood on her haunches, looming over me, neck twisted in an arc that pointed her face down at me. Every muscle under her scaly skin was drawn so tight she could have been carved out of obsidian. Smoke curled from her nostrils, and behind her snarl I could see the faint glow of barely suppressed fire. Her huge golden eyes were narrowed until they were little more than angry slits in her face.

"What in the seven hells do you think you were doing?" Her words slammed down in a gust of choking brimstone hot enough to melt the snow at my feet.

I heard a scream from behind me, and I realized that Evelyn had followed me out of the tavern. I glanced behind me at her; she was staring up at Lucille and fumbling at the doorway that had slammed shut behind her. Whoever was on the other side of that door wasn't opening it.

I placed my hand on my temple. I had misjudged how badly Lucille would react. "I'm sorry," I said, hoping to calm things down a bit. "I wanted—"

"You wanted? You're *sorry!?*" She bellowed that last word up into the sky. A good thing since it came out in a ball of flame so intense that it was briefly dawn in front of the tavern. The city guard dropped their halberds and ran, and to all appearances my personal guard wanted to join them. Evelyn dove to the ground and cowered behind me.

"Father has been working toward these negotiations for a decade! You risk disrupting them for what? For what!? What are you doing that's more important than years of diplomatic work and peace between our

neighbors? What's worth putting the princess and heir
to the Lendowyn throne at risk?"

While she had a point, I couldn't help thinking that
she was being more disruptive than anything I'd been
doing in the privacy of my rented room. I stepped forward and raised my hands. This needed to stop before
it went too far.

"Lucille, you're right. Just calm down and we—"

**"Don't patronize me! Don't tell me to calm down!
It's bad enough you're willing to upend talks with
Dermonica. What's worse is you did it just to degrade
yourself."**

I opened my mouth, but what she said sunk in and
left me in a brief stunned silence.

Wait a minute.

**"You're part of the noble house of Lendowyn. You
have responsibilities, duties. You need to behave in a
manner appropriate to your station."**

Is that *what this is about?* I stared at her in disbelief.
Of all the things to be angry with me about, she picked
this one? I thought she knew me ...

**"I not only find out you're missing, but I find out
that you abandoned your duties to have a cheap dalliance with a common whore!"**

"That's enough!" I shouted up at her in a voice that
hadn't been as commanding since I shouted down the
late Queen Fiona.

Her jaws snapped shut with an audible clack, and
her head withdrew, eyes widening. Lucille wasn't the
only one in shock from my outburst; the circle of
guards all turned their attention to me.

I pointed up at Lucille. "Don't talk to me about any

so-called 'nobility.' You're the *only* one of the bunch who's worth more than a bucket of warm ogre spit—"

"Frank—"

"And this woman has a *name!* It's Evelyn, and I'll take one of her over a dozen self-important lords from the noble houses of any kingdom you want to mention. You might forget that she's not the only one here who didn't have the good sense to properly pick the set of ancestors who were more adept at beating people into submission."

"Please—" The anger seemed to leak away from the dragon's voice. That was okay. I now had more than enough for both of us.

"Your noble 'obligations' are just a rationalization to convince yourself that you really are better than everyone else, and a desperate attempt to convince everyone else that they actually need to be subservient. Gods help us all if all the farmers in the land suddenly realized that they can survive a lot longer without the lords than the lords can survive without them."

"This isn't the place."

"No, of course not. Can't say such things before the unwashed masses." It was probably a bad idea to argue with her, though not for exactly the same reasons it was typically a bad reason to argue with a dragon. Exactly *why* it was didn't sink in. Not then.

"Why are you doing this to me? In my body?"

"Your body?" I screamed at her. "Your body?!"

"Please, Frank—" She must have heard what was coming in my voice, because she sounded more tentative than a dragon had a right to be.

"You lost your claim on this body when you decided you wanted to be Crown Prince Dragon. *Your body?* How much time have you and your dad spent trying to get it back? What kind of nerve do you have to claim control of something you don't even want?"

"I didn't mean—"

"And after what I've done for you, twisted my entire existence out of shape . . . this is the thanks I get? What kind of ungrateful bitch are you? Evelyn's beneath your station? *Well so am I!*"

I don't know where the line was, but somewhere along the way I had crossed it, kept going, and never looked back. Everyone fell silent, including her.

After a long moment she said, **"We should go."**

Maybe I should, I thought.

CHAPTER 3

We made it through the last couple of days in Dermonica and the journey back to Lendowyn without more than three words passing between us. I did everything I could to keep it that way, remaining sequestered alone in my rooms whenever my so-called "duty" didn't absolutely require my presence as window dressing. Lucille had been staying away from the talks themselves, for obvious reasons—her presence would have been distracting.

Still, I kept to myself even more than usual. Better to feel sorry for myself.

I did see her on our return trip. The draconic escort was a bit of pointless diplomatic swagger, the kind engaged in by kingdoms that had little to swagger about. I guess it was impressive to anyone who didn't realize that Lendowyn had no money and the dragon represented about half the kingdom's military prowess. Thus the importance of a peace treaty with neighboring Dermonica.

Before she took off to fly alongside the caravan home, she did catch my eye. I doubt anyone else noticed, but, as I said, I'd been around Lucille enough to understand a dragon's facial expression. I could tell that as she looked in my direction she was on the verge of tears.

It was a measure of how angry I was that I didn't walk over and try to smooth things over. I was at the point where I was mad at her for being upset. Why should she be? She had gotten what *she* wanted. She had become the Crown Prince of Lendowyn, and in a weird patriotic fervor, had become the most popular member of the royal court. And unlike my current experience as princess, she had some actual role in the running of the kingdom.

I was *not* about to feel sorry for her, and an apology was out of the question.

It was a long trip back to Lendowyn Castle, and as soon as I could free myself from the obligatory return ceremony I retired to my own private chambers and locked myself in.

After a side trip to the royal wine cellar.

I knew from experience that, in my case at least, alcohol and self-pity rarely mixed well. I think I convinced myself that I was more angry than anything else. When I leaned against the door and took a swig from some local vintage, I told myself that my vision was blurred by tears of rage.

I took another swig and thought I should have just left with Evelyn. I'd probably added a whole new layer to her fantasy mistress when I managed to argue a dragon into submission.

"Mistress," I whispered, half curse and half drunken giggle.

The "drunken" part of that didn't sink in until I took a half step, half stumble toward the bed and started toppling. Somehow I managed a pirouette that ended with my back flat on the bed, and more important, bottle high and unspilled.

"Mistress," I muttered again, with an unprincesslike snort.

I hadn't felt more powerless in my entire life. And, in addition to losing everything else, I had lost my tolerance for alcohol. That started me laughing and gasping, desperately trying to keep my bottle upright.

I'd figured out a while ago that I had become a lightweight when I inherited the princess's body, but I didn't remember three sips of wine putting me over the edge this quickly. I narrowed my eyes at the bottle, convinced there was something wrong.

There was. The bottle was half gone.

"I guess that's more'n three sips," I said, and started giggling. "There you go, Lucille, I'm acting beneath your station again."

I sat up and swayed a bit, lifting the bottle to the window in a toast. "Here's to the common folk."

I took another swig, downing a third of what was left.

"That's me," I whispered to the bottle. "Common. Nothing special about old Frank Blackthorne. Wasn't even the greatest thief." My hand tightened on the bottle and I watched my hand—the princess's hand—tremble as the knuckles whitened.

"But—" I forced out through clenched teeth.

"But that was who I am!" I threw the bottle. And despite the princess's lack of upper body strength it flew like a missile at the window, slamming into the

stone peak above it, sending red liquid and bits of bottle back into the room as if a small goblin with glass bones and a drinking problem had decided to climb into my room and explode.

"I want my life back!" I yelled at the remains of the wine goblin. I grabbed the neck of my dress and tore at it in frustration. "I don't want this! I want my own life! Something! A part of it back! Anything!"

I tore at my neckline, but, as I said, the princess didn't have the greatest upper body strength, and while I wanted to tear through chemise, bodice, and dress in a drunken rage, I just managed to strain my arm and give myself a friction burn on my neck.

The princess's neck. "Got to remember, like she said, it's her body."

A bad idea crossed my mind, and it stuck there. Holding my neck, angry, drunk, and self-pitying, I was ready to contemplate something I'd been avoiding since my "marriage" to Lucille. I stood up, steadier than I had a right to be, and walked toward the wardrobe that dominated one side of my room.

"Yeah, shouldn't even be thinking this," I slurred to myself.

I still opened the wardrobe. Inside, on the topmost shelf, it was still right where I had left it shortly after my wedding ceremony. I had done my best to forget it, because when I'm sober I do try to make a pretense of having good sense.

I pulled out a small box decorated in ornate carvings that were somewhat disturbing if examined too closely. I walked back to the bed with it.

I sat on the edge of the bed, ignoring the spots of

wine and pieces of glass. I traced the edges of the box with my fingertips, telling myself that it didn't look that bad. Not for a wedding present delivered by the Dark Lord Nâtlac himself.

I opened the box. Inside was a dark gem cut into facets that appeared to shift position when you didn't look directly at them, mounted in a twisted silver setting that could have represented vines, or tentacles, or veins wrapping a shrunken black heart. It was pretty in a somewhat mind-twisting way that made your eyes hurt after a while.

I still vividly remembered how the Dark Lord had appeared, wrapped in the voices of a million tortured souls, to present it to me. According to the Dark Lord Nâtlac, this evil-looking pendant could return me to a male form, if only temporarily. I had no idea what it cost, what I would sacrifice, as the Dark Lord had made his exit before I could ask any of the obvious questions.

In my inebriated state, it still seemed a good deal. I wanted nothing more than to stop being a princess right now.

If you're wondering why I hadn't used it before now, you probably should review the part where I said that this necklace was a personal gift from the Dark Lord Nâtlac.

If you're wondering why I was seriously contemplating it now, I should point out that the last time I was this drunk, desperate, and sorry for myself, I was picked up by an evil wizard in a dockside tavern and agreed to rescue a princess from a dragon.

Drunk me came up with a foolproof plan. If the

necklace did anything really objectionable, I could just take it off again. Also, how bad could it be if the effects were only temporary?

Drunk me couldn't muster any further objections, so I put the thing around my neck.

CHAPTER 4

Drunk me must have realized that he'd made a serious mistake, because he ran away immediately, leaving behind an angry invisible ogre to squeeze my brain in time to my pulse. The headache, nausea, and disorientation crashed over me like a devotion to the god of all hangovers. In a lifetime of unpleasant experiences with alcohol I had never produced a hangover this quickly or this severe.

Which isn't to say I'd never felt like this before.

The sudden abrupt change in every sensation I felt in my body, and the dizzying wave of disorientation that followed in their wake only increased the sense that I had been through this all before. I blinked my eyes and managed to make out a starry night sky as my blurred vision cleared. A cold night wind bit into my face.

"Oh Cra—" I began to mutter. I was interrupted when a weasel of a man strung together by leather, muscle, and hate decided to block the swing of his truncheon with my left kidney.

I decided that the proper response to that was to vomit up a meal I never remembered having. Weasel dodged easily to the side and I realized that I looked down on the top of his head. The vantage from on high sent my brain spinning. I would have collapsed to the ground if a pair of goons weren't holding my upper arms in a painful grip above the vomit-stained cobblestones of a back alley somewhere. I clenched my teeth to avoid heaving again.

Weasel spoke to me. At least I think I was the one being addressed. "Thought you'd put up more of a fight, Snake."

I didn't know who this guy was, and I had no idea who Snake was. All I was aware of was the fact that his voice ground broken shards of glass into my throbbing brain.

"How did you get this reputation? Look like just another punk in over his head, don't you?"

I kicked him just to get the noise to stop. I had aimed higher, but I hit him right under the kneecap. The guy gasped and twisted to the side, his other foot sliding on the slick of vomit. The goons holding me pulled me up and back away from Weasel, and the sudden motion ignited a new flare of agony inside my skull.

I kicked out again, this time at the goon to my right. I didn't expect much from the attack, I'd never been a brawler, even before I became a petite young girl. For me, a fight involved flailing around hoping to hit something vital.

Pain and panic must have fueled me because my boot—*I'm wearing boots?*—slammed into the goon's knee, bending it sideways with a soft crunch that I heard as well as felt through my leg. He lost his grip on me as that leg collapsed under his weight. He fell onto Weasel as the latter was trying to get back up, dropping him back onto the filthy cobbles.

The other goon still had hold of me and swung me so my back slammed into a wall. I gasped from another wave of shuddering pain that made my vision black out for a moment. I blinked in time to see three blurry fists descending on my head like a trio of falling trees. I half ducked, half slid, down the wall away from the blows. The goon still held my arm, so I only dropped about a foot. That was enough to take my throbbing head out of the path. I felt a single fist—still attached to a blurry set of goon triplets—brush the top of my head and crunch violently into the wall behind me. All three goons roared like a bull with his testicles caught in a thresher.

I threw the fist on my free arm toward the center goon, again to make the painful noises stop. I aimed at the face, but the goon's height and my position crouched against the wall meant I hit him low, in the throat. That still had the desired effect, shutting all three goons up. It also loosed the grip they had on my arm.

I pushed myself up from the wall, and stumble-ran out of the alley into an unfamiliar city.

I don't know how long I dodged through back alleys, but by the time my head cleared I realized I had lost Weasel and the goons. I also realized I was no longer Princess Frank . . .

Actually, I had known that as soon as the supernatural hangover had hit me. It had been exactly the same as the last time I had switched bodies, when I had become the princess in the first place.

Now, with my head clear and my pursuers nowhere in sight, it was the first time I had a chance to clearly think about it. Once I did think about it, I had to stop because suddenly I realized how much taller I was. It had taken some getting used to being the princess, being short and having everything in the world seem to grow in comparison. This was more disorientating. I looked down and felt a surge of vertigo staring down from a height about a foot above where I was used to. Every step my throbbing brain told me I was in danger of toppling over.

I stopped and leaned against a building, closing my eyes. I unconsciously reached up between my now nonexistent breasts for the necklace.

Nothing was there.

I opened my eyes and confirmed that the Dark Lord's wedding present was nowhere to be seen.

"Crap." My unfamiliar voice came out in a puff of fog.

The fullish moon stared back down at me. I repeated myself.

"Crap."

Of course it made sense now that I wasn't drunk off my ass. The enchanted necklace came from the Dark Lord Nâtlac, and the demon-god bastard dealt with souls as a specialty. There was a pretty good chance that he was responsible for the spell that originally displaced me in the princess's body in the first place. I didn't even need to imagine any particular malice on his part—and this was a deity who was made of malice and inconvenient suffering. If Nâtlac just wanted to give me the opportunity to be male again out of whatever goodness existed in his nonexistent heart, would he give me something that would magically transform the princess's body into a guy? Or would he give me something that just took me out of the princess and dropped me into some random victim?

The answer to that was distressingly clear to me now that I wasn't under the influence of two-thirds of a bottle of bad wine.

This goes on the list of my less intelligent decisions.

At least my demonic benefactor had made a point of telling me that the effects of the enchantment would be temporary.

I spent a moment feeling sympathy for the prior occupant of this body. He had probably just suffered a wrenching transition back into the princess's body back in Lendowyn. I can only imagine what the after-effects must have felt like when experienced in a body already saturated with alcohol.

I shuddered a bit.

But, now that I thought about it, I probably did the guy a favor. After all, he had been on the verge of being beaten to a pulp, and now he could be sick in the privacy of the princess's chambers, complete with featherbed. He may have gotten the good end of the deal. When things wore off and we switched back, he would be safely away from Weasel and company.

And, now that my head was clear, it sank in.

I was a man again.

I patted down my clothes, feeling my new body in near disbelief. I didn't seem any older than I had been before I'd been princessified, and if anything I felt bigger and more muscular—though that may have just been a contrast with the princess's body. The new parts certainly felt much larger than I remembered.

I found a belt pouch containing a small pile of coins.

"Well, stranger, you owe me for saving you from that fight."

If I was right in assuming this enchantment would last only as long as my opposite number wore the necklace, then I had only a limited amount of time to enjoy this.

I started looking for an open inn.

What else should I have done? I knew I had made a bad decision, but would it have become a better decision if I had ignored the main reason I'd made it?

One of the reasons, anyway.

Besides, if you were expecting to hear some tale of existential angst you're listening to the wrong story-teller, and the wrong story. I had already experienced my own identity crisis when I became a princess and had to kill of a wizard while he was wearing my body. Everything pales after watching your own body die.

Besides, while I had been a bit surprised at the particulars, Nâtlac's charm had worked as advertised. And now that my head had cleared a bit, I was back to being angry at Lucille—and I found it amusing to think she had to deal with some *other* guy in her discarded body. Maybe it would make her appreciate me when I came back.

I can be shallow like that.

Somehow, even after the shock of finding myself as someone else in a strange town, it was easy for my thoughts to return to Lucille, and my own anger. Enough so that, when I found an inn and used some-one else's gold to pay for a room and a woman, I was thinking less about my own long chastity than I was about how lying down with an *actual* whore was a perfect revenge for Lucille calling Evelyn one. It wasn't rational thinking, but if I had been thinking rationally I wouldn't have been there in the first place.

Any sane individual could tell you that such a tryst would turn out to be disappointing, and they would be correct.

I spent the balance of the evening with a young woman who knew her profession, but throughout the act, all I could think about was how angry Lucille had made me, and how stupidly I had reacted to it. My partner was willing, my borrowed body was functional and well equipped, and we successfully accomplished things that, for the last three months, had been little more than distant memory . . .

But I really wasn't there.

I began in anger, and somehow, as things progressed, the anger turned into guilt. My body ran on hormones, instinct, and muscle memory, while my brain kept thinking back to Lucille, my fading anger at her, and how, whatever I'd been feeling at the time, I'd really been kind of an ass.

I might be shallow, but I wasn't nearly shallow enough.

If my partner noticed the point where my actions became joyless and mechanical, she didn't show any sign. I suspect it was not uncommon in her line of work. Once her task was complete, she wordlessly gathered her clothes, dressed, and left me alone, lying naked on the bed.

Once sexual frustration was no longer at the fore of my mind, it began to occur to me that I had no idea how long the "temporary" effects of Nâtlac's artifact were going to last. I assumed that it would last until the former owner of this body removed the necklace from the princess's neck. But what if it didn't work like that?

I've been through this before, I told myself. *Just work it out logically and I'll sort it out . . .*

Because that had worked out so well last time.

"I'm ready for it to wear off now," I whispered up to the timbers above me.

I stared at the ceiling and wondered what was wrong with me. I had received in one night everything that I had felt was missing from my life over the past three months, and it just felt empty.

I could feel the Dark Lord Nâtlac and the whole pitiless universe laughing at me. Even when events conspire to give me exactly what I want—*especially* when events conspire to give me what I want—it never goes wrong the way I expect it to.

It may have been my growing familiarity with living in the princess's body, but I no longer felt comfortable in my own skin.

Someone else's skin.

I rubbed my chin and my hand recoiled at the feeling of stubble. I didn't even know what this guy looked like. I closed my eyes, made a fist, and pushed the knuckles against my forehead.

"I know it was a bad idea. I know."

Eventually I fell asleep.

CHAPTER 5

I had gone to sleep hanging on to two small optimistic thoughts.

The first, at least this time my foray into a new body was much less threatening to life and limb than the time I was displaced into Princess Lucille. Second, I had a small hope that when I did wake up I would find myself back in the princess's bed.

Wrong on both counts.

"Wakey, wakey," someone whispered into my ear.

The voice did not belong to the woman with whom I spent the night.

My eyes shot open and I tried to spring out of bed. That didn't work so well. As I sat up, my face collided with someone's fist, and I fell backward, head ringing. I shook my head and realized that my hands and feet were being held down by a quartet of very large men. Two of them were familiar. So was the man going, "Tsk, tsk," into my ear.

"Sloppy, Snake," Weasel said, holding a very sharp dagger up to my throat. "I'm disappointed."

"You're persistent," I said, spitting blood from a split lip.

The dagger withdrew and he began pacing around

the bed gesturing with it so occasionally it would reflect the cold winter sun from the window into my eyes. I could feel the icy draft on my naked skin. If they had come in that window, they must have been very quick, or very quiet, or both . . .

Or I'd slept too deeply for my own good.

"You've led me on a merry chase. Much farther north than I'm comfortable with. I've found you very annoying."

"Likewise."

He spun around and placed the dagger against my face. "I would like nothing better than to cut you into. Tiny. Little. Pieces."

The contrary self-destructive part of my brain decided to ask the guy, "Why don't you then?" I think that part of me was still trying to punish me for last night.

He drew the blade across my cheek, and I winced as it sliced a stinging cut under my eye.

He whispered, his breath hot and foul against my ear, "Because I love money more than I hate you." He stood up and said, "Bag him."

Unlike our prior encounter, I didn't have either luck or surprise on my side, and with four accomplices, Weasel could just lean back against the wall, paring his nails with the dagger. I would have shouted some questions, but the first thing his goons did was shove a rag in my mouth and tie the gag in place. They did a workmanlike job of tying me hand and foot before shoving me into a musty burlap sack.

I suspect Weasel didn't bother with my clothes just out of spite. The burlap was bad enough against my naked skin. But add to that the fact that whatever grain had occupied the bag before me had gone to mold and made the air incredibly unpleasant to breathe. And the less said about the weevils, the better.

They hefted the bag and carried me across the room. I felt a sharp cold draft though the weave of the burlap and had a brief moment to think, *They aren't going to throw me—*

Then they did.

There were only two stories to the inn, but it felt as if I tumbled forever in free fall. Bound as I was, all I could do was pull myself into a ball and hope I didn't land headfirst.

Someone caught me, then tossed me aside into a pile of something that was supposed to be yielding. Given the feeling of a hundred brittle stabby things trying to poke through the burlap, I suspected that it was a pile of straw that had been left outside to freeze. The little light that leaked through the weave in the burlap went away as someone tossed more straw on top of me.

At least it cut down on the draft.

I heard footsteps, creaking wood, and the snorting of a horse or three. I heard a muffled voice say, "You caught him finally."

Weasel's voice responded from farther away. "Your tone suggests a lack of faith in my skill."

"This ain't just some guy skipping out on his debt—"

"That's why the guild is paying us so much. Get on

the wagon, I want to get back to Delmark while we still have daylight."

Crap.

I knew Delmark, and it was much farther north than I wanted to be. That meant there were at least two kingdoms between me and Lendowyn—more if we were actually north of Delmark at this point. I felt the ground shift beneath me, more wood creaking and footsteps.

I figured that they were transporting me in a hay wagon piled with straw. It seemed reasonable camouflage, and it meant that—if there had been any doubt—these guys were not in league with the local city authorities. I heard reins snap, and suddenly we were racing down bumpy roads that jammed frozen straw into my skin with every bounce of the wagon.

Someone asked Weasel, "Think West River Guild would offer more for him?"

"Don't be a greedy sot. Playing West River against the White Rock Thieves' Guild was how our guest got a price on his head."

"Yeah, but he made off with how much from both of them?" I heard a thump. "Ow, why'd you—"

"Shut your trap." Weasel sounded pissed. "First, 'made off with' implies surviving to enjoy the fruits of your labor. Our friend Snake ain't going to, is he? Second, Snake's a lot smarter than you and he was only able to pull it off by sparking a bloody war as a distraction."

Again, crap.

Now I understood what was going on. Apparently Nâtlac's charm hadn't just found me a new body that matched my gender; it found one that matched my former profession. Weasel and company were talking about the two major thieves' guilds in Delmark, both of whom seemed to have an interest in seeing Mr. Snake.

As they bounced down the road, I heard more detail.

The former owner of this body had, somehow, conned both guilds out of a substantial share of their treasuries and managed to convince each guild that the other was responsible—escaping in the chaos that erupted. Weasel had been employed by the White Rock Thieves' Guild to find Snake and return him in a condition where they could extract the location of the missing horde from him.

I could only see this ending in pain and tears for everyone involved.

If I wasn't at that moment bound up in a sack, contemplating being tortured to reveal information I didn't have, I might have spent a bit more time worrying about the fact that I had released this "Snake" guy in the middle of the Lendowyn court disguised as the princess.

We rode an hour out of the city without my captors ever naming the place. Even though the city was long gone, for some reason I found it frustrating not knowing if we were traveling toward Lendowyn or away from it. Not that it really mattered. Unlike the popular stories, not every thief is an escape artist. That was a whole separate skill set unto itself. Sure I could pick locks and break in or out of most buildings people would think secure, but use of my hands was sort of a prerequisite. Tie me up and I was pretty useless.

My only chance at this point was to try to talk my way out of it when these guys delivered me to the White Rock Thieves' Guild in Delmark.

In other words, I was doomed.

To all appearance, the guild expected to be handed a con man. And one of the first rules of conning people is never try to con someone who's expecting to be conned. *Especially* someone who's already been conned.

It didn't matter now if I tried to tell them the whole unvarnished truth, the point stood.

About an hour out, the wagon came to a sudden stop.

I heard the horses scream and buck, followed by people shouting incoherently over each other. Then we were off again at a thundering gallop that tried to shake the wagon apart at every bump in the road. Then we slammed into a massive bump—a tree root or a crater in the road—and the wagon bounced up and didn't come down for way too long.

I felt the straw bedding tilt beneath me before the wagon finally slammed down. I was too disoriented to tell where the real ground was, but when we hit I heard a crunch of splintering wood, and everything continued tipping, flinging me out of the top of the wagon.

I tumbled blindly into snow that wasn't quite enough to cushion the blow from slamming into the frozen ground. I rolled downhill until I struck a small tree.

To my surprise, the tree kicked me so I rolled on my back. Through the coarse weave of the burlap, I saw the tree reach down and grab the material. A blade penetrated the burlap, an inch from my face, slitting the burlap from top to bottom. Sudden exposure to the frigid air made me appreciative of the weak protection the burlap sack had provided. I sucked in a breath and the cold stabbed like a knife. My lungs spasmed with nostalgia for warm mold and weevil dust. As I coughed into the gag in my mouth, the tree stared down at me.

He wore elaborately tooled black leather armor and a mask that covered the lower half of his face, half in leather and half in black cloth. Where the mouth should have been, my tree had an eye painted in a shade slightly less black.

The tree did not look like part of Weasel's crew.

He said, "You are a hard man to find."

"Not hard enough," I mumbled incoherently into the gag.

Mr. Tree raised his head and turned toward the actual trees surrounding us. He let out a high-pitched whistle that, I suspected, was to alert his compatriots that he had found his quarry, which given the circumstances, I assumed was yours truly—or, more accurately, the Snake gentleman whom I had displaced.

I began to suspect that Snake may have gotten the better side of my alcoholic decision-making skills.

Mr. Tree whistled again, and that proved to be once too many. Instead of alerting whatever allies he had in the forest, it apparently alerted one of Weasel's men, because a large black crossbow bolt sprouted from the man's shoulder just below the collarbone. His hand jerked, dropping his dagger on my chest—hilt-first fortunately—and he let loose with a litany of curses in a language I didn't understand as he dove for cover behind a fallen tree larger than he was.

I heard more whistles, short and long, and I saw shadows moving through the trees to the left and right.

I didn't pay much attention to the sound of fighting around me. Weasel's men had made one mistake. They had tied my hands at the wrists in front of me. It had been pure laziness on their part, not rolling me over on the bed to tie them behind me. But that error put the fallen dagger in my reach.

I might not be a professional escape artist, but put a dagger in my hand and I can fake it pretty well.

Once I cut my bonds I rolled out of the bag, toward the cover of the forest and away from the remains of the wagon where most of the sounds came from. I got to my feet halfway toward the densest part of the woods, and a bolt sprouted from a tree next to me.

I ran.

CHAPTER 6

By all rights, I shouldn't have been able to escape a pitched battle by running stark naked into the woods. However, it seemed Weasel's crew was more interested in fighting the guys in leather armor than they were in keeping me. At least I hope that was why the one leather-armored guy between me and the woods got a quarrel in the face. The other option was that it had been just too hard to hit a running target at that distance.

I was lucky.

Not really.

The last time I got displaced from my body, into the princess, I had found myself in a similar situation. Back then I had also found myself running off into the woods away from hostile people who wanted me—or who they thought I was—for less than pleasant reasons. But there were three very significant differences.

Last time had been midsummer. Last time had been daylight. And last time I'd been clothed. My feet were already growing numb from the cold, and blundering through the dark I had already lost my sense of direction.

It was a measure of how bad things were that I

found myself wishing Sir Forsythe was around. Say what you want about him, he had given me a ride the last time I was stuck alone in the forest. Of course, that time I was a princess in distress. This time I was a naked thief covered in blood that was mostly not my own—blood already freezing to my skin.

I stopped running because I was out of earshot from the battle.

"Another bad idea," I whispered to myself in a puff of fog. My muscles shuddered in the frigid air. Every small breeze felt like a knife flaying my skin. I probably only had a few more minutes before the cold finished me off.

I slowly turned around, trying to get my bearings. I needed some sign of civilization, a cave where I could take shelter, a sleeping bear that I could cut the skin off . . .

I wasn't thinking clearly anymore.

I turned around slowly, squinting into the woods. Everything looked the same. So much so that I wasn't quite sure when I had made a complete turn. I hugged myself and shivered. I knew it was the cold, but I felt a wave of fatigue wash over me.

I had to get moving again, if only to buy myself a few extra minutes.

But what direction?

I turned around again, not even opening my eyes, when I smelled something.

Smoke.

My eyes shot open, and I ran in the direction of the smell, against the wind. Smoke meant fire, and fire meant a place that might be warm enough to keep me from dying.

The smoke came from a large campfire. I emerged from the woods and ran right up to it, feeling the cold melt away from my skin in waves of agonizing pins and needles. I held my arms up, and had to pull back because the stench told me I was close enough to scorch the hair on them.

I turned around slowly so that each part of my body could face the fire as I squinted, looking for who it belonged to. At first I didn't see anyone. I saw logs drawn up to the fire, footprints, and a trio of tents that appeared empty.

I peered into the dark interior of one, wondering how likely it was that I could steal some winter clothing before everyone came back.

It wasn't more than a thought before I heard the crunch of a footstep. I spun around, afraid that either Weasel or one of his leather-clad opponents had chased me down.

Neither was the case, unless one side or the other had gotten into the habit of employing teenage girls.

"D-Don't you move," she said while pointing a shaking dagger in my direction. I exhaled a little, relieved that I wasn't about to experience a reprise of Weasel and company. The girl was maybe fourteen, it was hard to tell because she wore oversize clothes that had been made for a guy about twice her size.

But they looked warm.

"Okay," I said. "I'm not moving." I wasn't really

that inclined to move. I had spent long enough out in the cold. Until I had something to wear, I was happy to stay right where I was, next to the fire.

"You're n-naked," she stammered.

"You're observant."

"W-why are you naked?"

"Long story. Can you put down the dagger?"

"P-put down yours."

I glanced down and saw I was still armed. I sighed. I decided that, even with the dagger, the way she was shaking, she wasn't really a threat.

"Fair enough," I said and tossed my dagger down to thunk upright in a log next to the campfire.

The girl straightened and said, "That's better." The stammer and shaking were suddenly gone, and she asked again, "So why are you naked?"

After the sudden change in demeanor I thought, *Oh, you're good. Your dad's watching us from the trees with a crossbow, isn't he?*

"Because the guys who kidnapped me didn't let me get dressed first," I answered her. She reminded me a bit of a younger Lucille—the human version. I wondered if it was because she was a pale blonde with her hair tied back, or because she was beginning to annoy me.

As I spoke, I saw that I was only half right. There *had* been someone covering for my little con artist, but it wasn't her dad. Five girls emerged from the woods around the campfire, most no older than the girl facing me. The youngest may have been twelve or thirteen, the oldest could have been sixteen, or a tall fifteen. They all wore similarly ill-designed clothes that, despite alterations, were obviously meant for men of a much bigger stature. Though their clothes seemed to have been modified to the point where their movement wasn't affected.

The girl with the dagger gestured at the tall one, a lanky redhead who was apparently in the midst of a growth spurt, giving her the best-fitting clothes. Red ran up and pulled my dagger from the log next to me. Red gave me a sidelong glance as she did so. She blushed, unnecessarily reminding me I was naked.

Apparently the girl with the dagger was in charge.

I might have tried to stop Red, but one of the other girls, a dark-skinned fourteen-year-old with hair braided tightly to her scalp, had a crossbow pointed in my direction. I questioned whether someone that size could successfully wield a crossbow, but it didn't seem prudent to put that question to a practical test.

Once Red had retreated with my dagger, Fearless Leader asked me, "You were kidnapped? You worth a ransom?"

"More like a price on my head."

The youngest one, whose tight-curled hair was a shade between Red and Fearless Leader, frowned at me. "You hurt, mister?"

"Don't worry, it's not my blood."

Everyone withdrew from me and huddled around Fearless Leader, though the crossbow stayed pointed in my direction. I got more sidelong glances at my nakedness that probably should have embarrassed me, if it wasn't for the fact I still felt disconnected from this body.

As they whispered things to each other, I got a

good look at all of them. Six in all, outfitted with out-size garments and weapons. It made sense since there wasn't a booming market in chain mail and swords fitted for fourteen-year-old girls.

But, however large the garments had been, they had all been carefully altered. The alterations were rough, but skillful enough to suggest they'd been wearing this kind of thing for some time. All of them had some sort of weapon, and either had their hair tied or cut back. One of the girls had her hair cut so short that, if it wasn't for the context, I probably would have taken her for a slightly effeminate boy.

All of them had a lean and weathered look suggesting they'd been out here a while.

Their leader wasn't the obvious one. Any group of youngsters will invariably hand leadership to the biggest and most physically powerful. That's the way kids' minds worked. It took some maturity, and some experience, to hand the reins over to the most qualified to hold them. This group had been through something, multiple somethings, and the blonde with the vanishing stutter had been the one to get them through.

Fearless Leader pointed toward one of the tents, and a pair of girls ran off toward it, going around the side of the campfire opposite me.

"I seen it before, Grace." I turned my attention back to the main group because someone, Red, had raised her voice. All was not paradise in girltopia.

Fearless Leader, who was apparently named Grace, had sheathed her own dagger and was examining mine, turning it over in her hands. "I know, but they don't move this far north," she said.

"Not less someone pays them," Red responded.

"You think he . . ." Grace pointed the dagger in my direction and everyone turned their heads toward me. I had the sudden intuition that this might not be a good thing.

The two girls returned carrying boots, a cloak, a linen shirt, and a pair of breeches. No undergarments, but I wasn't choosy at this point, and I didn't know where these came from anyway. I tried a gracious, "Thank you," and a small bow toward them, and they both scurried away, giggling.

The conversation between Grace and Red continued in less audible tones, and I dressed myself. I tried to ignore the two bloodstained holes in the shirt.

After a bit longer, Grace broke ranks and walked up to me, holding my dagger. She stood just out of reach and held it up between us so that the elaborately engraved hilt reflected the campfire.

"So," she asked, "can you explain why a naked man is armed with a dagger belonging to the Assassins' Guild of Sanhom City?"

I shrugged. "The prior owner didn't need it anymore."

"You were kidnapped by the Assassins' Guild?"

"Not quite."

"What do you mean by that?"

"I was *kidnapped* by a group of thugs working for the White Rock Thieves' Guild out of Delmark. They were ambushed."

"By the Assassins' Guild?"

"By the dagger guy and his friends. We weren't properly introduced. I was busy removing myself from—"

"What you have to do with White Rock?" The red-head's shout interrupted my dialogue with Grace. The girl with the crossbow pointed it right at me. As she sighted down it, I got to view a long scar along the left side of her face.

Grace spun around and said, "Mary! No!"

"Have him say what he has to do with White Rock!" Mary spoke through clenched teeth. She was so tense I could almost see her muscles vibrating under her altered leather. "Now!"

"Mary! Remember the rules!"

"But—"

"We all agreed."

Mary took a deep breath.

Grace turned to the girl with the crossbow. "Laya?"

The crossbow lowered a fraction. As I watched her I noticed an accessory that I hadn't before. Laya wore a necklace whose primary component consisted of polished human teeth.

Grace turned back toward me and I saw that she wore similar jewelry. Only hers seemed to consist of finger bones and was a little less obvious.

"What rules?" I asked in a whisper.

Grace whipped the dagger up toward my throat. "Answer her question. Who are you and what do you have to do with White Rock?"

Teenage girls shouldn't be intimidating.

The question also put me in a tough spot. Should I tell her the whole truth? What *was* the truth at this point? I finally hedged and said, "Of late, they've been calling me 'Snake,' and I think both guilds in Delmark are upset with me at the moment."

She lowered the dagger and slowly shook her head. She stared at my face, as if she was looking for something.

"Apparently the Assassins of Sanhom as well," I added.

Everyone stared at me as if I'd announced that I was the Dark Lord Nâtlac. The entire group had fallen silent. Enough that I clearly heard Red whisper, *"You're the Snake?"*

Snake's reputation had preceded me again.

CHAPTER 7

To Grace's obvious irritation, Red's rhetorical question changed the character of the crowd facing me. A trio of the girls suddenly pushed forward, talking at once.

The young one with the curls asked, "Did you *really* steal the crown of Grimheld while the king still wore—"

The dark girl with the crossbow spoke over her. "—walked away with the golden idols of the Grey Dwarves of Blackstone Crag—"

The boyish one added to the din. "—actually you who emptied the treasury of—"

"—is it true that—"

"—both thieves' guilds in Delmark?"

I felt suddenly overwhelmed.

Grace didn't join the barrage of questions, and two of the other girls hung back with her, the tall redhead and a small mousy girl with almond eyes. As the three girls peppered me with questions I saw Grace's expression of irritation shift halfway toward amusement, as if she got some sort of satisfaction from my discomfort.

I would have called the expression predatory on

anyone other than a fourteen-year-old girl. Our eyes locked for a moment, and I could see she knew. She could read my face and saw that I had jumped in over my head just by implying I was "the Snake."

Whose skin was I wearing?

Whoever this Snake was, at least half the girls in this little band looked up to him. In the face of the youngest, I saw something like hero worship. Fearless Leader let the others obsess without doing a thing to correct them or rein them in.

Oh, you're a smart little girl, aren't you?

Grace could have stepped in, questioned who I was directly, but if she did, at least some of her girls would resent having their assumptions challenged. Better to let the prisoner stumble on his own feet of clay.

Yeah, there was a reason she was in charge.

She watched as the Snake fans questioned me non-stop. At least I had some time to think about what to do because I couldn't get a word in as the girls talked over each other and answered their own questions. She let it go on for a long time, enjoying my discomfort, *then* she cleared her throat.

Everyone stopped babbling.

Grace smiled all too sweetly at me, and asked a question that was way too perceptive.

"How does such an *effective* outlaw land naked by our campfire?"

I didn't even need to answer that. It went right at the heart of my implied claim, and I could see doubt cloud the two older girls' faces.

It irritated me because I hadn't even been *trying* to con anyone.

I wasn't about to be outmaneuvered by some brat. It was misplaced pride on my part, but I did a stupid thing.

I lied.

I rationalized it by telling myself that as long as at least some of Grace's girls thought I was actually Snake, it meant that I would have them on my side. So I decided to leap from lies of omission to full-blown fabrication.

It was not a craft I was unskilled in. Even before I opened my mouth to answer, I saw Grace's smile falter as she saw my own.

"Remember when I said that the blood was not my own?"

I had their attention.

"You know the town nearby here, about an hour's ride?"

"Westmark?" the youngest one offered.

"That's right," I said, having no idea if it was or not. "You know why I was there?"

Everyone shook their head as my mind raced to find an answer for that rhetorical question. "I had just finished up an accounting in Delmark, leaving both guilds there with a smaller treasury than they started with. I came here with my haul to pay a visit to a woman—"

"Your true love?" asked the young one.

Well, thank you, little girl. "There's no such thing in an outlaw's life," I said, shaping my lies to fit my new target audience. "Yes, she said she loved me, and I might have loved her ... but she had family in the White Rock Thieves' Guild, and while she'd helped

me take the guilds for their gold and jewels, when I
returned to give her share to her, she became greedy."

A tale of tragic love and betrayal and I had the girls
hooked. Half of them anyway. Even the small quiet
one who hung back with Grace and the redhead
started listening raptly. Grace herself wore an expression of growing disbelief. I couldn't tell if she was re-
acting to my story, or to the fact that her group was
buying my story.

I kept going, bringing all my skills to bear. I played
up Snake's reputation to the bleeding edge of what I
considered plausible, making him a tragic hero who
had suffered a lover's betrayal that cut worse than any
assassin's dagger. Weasel's goons became a squad of
armed mercenaries. The ambush by the Sanhom Assassins became an epic battle of evils where I escaped
clad only in my skin, carving my way out of the battle
with a stolen dagger.

I admit I overdid it. But the first two rules of spinning a falsehood were: Tell them what they want to
believe and tell them what they already expect to
hear. Most of the girls hung on my every word.

Grace was no longer smiling, and the gaze she gave
me could rival post-dragon Lucille in the smoldering
department. However well my narrative had gone, she
was the nominal leader of this little band—and given
that I now saw that about half these girls had accessories made from human remains I realized that alien-
ating her would be another in a long series of bad
decisions on my part.

I couldn't back up on the path I'd started down, but
I could take an abrupt left turn. I had just got to the

point where I'd been running naked through the woods clad only in assassin's blood, and I decided to change the subject.

"Now you know how I ended up here." I asked Grace, "Why don't you tell me how you came to be here?"

"It's not nearly as impressive as all that," Grace said. The smile returned, cold and hard. "But we're outlaws as well. Not that we've had a choice." She pointed the dagger at Red. "Mary here was sold to the White Rock Thieves' Guild when she was twelve. When she was fourteen, she was finally big enough to club her guard hard enough that he didn't get up again." Grace pointed the dagger at the quiet young girl that stood with her and Mary. "That's Rabbit. What we call her anyway. She can't talk because her tongue was cut out."

"Oh crap," I whispered, wincing a little.

"That's the punishment White Rock gives to anyone who rats on their members—even when it's telling someone what they're doing to their kids. Krys there—" Grace pointed at the boyish one with the brown hair cut close to the scalp. "She's been homeless since she was six and the Delmark watch took her dad to the dungeons. Laya there, with the crossbow, she ran away from an arranged marriage. And Thea—" Grace pointed to the girl with the strawberry curls. "Her parents had too many kids who weren't boys. They gave her half a loaf of bread and left her in the woods here two summers ago."

"What about you?" I asked.

"What about me?"

"Why are *you* here?"

She smiled and shook her head. "Least interesting of all. I'm just an outlaw from a long line of outlaws. Dad had no boys, so he taught me his trade. Unfortunately, the guilds in Delmark tend to think a girl's only good for one thing. Just ask Mary."

"So where's your dad?"

"The guild also doesn't take kindly to people teaching the trade to folks it doesn't approve of. The duke of White Rock himself took a hot poker—"

"I get the picture." One way or another, all these girls had lost their families. They became outlaws, but were outcasts even among outlaws.

A hard bloodless frown crossed Grace's face. She walked up to me, pushing past the three girls in front of me. She spoke in a harsh, shaking whisper. "Don't dare give us your pity."

"I wasn't—"

"I see your face. You're nowhere near as hard to read as you think you are."

"I just realized why you might have a grudge against White Rock."

She chuckled and stepped back. "Not a grudge, a debt."

I looked from her to the others, and the jewelry made from teeth and bone, and at the weapons and clothing they wore. "They sent men after you, didn't they? They wouldn't like anyone thieving without tribute."

"There's only one tribute they want from the likes of us," Grace said.

No wonder they looked up to Snake. My own embellishments aside, Snake hurt the guilds in Delmark. These girls would obviously take some pleasure in that. In some sense that put us on the same side.

But the way they dressed made me nervous.

"When Mary thought I might be part of the White Rock Thieves' Guild, you stopped her. You said something about rules. What rules?"

"It's simple," Grace said. "If someone doesn't try to take from us what we're unwilling to give, they get to live."

"And if they do?"

She looked at me with very cold blue eyes. "We need food and clothing."

Oh crap.

"They've sent a lot of men, but never figured out that rule."

I could have ignored the implications of what she was saying, but she made a point of stroking her necklace of finger bones to help drive home the point. It also explained why none of Snake's other admirers had followed me into this part of the woods. A pack of cannibal teenage girls might get a bit of a reputation that would even put off the assassins' guild.

I know it put me off.

Just because things weren't tense enough, the redhead Mary decided to add, "They've stopped coming, unfortunately."

CHAPTER 8

After giving due consideration to my terrifying admirers, and their terrifying leader, I decided that it wasn't all that cold out in the woods. I could see dawn starting to break. With a set of clothes, I probably wouldn't die out there.

"I should be going," I said.

My graceful exit was abruptly interrupted by a sharp point sticking me in my ribs above the kidney. I turned to see Grace holding the assassin's dagger up to my side. "You're not leaving."

"What?"

"You owe us for those clothes."

"Why don't you just keep the dagger?"

"Now," Grace said, "you are such a successful, talented, infamous outlaw. Surely you think your life is worth more than just a dagger. You can afford to be more gracious."

Even though they were probably responsible for saving my life—without the campfire and the clothing, winter would have made short work of me—I couldn't help hearing a threat. "What about your rules?"

She shook her head. "Snake, because you aren't a

rapist we let you live. Never said anything about letting you *go*."

"You saw me. The dagger's the only thing I have."

She withdrew the dagger and glared at me. "Do you take us for fools here? We've all heard the stories about 'the Snake.' For years you've stolen from kings, churches, wizards, even the guilds of Delmark. So after so many years, you have *nothing* stashed away? Or are you just not who you say you are?"

I could feel the audience wavering, and I didn't want to see what would happen if I lost their support. I couldn't back down now. Even though Fearless Leader Grace was operating at a level way beyond her age, I wasn't about to concede to a fourteen-year-old.

"Of course I have stuff stashed away, as in 'not here.'"

"Where then?"

"Westmark?" Red—Mary—prompted hopefully.

"Don't be an idiot," snapped the girl with the blond boy's hair, Krys. "They nabbed him there. Think White Rock'd leave anything for us?"

"Quiet you," Grace said. "Let the master talk. You leave money in Westmark?"

"I was a victim of a rather thorough betrayal." Grace did not like that for an answer. I saw her knuckles whiten as she gripped the dagger. "But—"

"But what?" she snapped.

"I do have a cache in the Kingdom of Lendowyn," I said.

She stared at me like I had just told her that I was the Elf King and my gold was on the Moon. She threw the dagger down in frustration. "I don't believe this crap! *Lendowyn?*" She turned and stormed off, for the first time looking her age.

Redhead Mary called after her, "Grace!" and followed.

I took a step, and Laya, of crossbows and arranged marriages, stepped in front of me, her loaded bolt pointed at my midsection. She shook her head and I stayed put.

Mary stopped Grace at the edge of the clearing. The two talked to each other in hushed tones. I strained to overhear, but couldn't make out anything even as the discussion between them became more and more animated. Whatever they discussed, I could tell Grace didn't like it. Mary pointed at me several times, as if someone might be confused about what they were arguing about.

The argument ended with their backs still toward us. After a long pause, Grace turned and walked back to the campfire. She tried to hide her expression, but her body language told me she wasn't the one who had won the argument. She stopped and picked up the dagger and slid the blade into her belt.

"You," she said, pointing at me. "You're taking us to Lendowyn."

I opened my mouth to say something, but Mary came up behind her, looking directly at me and shaking her head. I decided to quit while I was ahead.

Grace walked up to me and said, "But first, once dawn breaks, you're going to take us all to the scene of this massacre you described."

*　　*　　*

The ridiculousness of the situation did not escape me. Being held hostage by a group of teenage girls was the kind of thing that would prompt a guy to do something stupid just to assert his masculinity. It was easy for me to imagine how the men from the guild—men who'd categorically reject the idea of Grace being one of their number—would consistently tempt fate by trying to prove who the man was.

While I could understand how those men may have felt, it gave me no desire to emulate them. Having dealt with literal emasculation for months, the metaphorical kind didn't bother me nearly as much.

Grace was what really bothered me. The group's Fearless Leader filled her role well, but the way she'd snapped and stormed off in frustration showed she was still a teenage girl—not even the oldest one in the group. *That* was scary. Especially now that I was neck deep in a story that was barely half true. Inevitably they were going to find out I wasn't the legendary "Snake" no matter whose face I wore, and I doubt even the Dark Lord Nâtlac himself could predict her reaction—other than it likely would involve screaming and some form of pain.

What the hell was I thinking?

The answer was, as usual when I found myself in a situation like this, I hadn't been. I did what I always do. I improvised with whatever the situation handed me. My life being what it was, when the universe sees me flailing and tosses me a rope, more often than not there's a noose on the other end.

Fortunately for me, there was enough left at the site of the ambush to back up my story of epic escape.

The dead and wounded had been dragged away, but there were more than enough bloodstains in the snow. Several trees had splintered wounds caused by stray quarrels. Some still had the shaft embedded in them.

The wreckage of Weasel's hay wagon dominated the scene. Someone had tried to right it after the fight, but it had been damaged beyond repair. The side had caved in, leaving a good part of its wood members in pieces sticking up out of the half-frozen ground. The rear axle had snapped, releasing the right wheel to roll down the hillside. Scraps of leather, all that remained of the harness for the team that had pulled the wagon, had been scattered across the road.

Grace looked at the remains of the wagon as if it physically pained her. She turned to the others and said, "Spread out and search the area, see if anyone dropped anything useful." She pointed at crossbow-wielding Laya and said, "Keep an eye on him."

The rest scattered as Fearless Leader climbed up into the wagon and started tossing aside random bits of broken wood, canvas, and hay. I could hear her muttering, "Nothing? They left nothing?"

"So," I said to Laya, "arranged marriage?"

"Father couldn't pay his taxes," Laya said. "Gave me to the tax collector."

"That's rough."

She frowned, causing the scar on her face to crease and become more prominent. "Others had it worse."

I heard Grace cursing from above us, inside the wagon.

"She doesn't sound happy."

"It's how she is. She worries. Worry makes her angry."

In the wagon, I heard Grace say something like, "Bastards could have left some damn food!"

"How long have you been out here?" I asked.

Laya shrugged and nodded toward the wagon. "She was the first, then Mary. They've been out here two years, three maybe. I found them last fall."

If I really was as oblivious as I acted sometimes, I might have asked why she stayed. But I knew why she stayed, why all of them stayed even though it was clear that they were going hungry in the depths of winter. I understood the choice they'd made. In their case, the choice was much starker because of their age and their sex, but it was still the same choice I had faced long ago when I'd chosen life as an outlaw.

Die free, or live as a slave.

For some people, a full belly can never compensate for being someone's property.

"She's a good leader?"

"She knows what to do."

It was quiet, but I thought I heard a sob of frustration from the wagon. If Laya heard, she didn't give any sign of it. A few moments later, Grace climbed out of the remains of the wagon. I saw the instant before she realized I saw her, and her expression was wrenching.

By the time she jumped down to the ground and faced us, the pain was gone, replaced by the half-bored sardonic look she'd been giving me ever since I'd given up my dagger. Only I now had a sense of how brittle that hardness was.

"So," I said, "I guess you're going to want me to find you transportation to Lendowyn?"

Her expression didn't soften, but the way she narrowed her eyes slightly and cocked her head told me that she understood I was making an offer, and wasn't quite sure what it meant.

"Yeah," she said. "Something like that."

We returned to the campsite, and they packed everything up in a matter of minutes. We spent the rest of the day following the mute girl, Rabbit, who tracked the assassins from the ambush. I had my own reservations about that, but it did take us in the right direction, south. It was a pretty good assumption that those guys had some form of transportation since they were pretty far afield themselves.

Apparently no one had any doubt that the great master thief Snake could easily liberate whatever he wanted from a bunch of professional assassins.

For what it was worth, I agreed.

I just wished he was here.

We caught up with them before nightfall. There were seven or eight tents, at least a dozen horses, a carriage, and a pair of large covered wagons, all more than up to the task of transporting Grace's small band.

The campsite seemed larger and more opulent than I'd credit for a bunch of mercenary killers. I had a brief hope that we had come across a bunch of merchants who had coincidentally camped out in our path. I was able to believe that until I saw one of the sentries in the same elaborate patterned armor I'd seen on the Sanhom Assassins who had ambushed

Weasel and company, down to the mask covering the lower half of his face.

We watched from the woods as the sun dropped and Grace whispered, "We can take care of the guard, you take a wagon."

I shook my head.

"The master thief having second thoughts?"

"No," I said. "I'll take care of the sentry."

"Just you?"

"Just me."

It wasn't bravado on my part. I just saw the size of that campsite, and I knew Grace was not the best at calculating the odds. The numbers favored the home team at least two to one without taking into account that on one side we had a bunch of young girls, and on the other we had trained professional assassins.

Also, if things went wrong I'd feel better if the bad guys had no idea that the girls were here. I at least had the advantage that these guys didn't want to kill me. Even if I ended up where I'd started, tied up in a burlap sack, at *some* point this spell would wear off and I'd be back in Lendowyn Castle.

At least I hoped it would.

If that happened, I'd feel better if I didn't leave a pile of dead teenage girls in my wake.

I watched the campsite for a few hours as the night deepened and the cook fires burned low. At some point Grace whispered, "You staring them into submission?"

"There are two types of thief, young lady."

"Huh?"

"The first type is gone before you realize your purse is missing." I placed my hand on her shoulder and looked her in the eyes. "The second clubs you with a rock and swipes the boots off your corpse. There's probably twenty trained killers sleeping down there. Tell me which thief has the better chance of making it out alive?"

She sighed. "The first."

"Good choice," I said, holding up the dagger I'd lifted from her belt with my other hand. "Because that's the kind of thief you've got."

I wasn't kidding. That *was* the type of thief I was. It didn't matter if the camp was twenty people or two, the last thing I ever wanted was a physical confrontation. That kind of thing most likely ended in blood and humiliation even before I'd been princessified. Every fight I'd ever won had been through dumb luck.

Or cheating.

The sentry fell victim to the latter.

I studied his movements, and once the camp seemed mostly asleep, and the lone guard was deep in the middle of his watch, I waited in the shadows by a tree in the path of the circuit he walked around the camp. Just as he passed, I pulled a rope taut at ankle level. As he tumbled forward I took a large rock and helped his head into the forest floor.

While he was stunned, I tore his mask off and shoved it into his mouth. I used the rope to tie his ankles and wrists together behind his back, and to hold the makeshift gag in his mouth. By the time I was done, he was groaning and struggling ineffectively. After disarming him, I dragged him off into some brush so he was hidden from the camp.

Now I just had to swipe a wagon.

Sounds simple, right?

Strangely enough, these people didn't leave their horses tacked and harnessed to their wagons overnight while they camped. I guess they wanted their animals to rest and graze for some reason. That meant I had to quietly fetch a team and hitch them up to one of the wagons without alerting the camp.

Yeah. Simple.

It was already pretty clear what I had to take. There were a couple of large wagons that seemed capable of carrying most of the men and gear, but either one would have taken a four-horse team to move. Trying to hitch up four horses quietly in the dark pushed way past the bounds of sanity. So I just took my dagger and started cutting reins, bridles, and straps. It wouldn't permanently immobilize them, but after the damage I did it would probably be a good hour or two before they'd be able to hitch a team to either one again.

My target was a smaller, but much more opulent, vehicle. The carriage was all gilding and elaborate scrollwork, and bore a coat of arms that I couldn't make out in the dark. The girls might be cramped inside, but it only needed a two-horse team, and could probably get by with one.

Once I sabotaged the main wagons, I crept to the carriage and made sure all the tack was in place, unbuckled and ready for a team.

Okay, now the hard part.

I crept over to the clearing where the horses were tied. I had a moment of panic when I realized that I'd have to guess which ones were riding horses and which ones were trained as a team. Fortunately for me, it was clear after a moment which horses went with the carriage. There were two gray horses a hand or two smaller than the other shaggy draft animals, and both had their mane and tail tightly braided.

Just to complicate any pursuit, I untied the other animals and removed their halters, cutting a few critical straps with my dagger. If I was lucky, they'd also wander off.

After that, I took the first gray and coaxed him back toward the carriage. Lucky me, the horse was well trained and fairly docile. I managed to get him hitched up to the carriage without an incident or any undue noise.

I stepped back and briefly considered pushing my luck and fetching the other gray horse.

I wasn't nearly as lucky as I thought I was.

"Hey!" Across the campsite from me stood a gentleman with his arm in a sling. I guessed he was the same man who had taken a quarrel in the shoulder while bequeathing me my current dagger. At least from the bridge of the nose upward it could have been him. He spent a split second staring at me in open-mouthed surprise.

I ran.

The man started yelling to raise the camp.

Men began emerging from tents across the campsite, and I aimed my sprint toward the largest and most luxuriously appointed of the tents, intent on my secondary escape plan. I was halfway there when my escape plan emerged from the tent complaining about the ungodly racket. He wore a nightcap and long robe trimmed with ermine. He had a pale, pudgy, slightly annoyed look of someone who found physical activity distasteful and had either the money or power to avoid it as much as possible.

I grabbed him before he'd had a chance to turn his attention from the man raising the alarm. I swung him between me and everyone else and held a dagger up to his throat as I backed him away from the big tent.

"I suggest everyone stay calm," I yelled toward my acquaintance with the sling, "or our friend here gets a very brief lesson in how to breathe through a hole in his neck."

"Cur," Ermine boy said, "Do you know who I am?"

For an answer, I increased the pressure on the dagger and whispered at him, "Do you know who I am?" It was a lot easier to get an intimidating tone from my voice now that I wasn't a princess. He was about to say something, but he glanced back in my direction and—surprisingly for the type—shut up.

And I had to struggle to not lose my grip on the dagger because I *did* know who he was.

Prince Oliver?

I had just taken the prince of Dermonica hostage.

CHAPTER 9

I had headed for the opulent tent intending to take a hostage. Given that assassins were generally working stiffs, someone was probably paying them to be out here. The presence of a too-luxurious carriage and tent were obvious signs that their employer was along for the ride. And really, the best way to stop an assassin from doing anything is to threaten the source of his pay.

The fact that a dozen men had emerged from the tents around the campsite and none made a move toward me was a pretty good sign that my theory was sound.

I'd just never given consideration to exactly *who* might have been paying these guys. I backed my hostage up toward the carriage, keeping him in front of me. I whispered into his ear, "Now, good prince, if we're all calm and businesslike, we can all avoid a lot of pain. Understand?"

"Y-Yes."

"You hold the purse strings, correct?"

"Yes."

"Then you're going to order all these men back into their tents to wait quietly for your return."

"They will come after me," he said, an almost admirable note of royal steel returning to his voice.

"That's the point of a hostage, isn't it? If they do, their paymaster ends with a slit throat. That wouldn't be in their best interest, would it? Unless you hauled their gold with you all the way from Dermonica, and you don't appear to be that stupid."

"You won't get away with this."

"And you want to survive to see justice done, don't you?"

I felt him tense under my grip and I prodded him with the dagger.

"Do it. Things are messy enough."

For a moment I thought he was angry enough to risk his life just so his assassins would have a chance to take me out. But he shouted, "Everyone, back in your tents! Await my return. Do not interfere!"

They did as they were told, though they stared at me unnervingly as they did so. Each one of them was looking for some sort of opening. No way was I going to get that second horse. I kept from showing my back until everyone was back in their tents. Then I pushed Prince Oliver up into the carriage and followed him into the driver's seat.

"Pick up the reins."

He stared at me.

"Pick them up!" I prodded with the dagger.

He reached down and grabbed the reins for the one horse and held them up between us.

"Now drive us out of here!"

"How?"

We stared at each other. For a moment I was speechless.

After that moment I said, "You're kidding, right?"

He wasn't.

Of course the bloody prince has no idea how to drive a horse-drawn carriage.

Amazing how quickly a hostage can go from indispensable to completely useless. I reached up to his collar and yanked the robe down to his elbows, restraining his arms. Then I grabbed his nightcap and pulled it tightly over his eyes.

"Hey."

"Shut up and don't move." I grabbed the reins from him and did my best to drive our lone steed out on the road without putting the dagger away.

The question arises at this point, why didn't I just run?

I had safely disengaged myself from the group of feral teens, Weasel's crew, and a score of Dermonica-employed assassins. My first priority was getting back to Lendowyn to sort out the mess caused by my drunken decision to use the Dark Lord Nâtlac's jewel. I didn't owe anything to Fearless Leader and crew.

Well, I owed them for the clothes, but I figured that was outweighed by them pointing a crossbow in my direction.

Really, any thief worth his fingers would have been long gone by now.

But I was never a particularly good thief.

I stopped the carriage on the road over the hill from the assassins' campsite, and the girls emerged from the forest. Grace directed the other six silently to board the carriage and climbed up next to me. As the weight shifted below us, Fearless Leader paid me her first compliment, "That was impressive."

"Who's there?" Prince Oliver said.

"You don't want to know, Your Highness," I said.

I got the horse moving, but he strained against the weight.

"Your Highness?" Grace asked.

"Yes." I bent down to talk into the carriage. "We're overloaded, toss anything down there that isn't nailed down."

"Who is he?" Grace asked.

"Crown Prince Oliver of Dermonica."

"Prince? What is *he* doing here?"

"Other than weighing us down? Good question."

Below us the carriage doors opened and tapestries, cushions, and open chests sailed out into the road.

"What *are* you doing here?" she asked the prince.

"You know very well," he whispered.

"Bringing yourself and a score of hired assassins across the border," I said. "It looks like an act of war to me."

"Harboring *you* is an act of war."

The way Prince Oliver said that gave me a chill unrelated to the winter air. I knew I had a couple of thieves' guilds after me, but the prince implied something a slight bit more significant than conning a group of provincial outlaws out of their own ill-gotten gains.

"What did he do to you?" Grace asked.

"Ask your friend."

Way to put me on the spot, Your Highness.

I summoned up Snake's most intimidating tone and said, "She was asking *you*."

"Fine," he muttered with something like resignation. "I can think of worse uses for my last words than to condemn this villain for his crimes."

Grace snorted. "Don't preach to me the evils of thievery. I know the way the world works. You men in pretty robes are as much the thief as us, no less so because you do so at the point of a sword and some king's 'law.'"

Prince Oliver laughed, and there was so little humor in it that it began to terrify me what he might say next. I didn't want to hear.

I didn't want Grace to hear.

"This man is no simple thief, and his crimes extend far beyond the simple taking of property. Dermonica is peaceful, our people were prosperous from trade, trade that came through Fellhaven, our one navigable ocean port. For decades we had an agreement with the pirates of Darkblood Reef."

I knew where this was going, the use of the past tense was a big clue—as was the sudden diplomatic interest in trade routes through Lendowyn.

"Tribute," I whispered.

"You are aptly named," Prince Oliver said.

"What happened?" Grace asked.

"The legendary Snake won't elaborate for you?" The prince waited me to fill the silence. When I didn't, he continued. "For the safety of Fellhaven we paid the pirates a third of the gold from trade in a year. In return, we had safe passage, and our enemies did not.

But this prior year, our diplomats left on a ship bearing gold, and arrived on a ship bearing lead."

"A whole ship full of gold?" I heard a tone of awe in Grace's voice. Enough so that I knew that she hadn't yet thought through the consequences of such an act.

"Five days later, our ship returned to Fellhaven Bay. They had tied the crew to the masts, and once it reached the inner harbor, they set it aflame. As that ship crashed aground on the docks, the pirates came."

"What did they—"

"Fellhaven was sacked, burned to the ground. Thousands dead."

"You had no defenders?" I snapped.

"After five decades of peace, and no sign of the pirates breaking it? There was only the city watch, who massed to battle the fire on the docks. Every death there is on your hands." He turned toward me, nightcap still pulled over his eyes. "Do the courtesy of at least having the courage to look me in the eyes when you kill me."

"Yeah, about that?" I said. "Not going to happen."

I pushed him, and he tumbled off the bench into a snowdrift by the side of the road. We rode off to the sounds of him cursing Snake's name.

Grace stared at me with wide eyes, "Why did you do that?"

"He was weighing us down," I said. "And I can't kill him. Against the rules, right?"

CHAPTER 10

We rode the carriage into the dawn. Fearless Leader spent the time in uncharacteristic silence. While that wasn't unwelcome, she seemed to be spending her time digesting the confirmation of my identity by a credible witness.

I had some idea how she might have felt.

The more I heard about this Snake character, the less I liked him. It wasn't the thievery, I'm no hypocrite. Not about that at least. I held about the same opinion of the state of the world as Grace had elaborated to the prince. If the lords were entitled to tax the people, I felt entitled to tax particular lords back. And, at one point in my outlaw career, I would have literally given my right arm to have been able to pull off something of the brazen magnitude of what this Snake guy had managed. Maybe I still would.

But . . .

There was a deep ugliness about it. I'd always said, as I had to Fearless Leader, that there were two types of thieves. Thug and pickpocket, brawn or stealth.

Snake was something else. Yes, he seemed to slip in and out unseen, rather than beating people upside the head to swipe their purse. But when he left, chaos swirled in his wake. There was nothing subtle or low profile about his thefts, and they had deadly repercussions.

Beyond the skill, beyond the riches, Snake had a talent for leaving behind something more than a rich dullard with a lighter purse or some arrogant priest short one golden icon. The thieves' guilds he had conned had been left in a state just short of open war, and I couldn't help but think that Prince Oliver's thirst for blood, and his fear, were justified.

I know that if I had contemplated some of the jobs Snake had done, the potential consequences would have given me pause.

Even the snippets of other stories I heard about him from the feral girls' club had a similar unpleasant feel to them. His callousness was worthy of some of the most arrogant nobles I'd heard of.

It also raised the same question that Fearless Leader had raised to me when we had met: Snake had stolen a kingdom's worth of treasure a few times over.

Where was it?

Why did he continue to leave wreckage in his wake? This wasn't a line of work that encouraged longevity. If someone kept up the outlaw life after the kind of heists Snake had pulled, they'd have to be a special kind of insane.

Or the proceeds were going somewhere else.

I took a fork in the road and Grace quietly said, "Lendowyn is due south of here."

"I know, but so is Dermonica."

My dialogue with Prince Oliver had helped to determine the direction we needed to go. We were north and inland, while Lendowyn was south and on the coast. However, a straight-line course due south would cut right through the Kingdom of Dermonica, which didn't seem the greatest idea if I was ostensibly responsible for an act of war against them.

"So where are you going?"

The next worst option. "The other kingdom between us and Lendowyn."

Grünwald.

It was the last place I personally wanted to go, but I couldn't really explain my history with Grünwald without revealing the fact I wasn't quite the infamous Snake they thought I was. It didn't seem politic to dissuade Grace and company from the impression Prince Oliver had made. Besides, while the current King Dudley of Grünwald might have a grudge against the Princess Frank Blackthorne—since I was directly responsible for the death of his mother the Evil Queen Fiona—as far as I knew he had nothing against Snake and no way to connect Snake with Frank. It was probably more concerning that it was a hotbed for worship of the Dark Lord Nâtlac, but we were probably okay if we avoided running into the royal family.

So unless we wanted to go hundreds of miles out of the way, weaving our way to the coast, Grünwald it was.

Like most other consequential mistakes in my life, it made sense at the time.

We stripped the Dermonica coat of arms from the carriage and kept to the wilderness, avoiding towns, sleeping under the stars. I would have preferred an inn. But even if Snake wasn't a wanted man in Grünwald—and I had the sense not to just assume that—my traveling companions stood out for their salvaged armor and choice of jewelry, if nothing else. I was hoping to make it back within the borders of Lendowyn before I had to explain them to anyone.

Of course, I had no idea what to do about them once we crossed into Lendowyn. I barely had a coherent idea of what I was going to do about myself. I had no idea how to reverse what had happened, or even if it could be reversed. And while I was still feeling oddly disassociated with the body I wore, a feeling that got worse the more I learned about the prior occupant, what bothered me more was the idea of Snake running around in the princess's body.

It was wrong in a fundamental way that gave me a sour feeling in a stomach that didn't really belong to me.

That was my real mistake, unleashing this guy on the Lendowyn court. I had to do something to correct it, even if I didn't know right now what that was.

Fortunately, after the episode with Prince Oliver, the girls were a lot less aggressive about questioning me. I was able to sit down at the edge of the campsite and allow my mind to spin around in nonproductive circles without any interruption.

If anything, it made my mood worse.

The second night the girls had caught something and were cooking it over the campfire. Sometime after the sun went down, Mary, the tall redhead, came over to me and said, "You should eat something."

I grunted. I'd been begrudging the signals from Snake's body. Hunger, pain, fatigue—it wasn't really me that was feeling these things. It was some other guy. Someone I didn't particularly like.

Mary looked at me for a few moments, then sighed and turned around. There is something deeply unfair about someone twelve years your junior making you feel stupid.

"You're right," I said.

She turned around and said, "So you still talk. Thought you been struck mute."

"I've been preoccupied."

"With what?"

With the fact that I'm lying to you and there's nothing in Lendowyn other than a bunch more awkward questions . . .

"What are you cooking?" I asked.

"Half a rabbit."

I involuntarily glanced at the mute girl.

Mary laughed. "Not Rabbit, *rabbit.*"

"Glad you find that funny."

She walked up until she was uncomfortably close to me. She placed a hand on my arm and studied my face, and I remembered what Grace had said, "sold to the White Rock Thieves' Guild when she was twelve." That generally meant only one thing, and that knowledge made her proximity even worse.

Seeing this kid here, and knowing her history, made me start regretting the time I'd spent with a working girl back in Westmark. That regret meant that my time as "Snake" was a complete failure in every measure I could think of.

"Why you here?" she whispered.

"What?"

She leaned forward until her lips were nearly brushing my cheek. I froze out of fear that any movement might bring us into more inappropriate contact. "I asked, 'Why you here?'"

I stared past her, into the campfire. "Your Fearless Leader is holding me hostage, remember?"

She raised a hand to my cheek and turned my face toward her. "No."

"What do you—"

She placed her finger on my lips and continued. "You pretend she is. She pretends she is. She's acting because she doesn't know what else to do. *You're* acting because ..."

"I'm not acting."

She cradled my chin and shook her own head. "I'm not stupid."

Something about her proximity and body language became threatening for a whole host of other reasons.

"I don't know what game you're playing. But I know a man who let a whole city burn for the sake of some gold ain't going to help us wayward girls out of the goodness of his heart. What I hear, you don't have one."

"Maybe the stories are a bit overblown."

"And maybe there's some other reasons you have us along." She let go of my chin. "You were right, what you told Grace. Two types of people. When White Rock held me, I got to know both. The brutes, they were rough, violent—but they had no secrets, and you knew if you gave what they wanted you only hurt a little. But the smooth-talking ones, the ones with secrets, those were dangerous. I think you have too many secrets."

She made me wonder if Grace was the real one in charge here.

"You're overthinking this." I tried to sound disarming. "I just want to get to Lendowyn in one piece."

"I owe Grace my life."

"I gathered that."

"We all do."

"Yes?"

"And we—our group—is her life. All she has, her only family." She placed her hands on my shoulders and leaned forward to whisper in my ear. *"You do anything to take that away from her I will rip off your man-tackle with my bare hands and fry it up in a skillet with butter and onions."*

She stepped away from me.

"What about the rules?"

"I say anything about killing you?" She smiled and her voice resumed a normal tone. "So you want any of that rabbit?"

I shook my head. "I don't think I'm that hungry."

She walked back to the campfire.

At least the short confrontation managed to snap me out of the diminishing spiral of obsessive self-pity before I disappeared up my own backside. Ever since I'd thrown the prince of Dermonica into the roadside slush, I'd been half ignoring the girls. Now that I started paying attention again, I could see that any hero worship had evaporated. Even the youngest, Thea, seemed to peer from under her tightly wrapped curls with suspicion.

And I couldn't really blame them.

I considered telling them the truth, but I couldn't quite decide if that would make things worse or not.

*   *   *

We rode into Grünwald, avoiding towns and any concentrations of people. I sat above, and the girls took turns sharing a seat with me as I drove our horse over the ill-used back roads. The first day passed with Grace, then Mary, neither saying much to me. The second day, Laya sat next to me, crossbow riding across her knees.

For close to an hour, she said nothing, watching the road ahead. Unlike her elder companions the prior day, she didn't seem to be avoiding conversation. The silence didn't weigh so heavily.

"It is true, isn't it?"

"What?" I snapped upright. I had relaxed to the point that, when she finally spoke, it startled the hell out of me.

"What the man said about you?"

"Prince Oliver?"

"Yes."

To be honest, I didn't have a clue. "I'm not going to take issue with it."

"I see."

What I said earlier about the silence not being oppressive with Laya ceased to be applicable at this point.

"All those people . . . How?" she asked.

"How what?"

"How do you stop feeling that?"

I glanced at her, and she wasn't even facing my direction. Her eyes were unfocused as she stared ahead at something other than the road. I didn't think I wanted to know what she saw right then.

"You don't want to know that."

"Why not?" She sucked in a breath and I could hear her trying not to sob. "Why not?" she whispered again.

"Because it costs too much."

"It costs too much to feel. I want to be like you. I don't want to care any—"

"Stop it!" I snapped.

She faced me, cowering, eyes wide and shiny.

"You want to stop feeling for anyone but yourself, is that what you want? You want to be able to murder a man and sleep at night? You want to dispose of the few shreds of humanity you've been able to hold on to? Is that what you want? To become a heartless, merciless bastard like the legendary Snake?"

Her lower lip quivered, but she couldn't help but nod.

I leaned over and quietly said, "And if a man holds up a bag of gold and says, 'give me Thea,' you want to be able to say yes?"

"What? No—"

"And when the wolves are chasing you down, you want to be able to trip the mute girl to distract them while you escape?"

"Rabbit? That's not—"

"And if I held a knife to your throat and said, 'you or Grace,' you want to be able to say—"

"Stop it!" She was crying now and making no effort to hide it. *"Stop!"*

I sat upright and faced the road again. Laya quietly sobbed next to me. After making the poor abused kid cry, I felt as close to Snake as I was likely to get. "Being a heartless bastard is not as fun as it looks."

CHAPTER 11

"We should stop at the next town."

"What?" Grace's eyes narrowed in suspicion. "We're avoiding towns."

"Because you don't exactly blend in." I gestured at the girls surrounding the campfire, all busily eating pieces of some small game animal Laya had skewered with her crossbow. Between the mishmash armor and the grisly trophies they looked like a troop of slightly stunted goblins. "If we don't get you some more mundane clothing, there's no way we'll get close to Lendowyn Castle without attracting the wrong kind of attention."

The girl with the close-cropped hair objected. "You not getting me in no dress." After a moment I remembered her name.

"Krys—" I started.

"No! I'm not!"

"Listen to the man," Grace said. She gave me a sidelong glance, "He seems to have some clue what he's talking about."

"He's a man," Krys said. "Since when do we take orders from some man?"

"No one's giving any orders but me," Grace snapped.

"Don't look like it," Krys said. "What's the point of all this, if some guy comes in to make us all pretty little girls."

"This guy is taking us to a hoard that will mean we—"

Krys stood up. "Ogre crap!"

Grace stood up. "What?"

I noticed that Krys had her hand on the pommel of a dagger in her belt. I saw, across the campfire, Laya reaching for her crossbow.

"I said Snake isn't leading you anywhere he don't want to go."

"We're going where *I* want us to go."

I stood up myself and said, "Why don't we all calm down?"

Grace spun to glare at me with a look that was comprised entirely of the thought, "You're not helping."

Krys pulled her dagger and Mary scrambled to interpose herself between the two girls. But Mary had misjudged where Krys was headed. Krys moved around her and Grace to face me. "To the hells with you, master thief. I lost what I lost, suffered what I suffered, and all I won was a chance to be who I am. You ain't taking that. One of us dies first."

Grace yelled at her, "Put that down! We have rules!"

Krys kept moving toward me, and I took a couple of steps back to remove myself from the others. Krys was one of the taller girls, around Grace and Mary in age. If I had still been the princess we might have been more evenly matched. As it was, I had the advantage in weight and reach that meant she wasn't going to win a fight unless the other girls dove in after her.

Something in her eyes told me she didn't care.

I held up my hands and said, "All I was talking about is dressing in a way that won't draw attention, from the guilds or the militia, or the wat—"

"You want to make me into a little girl again!"

I opened my mouth. I was about to snap something about how it was just some clothes . . . But, to Krys, it wasn't. She said it was who she was.

Who she was.

I shook my head. "I don't want to change who you are."

"You said you want me to dress like a girl."

I crouched so I wasn't hovering over her anymore. "No, I just want you guys to stand out less."

She lowered the dagger and bit her lip. Her eyes were shiny, reflecting the campfire.

"All I want," I told her, "is for anyone seeing us to see what they expect to see. That could be a frilly little girl, or a farm boy."

"Y-you . . . you don't care if I dress like a boy?"

"No. Just look the part." I shrugged. "I was never too fond of wearing dresses myself."

"I . . ." Krys ran at me. I had a brief moment to see everyone tense before she tackled me. Then she had her arms around my neck and was sobbing into my shoulder. "Thank you."

"You're welcome." I patted her on the back. "Maybe you can let go of the knife now?"

"What?"

I winced. "You're stabbing me."

She sprang back from me, the dagger sailing off to my right, causing Mary and Grace to dodge aside. "Oh gods, I'm sorry. Are you all right?"

I rubbed my shoulder where the point of her dagger had jabbed me. "It's fine."

Mary picked up the wayward dagger and Grace stepped forward. She may have been about the same height as Krys, but she seemed to tower over the girl. "What were you thinking?"

"I—"

"This isn't just you!"

"S-sorry—"

"Of all the stupid things to get angry about—"

"Grace," I said.

She spun around to face me. "What?"

"Go easy on her."

She leveled a finger at me. "You're not in charge here!"

"No, but I know what it's like."

"Stay out of this!" Grace snapped. She marched across, grabbed Krys' arm, and marched her away from everyone else. Krys went meekly, letting Grace berate her until they were out of earshot.

I stood and rubbed my shoulder again. I could feel some warm wetness smearing my skin under my shirt.

Great.

Mary walked up to me, twirling Krys's discarded dagger in her right hand. "You handled that well."

"Then why am I bleeding?"

"What you mean, Mr. Snake?"

"What did I mean?"

"You 'know what it's like.'" The dagger stopped twirling, hilt toward me. "What what's like?"

"I just know what she's going through."

"You do?"

I didn't answer her. I just watched the shadows of Grace and Krys across the clearing from the campfire. I couldn't really go into why I empathized with Krys right now. How it was that the legendary thief Snake, cold heartless bastard that he was, could be moved by the fact that a young girl felt as if she was trapped in the wrong body.

My logic won out and we headed for the last Grünwald town before the border with Lendowyn. As we packed up and departed, the looks I got from half the girls suggested that Snake's façade was beginning to crumble. Only in Krys's case did this seem a good thing. She smiled at me, and it seemed genuine, but Laya wouldn't even meet my gaze. Grace was obviously angry, and Mary stared at me in a way that gave the impression that she knew exactly how out of character my reaction to Krys had been.

As I drove the single horse, the mute girl, Rabbit, sat next to me. She was one of the youngest girls aside from curly-haired Thea, and almost as small, a tiny bundle of bone and wiry muscle topped by a cap of straight jet-black hair. She scrambled effortlessly into the bench next to me and shrugged as if to apologize for being a lousy conversationalist.

After we were on the road for about half an hour, she curled up next to me like a cat and fell asleep.

I appreciated the lack of drama.

It gave me time to think, which may not have been the best idea. The closer I got to Lendowyn, the closer I was coming to an inevitable decision. I was going to have to tell these girls the truth, or I was going to have to abandon them somewhere. I was leaning toward the truth, since it didn't seem fair to take them all this way just to ditch them. At this point the only reason I hesitated was because that would also mean admitting there was no treasure to share, and I suspected the news would be taken badly.

Slipping away felt wrong, but I'd seen enough evidence to tell me that these girls were quite able to take care of themselves, and I'd at least be leaving them in a climate a bit warmer than where I'd found them.

As usual, I couldn't come to a firm conclusion.

"Yeah," I whispered, "I'll think of something when the time comes." *Because improvisation has worked so well for me so far.*

Rabbit surprised me by suddenly grabbing my knee and squeezing a lot harder than someone her size should have been able to do.

I winced. She was now wide awake and staring down the road ahead of us. Her nostrils flared and she shook her head.

"What?"

She made a grunt and started waving her hand, palm flat toward my chest. I stared, not understanding, and her gestures got more forceful until her palm struck my chest. She held her hand there and shook her head violently.

I drew the horse to a stop, rolling the carriage to

the edge of the road. She exhaled and nodded, removing both her hands.

"What's the matter?" I asked. She had already scrambled to the ground before the entire question was out of my mouth. I hung up the reins and climbed down myself.

She walked about ten yards ahead, and stood in the middle of the road, looking upward and slowly turning around.

Grace stuck her head out of the carriage. "Why are we stopping?"

"I don't know," I told her.

I walked up next to Rabbit and saw her nostrils flare as she froze and looked up at the sky. I followed her gaze and didn't see anything. I started to ask again, "What—"

Then I smelled it.

Smoke.

Not just the smell of something burning. There was a familiar character to what I smelled. "No, it can't be what I think . . ."

Rabbit turned to look at me with a furrowed brow.

"No," I repeated.

" 'No' what?" Grace asked as she jumped out of the carriage. Mary and Krys followed her out.

"Nothing. I'm imagining things."

She asked Rabbit, "What's going on?" Behind her, the rest of the girls had dismounted and were looking around. Mary and Laya were giving me a few suspicious glances.

Rabbit pointed at her nose then swept her hand toward the road in front of us.

"Something's burning ahead of us," I said. "We should probably check it out before we go on."

"Rabbit?"

Rabbit nodded, agreeing with me I suppose.

"Fine." Grace sounded irritated. She turned around and said, "Mary, go with them and check out what's going on. The rest of you get back in, in case we have to leave in a hurry. Laya, you keep watch with me." She climbed up next to the reins and Laya followed with her crossbow.

Mary walked up next to us and told Rabbit, "You lead."

We weren't going to get the girls a change of clothes at the next town.

Mary and I followed Rabbit through the woods, along game trails that were barely visible under a fresh snow cover. As we went on, the woods became deathly quiet. Even the wind fell silent, leaving only the sound of our own breathing and our footsteps crunching through the snow.

The smell got worse, almost choking in intensity. Our footsteps grew silent as the snow melted away to soft forest loam under our feet.

We were upon the scene before I was prepared for it—even though I had half expected it ever since I caught the first whiff of what had happened here.

Mary gasped as we emerged from the tree line about a hundred strides downhill from the town we'd been approaching.

The remains of the town.

It had burned so badly that no snow remained on

the hillside or the trees surrounding it. There had been a wall, but all that remained were a few random logs pointing black fingers at the sky. The remains steamed in the cold air.

"What happened here?" Mary asked.

I started walking toward the ruin. There was no ignoring the familiar scent of sulfur and brimstone. I felt my chest tighten as I whispered, "Dragon fire."

"Dragon?" Mary ran up next to me. "You say 'dragon'?"

I kept walking up toward the smoldering corpse of the town. No recognizable building remained standing, and I began to smell ugly things underneath the dragon fire, other things that had burned. "No. No. No! Damn it, Lucille! What did you do? *What did you do?!*"

Mary grabbed my arm, and I realized that I'd been shouting. "Dragon? *What dragon?*" she yelled at me. "We have to get out of here!"

I shook my head. I couldn't bring myself to move. I couldn't force the idea that Lucille might have done this into what I knew of the world. Not *my* Lucille.

But I'd seen her in combat. I saw what she could do when she was angry. What would she be capable of if she wasn't near death from dozens of arrow wounds and facing a guy with a magic sword? Even before that, when we'd suffered the enchantment that swapped us around in the first place, in the first few minutes in her new draconic body she set another town on fire. That might have been an accident, but . . .

"Move," Mary screamed at me, tugging at my arm.

She turned toward Rabbit and yelled, "Run! Get back to the others!"

Rabbit didn't move. She faced back the way we'd come.

Mary let go of me and ran toward her. "What are you doing? We need to . . ." Her voice trailed off with a weak strangled sound that turned into something that sounded like an obscenity that would have been harsh and inappropriate coming from an old goblin sailor, much less a teenage girl. I turned away from the ruined town and saw Mary and Rabbit staring back toward the woods. I followed their gaze and repeated Mary's curse.

A line of black-armored Grünwald militia had emerged from the tree line.

I stepped between the approaching troops and the two girls and raised my hands in what I hoped was a nonthreatening gesture. A bull of a man broke ranks to walk up toward me. He had the typically elaborate Grünwald armor, all black leather, spikes, and embossed skulls. He wore a helmet with a visor in the shape of a screaming demon.

We weren't going to run away or fight our way out of it, so we were left with trying to negotiate. Fortunately, of the three, that was my strength. I just hoped Mary would catch on and play along.

I faced the approaching commander and said, "Thank the black soul of the Dark Lord Nâtlac you've arrived. You won't believe what we've had to—"

The guy interrupted me with a gauntleted hand slamming me in the side of the head.

The world went black.

CHAPTER 12

"Okay," I groaned some interminable time later. After the pain of the word sank into my skull, I added, "Talking is bad."

"Ahh, the prodigal wakes!"

My eyes shot open. I knew that voice.

A fuzzy smear almost the size of a man dominated my blurry field of vision. I shook my head to try and clear it, and my consciousness rattled around like a dried pea in a coconut husk. The blur defined itself as I squinted.

"Dudley?"

The recently elevated king of Grünwald stared down at me, smiling. "It has been a long, long time, hasn't it?"

He knows! Somehow the bastard knows who I am.

It was clear to me from the predatory grin on that pudgy face that Dudley knew that inside the body of the grandmaster thief Snake resided the soul of his nemesis, Frank Blackthorne.

As that thought crossed my mind, I completely forgot the first principle of how the universe expresses its hate for me; things *never* go wrong in exactly the way I expect. In fact, the more certain I am of any one ill outcome, the more severely the reality diverges. The idea he knew I was Frank hit me with such certainty that I almost missed when Dudley took me off the main trail and headed off into uncharted woods.

"What did you say?" I asked, because I didn't believe what I'd thought I'd heard.

"I said that I always knew you'd come back here, brother. I never stopped watching for you."

Brother?

Dudley leaned forward so we were almost nose-to-nose. "The life of an outlaw never did quite suit you, did it, Bartholomew? Or should I call you 'Snake' now?"

Oh crap.

Dudley gave me a self-satisfied smile as he congratulated himself on outsmarting me. "You're our father's son, Bartholomew. I knew, as soon as Mother died, that I would see you return. Just like him, you could never accept the shift of power to Mother's line. But I'm afraid your claim on this crown died with him."

Dudley backed away from me, giving me the first clear view of where I was. I sat on a wooden chair in a windowless stone room. I saw a cot and a table bearing a small oil lantern that provided the only light in the room. Two large men in Grünwald armor flanked a rusty iron door a couple of short strides behind Dudley.

"So if I renounce my claim to the crown you'll let us all go?"

Dudley laughed. "I see you still have your sense of humor."

"You're too established; I would need an army to challenge you."

He spun around and backhanded me. I'll give the twerp credit, he was able to muster a lot more force than I expected from someone with the constitution of day-old pea soup. "Do not mock me. Don't pretend I'm a fool, even in jest."

"No, Dudley. You are no fool."

Some of my true feelings must have leaked out in my voice, and he struck me again. Between that, and still being dizzy from waking up, I lost my balance and tumbled out of the chair.

"You think I don't know what you've been doing?" He yelled down at me. *"You think I don't know?"* He threw a kick into my stomach. It was weak but elicited a groan. "Why else would you amass such wealth if not to raise an army against me?" He placed his boot on my shoulder and rolled me onto my back. "And why bring six maidens into my demesne all by yourself, if not to make a sacrifice to gain the Dark Lord's favor and seal your victory?"

I couldn't help myself. I started laughing.

It was just so perfectly *wrong.* I couldn't even stop when he started kicking me again. I wheezed and spat out, "They aren't maidens." But it was so low I don't think he heard me. After a few kicks, he finally landed a lucky shot that slammed the breath from me. I gasped, my giggle fit broken.

He leaned over me, panting from his exertion. "Funny now? Is it? Well here's . . . the punch line." He took another deep breath. "The Dark Lord's . . . getting his sacrifice. But I'm going . . . to officiate. And you're . . . the prize offering."

He straightened up and waved at the two guards. One opened the iron door.

I sat up as Dudley walked away.

"Royal blood . . . and my own flesh. Going to count . . . for something." He turned around as he reached the door. "Enjoy the accommodations . . . the King's Suite is . . . the most palatial . . . cell in the dungeon."

The door shut me in with a slam, creaking as it locked.

"I don't believe this," I whispered. I stood with a groan, Snake's bruised body creaking almost as much as the door had.

I hadn't thought my opinion of my body's prior occupant could sink any lower, but finding out that he was a bastard prince of the Grünwald court . . .

"Bartholomew? *Really?* No wonder you went by 'Snake.'"

I had only a vague idea of the history of the Grünwald royals. But I was clear on a few points: the past king had a few bastard children, of which Snake must be one. And given Dudley's little rant, it was obvious that Snake's relation with his stepmom was strained at best. Especially since Queen Fiona had assassinated her husband. Given that Grünwald traced royal lines via paternal descent, if Snake was Dudley's older brother, he'd have a more legitimate claim to the crown than Dudley did. I suppose desperation helped give Dudley a rudimentary spine.

And I had unleashed this—literal—bastard on the Lendowyn court; a completely amoral royal with a grudge; a *Grünwald* royal, which earned him bonus points in the ruthless evil department; someone who had the ability to finance his own army.

That suddenly placed a more sinister spin—if one was needed—on the fact that a dragon had obliterated a Grünwald border town. In isolation it made no sense. But if Snake—aka Prince Bartholomew—was influencing Lendowyn, it could be a feint in a coming invasion.

I sat on the cot, buried my face in my hands, and marveled at the infinite capacity of things to get worse.

As always, "worse" is a relative term.

After confirming that my skills weren't up to opening the door from the inside, I collapsed on the cot and contemplated exactly how bad things had gotten. One bad decision on my part, and it wasn't just me suffering for it: I bore responsibility for the six girls who had followed me into this dark hole. Lucille may have become the spearpoint in a war against Grünwald because of someone she thought was me. Then there were the victims who died in that attack, and the thousands who would die in a war between Lendowyn and Grünwald.

I think I had a good grasp on what Laya must have felt when she asked me how to *not* feel. "I don't know," I whispered, my eyes blurred for reasons other than a blow to the head.

A voice answered me. "This is amusing."

"Who's there?" I bolted upright, looking for the

source of the voice. The door remained shut, and the small oil lamp shone into every corner of the stone cell. As I frantically looked for the speaker, the lamp guttered and started burning with a dimmer, redder light. As the shadows in the room darkened, the voice laughed.

The sound dug into my skin like tiny needles pulling spools of barbed thread behind them.

I got unsteadily to my feet as the cell plunged into a flickering ruddy twilight.

"Enjoying my wedding gift, Frank?" The voice asked.

"You?" My mouth had gone so dry my voice cracked.

"Me."

My eyes adjusted to the dimness. The walls of the cell were gone, replaced by a plain of living flagstones that receded into the darkness, broken only by veiny stalactites vanishing upward into more darkness. I looked down at myself and I was no longer wearing Snake/Bartholomew's skin. I stood in the long-dead body of Frank Blackthorne, just as I had the last time I stood before this red-tinted landscape of pulsing pillars and flagstones made of eyes, teeth, and oddly placed fingers.

I looked back up because the floor was staring at me.

I turned around, and faced the handsome figure of a man sitting on a throne of bone and sinew.

The Dark Lord Nâtlac said, "Boo."

CHAPTER 13

He appeared just as I remembered him, much as I'd tried to forget. He wore the perfect form of a man, perfect enough that looking at him caused an itch in the back of the eyes that told you that what you saw and what was really there were two very different things. He still wore a midnight black cloak whose stitched leather bore the outlines of human faces, faces whose lips twitched against the stitching binding them closed, and whose eyes moved behind eyelids that had been sewn shut.

"You planned this," I said when I could find my voice again.

"Oh, far from it." He chuckled with a sound like someone sprinkling tiny splinters of broken glass into my ears. "You *earned* that token. But it is only what it is. Your own snarled fate led you here."

"So you're here to gloat?"

"No, Frank. The rituals to consecrate sacrifices in my name brought you all into my presence."

"'You all?'"

He gestured and I saw we weren't alone. I saw a huddled form and involuntarily snapped, "What are you doing to her?"

"Nothing, Frank. They are not yet mine. What they bring here now, as with you, is solely their own."

I ran to the cowering body. It was Rabbit. She seemed smaller and less gaunt, but I recognized her face as she huddled shivering against the cobblestones. I bent down and touched her bare shoulder and she winced.

"Daddy, please, no," she whispered, and the sound of her voice was so unexpected that I jerked my hand away.

"Rabbit?"

"Please," she sobbed. "No."

"She may be here." Nâtlac's voice burrowed into my ears. "But what she sees is what she brought with her. Your privileged history with me allows you to see partly through the veil."

"But she's a mute," I said.

"And what are you?"

I opened my mouth, but nothing came out. If I strode here in my original body, a body that had been worm food for months, of course poor Rabbit could regain her tongue. But, as I watched her cower, naked, from her invisible father, I couldn't think the return of her speech was worth it.

Several steps away Laya sat on the ground, legs crossed. She appeared mostly as I remembered, except for the blood covering her hands and arms, and the scar on her face was a fresh wound. "Laya? Are you all right?"

She didn't respond. She stared glassy-eyed into a pile of shiny entrails heaped in her lap.

Even though I knew what I saw was some sort of

illusion, I shouted, *"Laya?"* afraid that she'd been disemboweled.

She hadn't.

I saw, though she was about the same age as the Laya I knew, she was much more gaunt—starvation-thin, showing the edges of her skull and the knobs on her wrist as she slowly brought a bloody flap of meat from the pile on her lap up to her lips. I turned away as she opened a ghoulish mouth of red-stained teeth and began to chew.

My own nightmares are sort of tame, I thought.

"Hello, have you seen my daddy?" I spun around and saw a small boy, maybe about five years old, dressed in crusty rags. His face was smeared with filth except where tears had washed stripes of white against the skin.

"I lost my daddy."

The boy didn't wait for an answer. He turned away from me and wandered off, asking the darkness, "Have you seen my daddy? Where's my daddy?"

It took me a moment before I realized I was watching a much younger Krys. *"She's been homeless since she was six and the Delmark watch took her dad to the dungeons."* I watched her disappear into the darkness.

"Why put them through this?"

His laugh sliced through my skull. "Suffering needs no reason. It just *is*. I find it admirable."

"Admirable?"

"Each soul is unique in its particular pain. There is beauty in it."

A baby cried in the darkness and I ran toward it. When I came upon her, the tiny body was blue, cold, and stiff. I recognized the strawberry-blond curls plastered against her scalp. "Thea?"

"I turn away no offerings. And children can bear so much more before they're broken."

I placed a hand on the cold body, and it sucked in a breath and began screaming bloody murder again. The skin was suddenly warm and pink. "What?"

"You're walking through their dreams, their fears, their pain. They honor you by presenting their wounds."

I didn't feel honored.

I glanced up as I touched the infant Thea and I could see another scene dimly through the low red light, woods that seemed familiar. "But ... they said she was abandoned in the woods ... she would have been nine or ten."

"The little one was abandoned long before her family left her in the woods."

The baby stopped crying. The skin had gone cold again.

I shook my head. "I don't want to see any more."

"Yes," Nâtlac said, his words burrowing into my brain like a thousand hungry beetles. "You do."

I turned to look at the Dark Lord, and his smile was a knife slash across my eyes. I looked away, and baby Thea was gone, replaced by Mary, equally naked. She lay on her back, staring upward, not seeing me. Her body was roped with bruises, and blood stained her legs.

"No," I said, closing my eyes. "I don't want to see this."

I started getting to my feet, and something grabbed

my wrist. My eyes shot open and I was looking directly into Mary's staring eyes. Nâtlac's realm was gone, replaced by a shabby room with a bed and a few sticks of furniture. Mary stared into my eyes, but somehow I also saw the scene from outside myself as well. I wasn't myself or Snake, I was someone else with shaggy gray hair growing everywhere but my scalp. Mary had sprung from the bed and had grabbed my/his wrist.

"You like it rough?" she whispered.

I/he tried to pull my/his arm away, and Mary's other hand came down, clawing at my/his eyes. My own eyes burned as I watched the stranger scream and cover his bloody face. He tried to block her, but she leaped on him. Despite the fact she was little more than half his size, he was slow and blinded and wasn't able to block it as she sank her teeth into the side of his face, coming away with pieces of his ear and cheek.

He threw her off of him and stumbled for the door.

That just gave her the chance to find a weapon.

He collapsed to his knees as a chair splintered across his back. He tried to get up and a splintered chair leg stabbed into the soft part of his back above the right kidney.

He bellowed, and Mary spat at him. "Rough? You like it rough?"

She pulled the chair leg out and stabbed him with it again, and again, and a third time before the wood broke off in the wound. I watched as she kept beating him, venting years of rage and anger in a few minutes. When it was done, she was as bloody as the corpse smeared on the ground, and most of the blood wasn't hers.

I backed away at the same time I realized I could back away.

Nâtlac's realm reasserted itself, and it was almost a relief.

Part of me wondered what was different about that guy, how awful he must have been to trigger that response. Another part of me knew that the only thing that marked him from any of the others the White Rock Thieves' Guild had given Mary to was the fact he was the *last* one.

I already felt a few qualms about how I had spent the first night in Snake's body. Now those qualms had blossomed into a full-blown self-loathing. Sure, I had *assumed* that I had been dealing with a willing businesswoman, but did I *know*? When I'd had to deal with a guild in the past, I know quite a number of my jobs had been less than voluntary . . .

Of all the times before, when I'd paid for my companionship, how many times had it been coerced?

And why had I waited until now to care?

"That's enough," I whispered.

"No, there are two more."

Mary disappeared, and I asked, "*Two* more?"

"No, I didn't mean this . . ." I turned toward the new voice, and saw Grace, Fearless Leader, on her knees, shaking her head. Unlike the others, her appearance in the world of nightmares hadn't changed. Body and clothing were pretty much as I had last seen her.

But her attitude . . .

Grace seemed to have collapsed inside herself. I

had seen some stress fractures in her commanding demeanor here and there as she struggled to keep rein on her little band. What I saw now was a complete collapse of the mask she wore. She shook as she wept uncontrollably.

I walked up to her, and she seemed tiny and much younger, kneeling on the ground. I reached out and touched her shoulder—

—she peered in through a window at a quartet of black-clad thugs. A woman was obviously dead at their feet, a pool of blood spreading beneath her. They held another man down on his knees, knife to his throat. One of the thugs asked, "Where's the brat you been givin' our secrets to?"

Another chimed in. "Give her up, we may just hurt you some."

Next to me, Grace whispered, "Father, don't."

The man on his knees moved only his eyes to look directly at us. He may have smiled slightly before he raised his head and spat in the face of the lead thug.

They slit his throat without any ceremony.

Grace gasped as his body fell face first onto the floor next to his wife. I squeezed her shoulder, but I wasn't really part of this vision, and she ignored me. She shook her head, sucking in breathless sobs and saying near silent words.

"Not . . . my . . . fault . . ."

Then her breath caught. I saw her eyes widen and the color drain from her face, and I turned to look at what new horror she was seeing.

"Oh no, Grace," I whispered, "don't do this to yourself."

The window was gone, and we faced a blasted plain under a moonless night sky. Five bodies were strewn in the mud, bodies broken, sightless eyes staring at the endless blackness above us. Mary, Laya, Krys, Rabbit, Thea ...

"This hasn't happened," I told her.

But I wasn't there, and she just kept shaking her head. "Not my fault."

I let go of her shoulder. "She shouldn't have to bear that weight."

"It is her weight to bear, Frank." I winced at the Dark Lord's voice.

"Why are you showing me this?"

"I am not showing you anything. These are their secrets to reveal."

I got slowly to my feet.

"One more, Frank."

"That was all the girls. There's no one left."

"No. There is one more sacrifice. Someone you want to meet."

"Who?" I said, even as a shadow coalesced out of the darkness, forming into an armored figure kneeling in supplication. The plate mail shone despite the dark ruddy light, the cascade of blond hair only slightly less so.

For several moments I stared, unbelieving.

"You must be kidding."

Unlike the others, this apparition heard me.

Sir Forsythe the Good turned to face me and smiled. "My Liege! The Dark Lord has truly answered my prayers."

CHAPTER 14

My first thought on seeing Sir Forsythe was that it was time for me to undergo my own trial by nightmare. That was only slightly unfair to him, since while he had pledged fealty to me, that was only *after* trying to kill me a few times. It was hard to completely trust anyone who had managed to somehow reconcile maiden-saving and monster-slaying with the worship of the Dark Lord Nâtlac. It was a bizarre bit of mental legerdemain that, frankly, made him look as crazy as a rabid goblin drunk on fermented mushrooms.

But he was also one of the few people around who knew me as I originally appeared, pre-princess.

"What are you doing here?"

"A final devotion before the usurper offers me to the Dark Lord." He shook his head sadly. "I had always expected my end would be on the battlefield fighting the forces of darkness."

You are *the forces of darkness.*

"No, why are you in Grünwald?"

"To find you, My Liege."

"What? How?" I had a brief surge of optimism that they had figured out what had happened.

"When you disappeared, suspicion immediately fell to your main rival for the Dark One's favor."

"When I . . . disappeared?" Something about the way Sir Forsythe spoke suggested something else was going on.

"The Dragon Prince was inconsolable when you were abducted from your chambers. Without a ransom demand there was no evidence of who took you and where."

The coward just ran away, great.

"Of your retainers, I am the one who knows the most of the secret ways through Grünwald, and the passages to enter their keep unseen. It was my sacred duty to find proof that Grünwald was behind your disappearance."

"That doesn't seem to have worked very well."

"I was betrayed, My Liege," he said. "I had barely slipped across the border and King Dudley's soldiers were waiting for me. I battled valiantly, but there were too many. I was overwhelmed."

I didn't say anything, but I suspected that his capture had less to do with any betrayal than it did with the fact that it was implausible that Sir Forsythe could sneak anywhere. The man was normally as subtle as a brick to the face.

"But I see that the Dragon Prince's suspicions have been vindicated. You are here—"

"Not exactly. Dudley doesn't even know he has me prisoner."

"My Liege?"

"You served Grünwald for a long time. I suppose you are familiar with the Bastard Prince Bartholomew?"

"Of course, a horrid man, exiled and driven to be a petty outlaw." Sir Forsythe shook his head. "Forgive me, My Liege, but what does Prince Bartholomew have to do with what is happening?"

"Everything, unfortunately."

It felt like hours later when I opened my eyes and found myself back on the cot in the dungeon cell that Dudley had left me in. However, from what I had experienced before in the Dark Lord's realm, I knew that it had only been a few minutes.

I took a few breaths to help the sense of disorientation pass. Being in Nâtlac's presence too long left a feeling like sharp gravel abrading the inside of my brain. I rubbed my temples, remembering that at some point I had heard the Dark Lord mentioning something suggesting that what his mother lacked in ambition, King Dudley made up for in stupidity.

I found it impossible to fault the sentiment.

King Dudley apparently hadn't known, thought of, or cared about the fact that the mass consecration in Nâtlac's presence would give the offerings a chance to communicate. Of course, most victims would be paralyzed by the inherent wrongness of the Dark Lord's presence and escape into their own nightmares like the girls had.

However, Sir Forsythe was an acolyte of Nâtlac, and the Dark Lord had actually crashed my wedding. We were both about as used to it as you could be. Even if I had been the Bastard Prince Bartholomew, Dudley expected his half brother to be familiar enough with the family religion to bring six girls into Grünwald specifically to sacrifice them.

Even if King Dudley the Dim thought it didn't matter because we were all locked up in the dungeons, it was a stupid risk.

Especially since it *did* matter.

Sir Forsythe was here specifically because he was aware of just about every secret passage in this keep. There were very few in the dungeons, which was why he was still chained in a hole. But, given the fratricidal history of the Grünwald royal family, it didn't take a genius to realize that if there was going to be a secret passage in the dungeons, it would be installed in the so-called "King's Suite," and that the king who installed it might have been less than forthcoming about its existence to his immediate family.

It was just too bad for King Dudley's father that the queen had him assassinated rather than imprisoned. Then again, one man's ironic regicide is another's escape hatch.

It took me a bit of searching to find the false stone in the base of the wall and pry it free. Beyond was an unlit tunnel, dark as the Lord Nâtlac's soul. I grabbed the oil lamp from the table and shone it into the hole. Beyond the wall, the hole opened up into a narrow corridor that snaked between this cell and the next. The space was rough and unfinished and barely wide enough to accommodate me in my current incarnation. I crawled and wedged myself in.

Even with a bustline, I would have fit better as a princess.

There were handles on the inner side of the false stone, but I only made a token effort to pull it shut behind myself. Tight as the space was, I couldn't bend myself to get the leverage to grab it, and there were other things higher on my priority list.

I crept along, sandwiched between two stone walls, holding the lamp in front of me. It felt like hours. Then I came to the end.

I stared ahead of me. Several feet in front of the lamp, the void between the walls was filled top to bottom with loose stone and gravel. I suspected that was how the walls were naturally constructed, two stone surfaces with a void filled with debris. It certainly would make it harder to dig out, and it made the "secret" passage easy to hide, since the wall with the passage wouldn't be any thicker than any other wall.

That was a point in the designer's favor.

However, that was outweighed by the complete absence of any obvious exit. I stood there, dumbfounded, wondering if some sort of cave-in had blocked my escape. That seemed unlikely, since the debris blocking my escape was packed too flat and evenly to have happened by accident.

Did Dudley discover the passage and block it off?

Then why block it off here and not back at the cell itself? It seemed a lot of trouble to go to just to have a laugh at my expense.

The flame from the oil lamp flickered, and I realized that I felt a slight draft on my face.

"What?" I whispered.

I did my best, one-handed, to shutter the lamp. I fumbled with it and it slipped out of my hand. It clattered on the floor and guttered out, plunging me into almost complete darkness.

After several long moments freezing in place, my eyes began adjusting to a dim light that seemed to shine up from the floor in front of me. I lowered my arm, no longer holding the lamp, so I could lean over and look down at the light source.

It was a good thing I had stopped where I had. Barely a hand's-breadth from my right boot, the floor dropped away. From there to the wall of debris, there was no floor, just a drop into a corridor somewhere in the dungeons. The wall behind me continued to descend until it reached a stone floor about ten feet below, and the flickering light came from what I assumed was a torch hiding behind a pillar that hugged the wall and supported the end of the passage before me.

I heard footsteps below. I held my breath and quietly inched forward to lean in and get a better view of the hallway beneath me. That proved a mistake. My right foot slid on spilled lamp oil and shot out from under me. I fell forward, and almost completely through the hole. My descent was only stopped by instinctively grabbing the top of the pillar in front of me and pushing my left foot against the edge of the hole. I fought to remain silent as my naked hands slapped against the stone and pressed in.

Snake was just tall enough for the maneuver to work.

I held myself there, muscles vibrating, as one of the dungeon guards sauntered by below me. His pace was leisurely. So much so that it felt deliberate as my lungs screamed for air and my legs, arms, and hands stung from the effort of holding me suspended.

After a short eternity, he passed out of sight behind the pillar in front of me.

I slowly exhaled, and when no one came running, I shifted my grip on the top of the pillar and let go with my legs to swing down to between the pillar and the wall. I dangled for a moment, then dropped the last four feet or so. It would have been a graceful dismount if not for the fact my right boot was still slick from lamp oil and slid away from me again, dropping me on my ass.

I sat there, not daring to move. After it became clear I hadn't made enough of a commotion to warrant the attention of the guard ahead of me, I got slowly to my feet and peeked around the pillar.

I stood in the middle of a long corridor dominated by rough stone pillars supporting squat vaults every ten paces or so. Every other pair of pillars had a torch burning in a sconce between them. The torches were all on the same side of the corridor I was, meaning that the space where I stood, between a torchless pair of pillars, was the most shadowed spot available. Looking up, the gap in the ceiling I had fallen through was completely wrapped in the shadows from the pillars and the vaults they supported. Even standing directly beneath it, I couldn't distinguish between the gap and the shadows surrounding it.

"So far, so good," I whispered.

I had some basic information on the dungeons from Sir Forsythe, but he could impart only so much in the time we'd had. Also, he had no knowledge of the girls or where they might be locked away. There were five levels of cells where they could be hidden.

However, there were other sources for that information.

I followed my quarry past two twisting corridors while he made his rounds, and I made my move when he passed near a cell that was open and empty.

I'm normally not bloodthirsty, but people guarding more-or-less innocent sacrifices to the Dark Lord Nâtlac are fair game. Also, when you're armed only with a torch and the element of surprise, you can't really hold back and wait for the other guy to draw a sword. So one burning torch across a face later, I stood over the unlucky guard holding his own sword to his neck.

"My face!" he yelled at me through a still-smoldering beard.

"Shut up," I said, "or the pain is going to come to a very abrupt stop." I prodded his neck to emphasize the point.

The guard whimpered, but he sucked it up and stopped screaming.

"Now," I said, "you're going to tell me where you're holding all the sacrifices."

"I don't know what—"

He stopped when I pressed the sword point down. "Try again. Six teenage girls and a pretentious knight. I'd think that'd stick in your mind."

"Oh, them."

"Where?" I repeated.

CHAPTER 15

I left my singed adversary in the unused dungeon cell after divesting him of his weapons and armor. Unfortunately, it was too ill-fitting to be a disguise. I had to leave half the fittings unbuckled, and I had to abandon the boots and helmet. But it did give me more protection than I started with.

I did have one lucky break—assuming he'd been telling me the truth. According to him, my girls were all chained in a single cell only a few hundred yards from Sir Forsythe.

I just had to sneak down one more level to the deepest part of the dungeon. Unfortunately, there was only one narrow stairway down, protected by a guardsman who rivaled my barbarian friend Brock for sheer size. I suspected that he was on guard duty here because he wouldn't fit in the stairwell.

Unlike Brock, I felt a sense of physical competence about the guy that suggested walking up to him and swinging a sword would just be adding to my personal list of bad ideas.

As I hid in the shadows, trying to come up with an effective way to get around this guy, the involuntary fire-eater I had locked up behind me decided to start screaming. While I had chained the semi-flammable guard to the wall with the available manacles, apparently balling up the end of his shirt and shoving it in his mouth did not make an effective gag.

But that oversight made an effective distraction.

The main obstacle to my descent ran off to investigate the screaming. He ran by the pillar I hid behind without even looking in my direction.

Once he passed, I bolted for the stairwell.

It was a good thing my immediate nemesis was distracted by my lightly toasted victim, because my oil-slick boot squeaked loudly on the stone as I ran. I stopped running when I hit the stairway.

The steps downward were narrow, steep, irregular, and corkscrewed down into complete darkness. If I tried to run down the stairs, my slick boot would probably try to kill me.

I sheathed the sword I'd been holding and grabbed the nearest burning torch from its sconce and began a slow, careful descent. I finished two complete circuits before I reached the bottom, where the stairway emptied into a closetlike antechamber dominated by a heavy oak door banded in iron.

The door would have been close to impenetrable, if it wasn't for the fact that the heavy iron bolts were all on this side. I slid the bolts aside with my free hand and stepped back as the door slowly creaked open toward me, pulled by its own weight.

I saw flickering light beyond, and I took a step to keep behind the opening door. I heard a horrible guttural sound and for a second believed that some demonic creature had been set to guard the lower depths of the dungeon.

Then the sound cut itself short with a sucking breath and I realized it was someone snoring. I heard a clatter and a groan, then a deep voice say, "Gryod?" Followed by a long yawn. "Can't be time yet, is it?"

The door now hung fully open, pressing me against the wall. I couldn't see the speaker, but I heard his footsteps, large and heavy, as imposing as the man above had been.

"Gryod? You there?"

The footsteps approached me. I heard jingling that might have been mail, or keys. I also heard a sound unmistakably like a blade being drawn from its scabbard. "Who's there?"

I said nothing and kept my gaze focused on the gap between the door and the floor. I saw a shadow pass on the other side as I heard the man, very close now, say, "Show yourself!"

I decided to oblige him by bracing against the wall behind me and shouldering the door closed with all the force I could muster.

I can say this about the body Snake bequeathed me, it made such a move a lot more plausible than it would have been if I still had Lucille's mass and upper body strength. The massive door had quite a bit of momentum as it slammed into the unseen guardsman. It came to a stop with a bone-jarring impact that stopped me cold and sent a dagger of pain shooting down the right side of my body. I heard cursing and a thud, and I ducked around the door to point my weapon at the prostrate guard.

I cursed myself as I realized that the weapon I pointed at his bloody face was the guttering torch.

"My nobe!" The man below me bellowed, swinging his own sword up to knock the burning torch out of my hands. *"You buhded my nobe!"*

I jumped back and drew my sword as the man unsteadily got to his feet.

"Imb goind to cud your fabe off!"

The massive guard had about a foot's reach on me. He swung his sword back, and before he brought it to bear, I hooked my foot around the door and slammed it shut on him again. It hit with a solid crack, and I heard the sword clatter to the ground.

"Ag! I'll gill you."

The door swung back toward me, and I saw the guy, on his knees, holding his bloodied face in his hand as he groped behind him for his sword.

You don't change a winning strategy. I slammed the door on him again. Since he was leaning forward slightly, it was brought to a solid halt by his forehead. The door swung inward again, forced by the full weight of the guy falling against it. He flopped, unconscious, facedown in front of me.

Armed with keys liberated from the man who lost his argument with a door, I started opening cells. The first few were people I didn't recognize, but I freed them anyway. The logic was simple and self-serving. There were at least two guards upstairs free to come after me or sound an alarm, and it would be a bit more difficult for them if a bunch of former prisoners were coming up out of the lower levels of the dungeons.

If you can't remove the opposition, distract them.

The girls had been stripped of their armor and placed in one large cell together. I opened the door and six pairs of eyes focused on me. I heard Grace's voice, raw as if she'd been screaming, "You bastard."

"I . . ." They all sat on the straw-covered floor, chained, dressed only in the oversize male chemises they'd worn under their salvaged armor. Without the outward trappings of their independence—the armor, weapons, even their grotesque jewelry—they appeared much smaller than they had before. "I'm getting you out of here."

"You got us in here!" Grace spat.

I started with Thea who stared at me with shiny eyes and shook. The chains came off her legs with a clatter, and she leaped up to run across the room to cower behind Grace and Mary. Rabbit didn't cower, but she didn't look me in the eye as she got up and walked over to Grace and Mary.

When I unlocked Laya, she whispered as she stood, "You were right. It can't be worth it."

Of them all, only Krys looked at me as if I wasn't the guard come to haul them away to sacrifice them to Nâtlac.

I finished freeing them and said, "Now let's get you all out of here."

My statement was met by a thundering silence.

"Come on, we don't have much time before the guards—"

Grace stepped forward. "Why should we go anywhere with you, Bartholomew?"

Crap.

"Can we talk about that when we're not in the middle of escaping?"

The band of girls crowded together, Mary and Grace at the front.

"Escape to what?" Grace said. "What do you want us for?"

"I'm trying to save you!"

"So you can use us before your brother does?"

I rubbed my forehead. I always knew that everything would unravel at some point. I had just naïvely hoped that it would happen at a more convenient moment. Behind me, I heard the sounds of commotion, running feet, things thudding into walls, people cursing and shouting.

The other escapees must have introduced themselves to the guards.

"You really should come with me."

"Why should we trust you?" Mary said.

I had two swords and scabbards I had liberated from the guards I'd fought. I pulled both of them off and tossed them on the ground in front of the girls.

"Because I'm trusting you," I said. "I'm sorry. Things got out of hand. I can't explain everything now. Too many angry guards coming after us. We still have to find the guy who knows how to get out of here."

"I don't think—" Mary started to say.

I didn't hear the rest of her statement because someone tackled me from behind, screaming, *"Gill you!"*

I hit the floor as I turned toward my assailant. A huge bloody moon face with a nose swollen like a lumpy black potato snarled and drooled down at me.

"Gill you!" he shouted again, spraying me with blood, phlegm, and broken teeth. I couldn't respond since words were hard to come by while this guy squeezed my trachea shut.

"I'll teah you do slam a door in my fabe!" He pounded the back of my head into the floor for emphasis. Fortunately the stone floor was covered by a layer of filthy straw and fecal matter, so I probably only got lice and some sort of disease rather than a concussion.

He yelled something inarticulate that trailed off into an incoherent sputtering. His hands loosened and he turned his head to look off toward the girls.

"Ah you gibbing me?" he said as he fell off to the side.

Above us, Grace held my recently abandoned sword.

I sat up, rubbing my neck. "What about the rules?" I asked.

Grace looked down at me and said, "Don't press your luck. You said that there's someone who can get us out of here?"

I let Grace and Mary bear the swords. One less thing for me to worry about. Despite the change of heart that saved my life, I could still tell that I had exhausted the reservoir of trust I had with them. Better to let Fearless Leader take her natural role and not even pretend I was in charge. Once all of us were out of this place, we could part ways.

Just a bit deeper in the dungeon we found Sir Forsythe. I opened a heavy iron door, and it was unquestionably him. He was the only man I knew who could be stripped and thrown in a dungeon hole and still appear as if he'd stepped fresh off the parade grounds. Despite the black manacles holding him to the wall, the filthy bedding in the stall, he appeared unsullied, his long blond hair shining in the torchlight.

"Is it you, My Liege?"

"Yes." I ran up and started unlocking the chains that bound him to the wall. "You're going to lead us out of this dungeon."

He stepped free and looked me up and down. "You *are* wearing the body of Prince Bartholomew."

"Yeah, he goes by 'Snake' now."

From outside the cell I heard Grace. "Who's the pretty boy, and what is he talking about?"

He drew himself up and walked out, intoning, "I am Sir Forsythe the Good, fair maiden. I am here in service to my liege, Frank Blackthorne, Princess of Lendowyn, and the rightful Dark Queen of Nâtlac. And I am going to save you."

There was a chorus of "what?" as Sir Forsythe strode through their midst. Mary gaped at him, and he bent down to kiss her hand. "Thank you, My Lady," he said. Somehow he had taken the sword Mary had been holding.

Sir Forsythe raised the sword above his head and said, "Now, follow me." He charged back the way we had come.

Grace sputtered, "What the f—"

"We better follow him," I said. "He knows the way out."

Everyone started chasing the charging knight. As we ran, Grace asked, "Who is Frank Blackthorne?"

"That would be me."

"What?"

"Princess of Lendowyn? Dark Queen?" Mary sounded the words as if she had lost track of what they actually meant.

"Long story," I responded.

Behind us I heard Laya say, "Aren't we running back toward—"

She didn't manage to finish the thought, because she was interrupted by Sir Forsythe bellowing, "Servants of the Usurper! Cower before the might of he who serves the true Queen of the Dark One!"

The statement was punctuated by a high-pitched scream as a flailing body sailed through the corridor toward us. Everyone dodged to hug the wall as a guardsman crumpled limp between us. After a moment of shock, Rabbit, Krys, and Laya descended on the body, stripping it of weapons and armor quicker than I thought possible.

Sir Forsythe, for all his bluster, seemed to have a hint of tactical competence, if not subtlety. He stood before the doorway to the upper levels, but not so close that anyone could fight him with the door. But that meant that the guards—and I couldn't even see how many there were past the door—were forced to engage him one-on-one. That was not a winning proposition.

A guard took a step toward him and swung his weapon. Sir Forsythe effortlessly blocked it and grabbed the faceguard of the man's helmet with his free hand. Sir Forsythe pulled the man's head forward. As his opponent fell, Sir Forsythe bellowed, "Brilliant! Future generations will sing ballads of how bravely you stepped up and met your doom!"

The guard continued stumbling forward, and Sir Forsythe dropped his block and introduced his weapon to the back of the falling man's neck. The result was not pretty.

By the time the body hit the ground, the guard was permanently out of the fight and Sir Forsythe was blocking the next attacker.

"I am amazed at the ferocity one can muster in the service of someone like King Dudley. Such valor," he said as he ran through the next man. "So misplaced." Rather than spend time freeing the sword from the corpse's chest, Sir Forsythe grabbed his latest victim's weapon before he hit the ground. By then the girls had dragged away the guy Sir Forsythe had partially decapitated and were stripping weapons and armor off of him.

By the time the other guards realized that Sir Forsythe was homicidally insane and slammed the door on us, all the girls had some form of armor, and everyone but Thea had a weapon.

Grace said, "Great, now they've locked us in."

Sir Forsythe turned around with a somewhat unnerving grin. "No, My Lady. They've locked themselves out."

CHAPTER 16

I have to admit that when it came to rescuing damsels in distress, Sir Forsythe was the professional. Despite a nonchalant attitude toward bloodshed that bordered on the psychotic, there had been a method in his unnerving madness.

By forcing the defenders back, and convincing them the better part of valor was shutting the door on the crazy man with a sword, Sir Forsythe had insured that our exit from the dungeons would be relatively unimpeded.

This did not translate into "pleasant."

Our secret passage out of the dungeons had to be accessed through a drainage tunnel that received all the excreta from the lowest dungeons. Reaching said egress was to be accomplished via the obvious method.

"In *there*?" Mary echoed my own thoughts as Sir Forsythe led us to a stinking alcove set a distance from where the guards kept watch. The privy was a dark hole set in the stone floor, emitting a slightly foul breeze.

"I apologize for the unwholesome venue," Sir Forsythe said, "but we are escaping a dungeon."

"Eeew!" Thea said.

I heard a grunt and someone pushed me aside from behind. Rabbit passed me and leaped up, straddling the hole, facing all of us. She looked down, wrinkling her nose. She held out her hand.

After standing there a moment, staring into the foul-smelling abyss, she glanced up, turned to Mary, and made a "gimmie" gesture with her outstretched hand. Mary reached for the sword tied at her side and Rabbit furrowed her brow, frowning in a "you're kidding me" expression. Mary froze a moment, one hand on her sword. Then she looked up at her other hand, which held a torch that she'd liberated from one of the wall sconces.

"Oh," she said meekly, and handed the torch over.

Rabbit snatched the offered torch and held it over the hole and looked back down. She frowned and shook her head, then she gave Sir Forsythe a pained expression. She arched an eyebrow and cocked her head in a way that I could almost hear her say, *"Really?"*

"A tunnel leads out of the cistern, we can crawl for fifty yards—"

"Crawl?" someone, Krys I think, interrupted from behind me.

"—before we reach the spot in the wall where we can push through."

Rabbit sucked in a breath, straightened herself, and jumped into the hole.

"Rabbit!" Grace yelled, running to the edge of the hole just as I heard an unpleasant squishy noise from below. Grace covered her mouth and made a strangled gagging noise and I ran up next to her, fearing the worst.

Fortunately, Rabbit was fine. Grace was gagging at the now torch-lit pile of filth that Rabbit stood shin-deep in. It glistened brown, black, and gray around her, while streams of greenish-yellow water slid in rivulets between the lumpy piles.

I came perilously close to gagging myself.

Rabbit took a few steps back from under the hole and waved us down.

I couldn't in good conscience let any more of the girls precede me. I at least still had my boots.

It took me a little more effort than Rabbit, as Snake's shoulders were almost too broad to slip through. I had to push myself back up twice before I could swing my left shoulder lower than my right and slide it below the lip of the hole first. I dangled from my right arm for a few seconds before I gathered the will to let go.

I dropped the last two or three feet into the vile slurry below. I hit with a splash that sent a spray of filth in Rabbit's direction, causing me to wince in sympathy. Then I realized that my boots were not as much an asset as I supposed. My feet sank into the semisolid mess below to a depth higher than the tops of my boots, and I felt the slick mass ooze inside until my toes squished.

I stared at Rabbit, and despite her bravery taking the lead, I could now see a green cast to her face that was stark even in the flickering torchlight. I suspect I wore the same expression. The air down here oozed into my lungs the way the crap I stood in oozed into my boots, almost as viscous and just as foul.

Holding down my bile, I slugged across the floor to stand in front of her to shield her from further splashing.

Grace followed, then Mary, Krys, and Laya. Lastly, Sir Forsythe lowered Thea down into my arms. She sobbed and buried her face in my neck.

I guess I smelled better than the wrong end of a latrine. Though, standing where I was, I wondered how long that would last.

Sir Forsythe slid down last, somehow landing without throwing up waves of black foulness. He waved his own torch around as he circled, until he faced a stone wall with an opening that rose about three feet above the muck.

"This way," he said.

Of course . . .

Most of the girls were lucky, they were short enough that they could crouch and walk through the tunnel. Mary, Sir Forsythe, and I were not so lucky. We three had to go forward on our hands and knees. Sir Forsythe took the lead while Mary and I stayed to the rear. Thea stayed with me, on my back, because I couldn't bring myself to put her down.

That meant I had to crawl lower than the others, leaving my face a bare inch from the sludge in the bottom of the sewer.

At least, if I throw up now, no one will even notice.

Sir Forsythe had said we'd only go fifty yards in this, but it felt like we easily went a few miles. By the time we came to a halt, my elbows were trembling from the extra weight on my shoulders.

"Here we are," I heard Sir Forsythe call from ahead. I couldn't really raise my head to see where he was, but I heard a couple of thuds, and the sound of crumbling stone. A moment later, I felt a breeze cooler than the steaming odor we'd been crawling through.

The girls ahead started moving again, and I followed. Soon I reached a hole in the side of the sewer and someone lifted Thea off my back. I straightened my neck and saw that a portion of the sewer wall had been built without mortar, so Sir Forsythe had been able to just push the stones out into a larger chamber. I scrambled through the hole and into a room that, while having claustrophobically low ceilings, was just tall enough for me to stand upright.

I turned around to look at the hole we had come through as Mary pulled herself out of the mire. Something sailed out from the edge of the torchlight at me and I caught it without thinking. "Good catch," Krys said with a chuckle.

I'd caught a human skull.

"Gah," I said, dropping the thing to clatter on the stones by my feet.

My reaction brought a few more chuckles.

"Okay, this is an improvement," Grace said to Sir Forsythe, "but where are we?"

"We have entered the lowest catacombs of the Royal Ossuary, My Lady. Here rest the bones of all the prior generations who gave themselves to the Dark Lord."

Rabbit, who still held a torch, stood up against one wall, and I could see niches of neatly stacked bones. It gave me a shudder, but didn't seem to faze any of the girls aside from Laya, who had edged into the center of the chamber, far from the piles of stacked bones.

Thea picked up a dusty old femur and started swinging it around like a wooden sword.

The bones didn't bother me so much as the thought that these were sacrifices to Nâtlac, and I was sure that those who "gave themselves" had not done so voluntarily. I bent down and picked up the skull I had dropped, and squinted until I saw a small pyramid of skulls missing its top member. I replaced it and asked Sir Forsythe, "Which way out?"

The ossuary gave way to more typical catacombs as we followed Sir Forsythe through tunnels bearing generations of Grünwald's dead. We walked down a narrow tunnel that bore niches on either side where the dead were laid out. Unlike the ossuary, these niches held more than bone. The occupants here were laid out in shrouds, fully clothed, to await their return to dust. Ahead of us, waves of rats scampered away from the approaching torchlight.

Our path remained generally a straight line away from the sewers, so I was certain that we had long passed out from under the walls of the main keep. The catacombs probably spread out underneath most of the surrounding city.

Sir Forsythe finally led us up a steep stone staircase that emerged behind a vine-covered iron gate. He pushed through the gate and we emerged out into the cold night air. It wasn't until I stepped outside that I realized that we all smelled as if we'd been rolling in the aging vomit of a coprophagous ogre with hygiene issues. I took a few steps upwind so the only airborne contaminants I breathed came from my own sewage-saturated clothing.

"Where are we?" I heard Grace ask.

I didn't need to hear Sir Forsythe's answer. We were in a lonely wooded corner, but the night was clear and the moon was high and illuminated the ground beyond our torches. Beyond the cluster of trees that shielded us, ranks of memorials and tombs marched up toward a ruined temple on a small rise.

Sir Forsythe stepped up next to me and said, "These are the Gardens of Lysea."

I heard the sound of a dozen feet crunching the snow as they approached behind me. Mary asked, "The Goddess Lysea?"

I said, "That seems a bit out of character for Grünwald." Even if Nâtlac worship was confined to the aristocracy, the Goddess Lysea was a patron of love, beauty, poetry, and a half-dozen other things that wouldn't help you in a bar fight. In other words, not nearly martial enough for the Grünwald hoi polloi.

"This is an *old* graveyard," Sir Forsythe said.

That was obvious. Many of the memorials were visible only because the vegetation covering them had withered away for the winter. Many were half ruined, and as I looked closer I could see some of the statues and religious symbols had been broken deliberately.

Thea walked past me still carrying her femur. She hugged herself and said, "I'm cold," in a puff of fog.

Of the girls, outside a few hastily scavenged bits of armor, no one was properly dressed for the winter cold. No one even had shoes. I pointed up to the ruined temple. "We can take shelter up there."

Grace glared at me and I realized she resented me taking the initiative again. Not that I could blame her.

"Unless you have a better idea," I said.

She stomped off in the direction of the temple, so I suppose she didn't. The others followed her single file between the ranks of broken tombs in an unpleasantly spectral procession. Sir Forsythe stood next to me, holding his torch, staring after them.

I followed the girls, and after a few steps I realized that Sir Forsythe wasn't with me. I turned around and asked him, "You coming?"

He blinked and said, "Of course, My Liege." Something about the way he said that was way more tentative than anything that had a right to come out of Sir Forsythe's mouth. The word "tentative," didn't even belong in the same paragraph as Sir Forsythe the Good. I considered asking him what was the matter, but I had a suspicion that I didn't really want to know.

The temple's damage had been confined mostly to the front. Again, statues and pillars had been deliberately toppled, frescos defaced by more than age and neglect. We climbed broken steps into an entryway whose roof had caved in, but beyond a pair of heavy bronze doors, the inner sanctum remained intact and sheltered from the elements. Whoever had wrecked the outside apparently had never come in here.

We entered an octagonal room with an elaborate mosaic floor. More frescos on the interior walls depicted artists and lovers engaged in the various activities generally ascribed to artists and lovers. Opposite the doors sat an elaborate marble altar set before a statue of a smiling nude woman.

Flanking the altar were a pair of low copper braziers heaped with wood and coal, as if just waiting for someone to arrive. Grace, who still carried a torch, touched the flame to one of the braziers, and the contents almost exploded as they erupted into a rolling fire that sent sparks up into the domed ceiling.

The sudden heat was very welcome, even though the ancient wood was so heavily scented with herbs and perfume that the room suddenly smelled like a burning whorehouse. The heat also made me aware of a chill draft coming from behind me. I turned around and saw Sir Forsythe standing in the doorway.

"Would you close the door?" Mary asked him before I could.

He shut the door as Grace set the other brazier alight. If it was me, I would have saved that one for later. The fuel was so old and dry that I suspected it would burn down rather quickly. But I held my tongue. There was wood outside, and I didn't need to do any more to alienate her.

Everyone gathered around the fires as I examined the larger-than-life statue above the altar. I had some nostalgic thoughts about Evelyn the tavern wench. I was sorry we hadn't gone much further with the awkward assignation before we had been interrupted. Then, since I was indulging in impossible thoughts, I felt regret that I hadn't gotten the chance to know Lucille back when we were more . . . compatible.

Where'd that come from?

"Now," Grace said behind me, interrupting a half-formed thought.

I turned to face her as she spoke, and I realized that I was surrounded with my back to the altar. I glanced from her to Sir Forsythe, who was still across the room by the doorway.

"Now?" I repeated.

"Care to explain 'Frank Blackthorne, Princess of Lendowyn, and the rightful Dark Queen of Nâtlac?'"

"Like I said, it's a long story."

"We seem to have the time now."

I guess we did.

I backed up and sat on the altar, facing everyone.

"Well . . . My name is Frank Blackthorne, and I'm going to tell you a story."

Frank Blackthorne, Princess of Lendowyn, and the rightful Dark Queen of Nâtlac . . . also add, somewhat mediocre thief.

I found it an immense relief to finally admit to who I was. I felt no small gratification in taking Snake Bartholomew's identity and metaphorically crumpling it up and tossing it into one of the hotly burning braziers. I unloaded my whole sorry story starting with my accidental liberation of a virgin sacrifice to the Dark Lord Nâtlac, to the somewhat less than epic battle between Weasel and the assassins. No one interrupted me, not even Sir Forsythe who probably could have offered some alternate explanations of his behavior before Queen Fiona's demise.

When I finished, Grace muttered, "Of all the idiot—"

"You were royalty and you gave that up?" Mary snapped, echoing what Grace must have been thinking. "What kind of fool—"

"The kind of fool who gets drunk and wears evil enchanted jewelry," Laya finished.

"And you just let us think you were the legendary Snake," Grace said, "dragging us all the way down here. Nearly getting us all killed."

Thea peered up at me. "You were really a girl?"

Mary turned to Sir Forsythe, who still hung by the doors. "So is this all true? This twit killed off your Dark Queen Fiona?"

I shook my head. The girls were arguing to themselves, venting. That didn't really require any response from me. I sighed and waited for things to subside. As I did, I noticed three things.

First, Krys didn't contribute anything to the conversation. She looked at me in a way that, unlike everyone else, wasn't tainted by anger or contempt— sad, more than anything else.

Second, Rabbit wasn't paying attention to any of the others. She was looking in my direction, but seemed to be staring through me with widening eyes. She grabbed the edge of Grace's befouled shirt and was yanking it, and her mouth opened to emit a sharp, almost barking sound for attention.

Third, Mary was still shouting at Sir Forsythe and Sir Forsythe quietly whispered, "My Lady," and fell to one knee, looking not at Mary, but toward me.

Actually, like Rabbit, *past* me.

I turned around, sliding off the altar at the same time, to stand in front, facing the statue behind it. A statue that had changed from a marble nude to a flesh-and-blood woman, a woman with the same epic proportion as the statue, half again as tall as Sir Forsythe, clad only with a flowered garland in her hair. She smiled and rolled her head, and I could hear the vertebrae cracking as she yawned and stretched her arms, touching the ceiling above us.

"You're kidding me," I whispered.

CHAPTER 17

"Well no one's been here for a while," she said when she was done stretching. She walked out from behind the altar, tracing the tops of the frescos with one hand. The girls fell silent as they all realized we had a visitor. She towered over all of them, offering a bemused smile. She stopped a few paces from where Sir Forsythe was genuflecting.

"Oh dear," she said. "Are you afraid of *me?*" She reached down and lifted his chin with her hand. Her hand was delicate and beautiful, but large enough to wrap halfway around Sir Forsythe's face. "You aren't afraid of anything."

"My Lady, I—I—"

This was a first. I had never seen Sir Forsythe at a loss for words before. She stopped his stammering by placing a finger against his lips and clucking a tongue at him.

"Don't embarrass yourself, Sir Forsythe. You have a reputation to uphold." She brushed an errant hair from his forehead. "Why would I harm you? Just because you pledge yourself to a rival deity whose followers desecrated my temples and enslaved my priestesses?" She reached and grabbed hold of the hair on the top of his head and yanked his head back. "Just because your Dark Lord raped my church?"

"Stop it," I called out. I think I've mentioned that I am more impulsive than is generally wise. So the words came out before I had time to realize that interrupting an annoyed deity was not the best course of action. Especially since, by some lights, I was higher in the Nâtlac hierarchy than Sir Forsythe—Dark Queen and all that.

She let go of Sir Forsythe's hair and turned to face me. She smiled and her expression was beautiful and terrifying. "Stop what, Frank?"

She strode toward me, and the girls parted between us.

"You think I might do some sort of damage to your loyal minion? Look at me. Excessive displays of violence are not my forte." She strode toward me, and it was impossible for me to take my eyes from her. Every curve of her towering body carved itself into my consciousness, as if some tiny artist was sculpting my brain into a likeness of the statue that had spawned her. She stopped less than an arm's length from me and placed a hand on a cocked hip. "I have other weapons."

"I see."

She laughed at me. "No, Frank, you don't. You think somehow I've not already had my revenge on that babbling idiot? If you don't realize that, you're a bigger fool than he is."

"What revenge?"

She laughed again, shaking her head. "You, now." She reached out and placed a finger on my chest, and just her proximity set my body into overload and I had trouble keeping my knees from wobbling. "I should be furious at you, shouldn't I?"

"Uh," I said with an eloquence I usually found only while drunk.

"After all, someone so close to the Dark Lord walks into a temple that was desecrated in his name ... But ..." She trailed off as she removed her finger and sighed. She shook her head and turned away. "Get up," she told Sir Forsythe.

"But what?" I said, once I had caught my breath again.

She paused, her back still toward me, just as mesmerizing as the rest of her. "But you had to give me an offering, didn't you?"

"An offering?"

She sighed. "You do know that's what the altar and those braziers of incense and perfumed wood are for."

Oh. It was probably what summoned her too.

"Of course, if some man comes into one of my temples with six young women, I generally expect a slightly *different* sort of offering. My rival Dark Lord to the contrary, there is more than one way to offer a virgin sacrifice."

She turned around to face me again. "But that gets *so* tedious. The same thing, over and over and over and over ... *booooring*. And look—" She gestured down at herself and spread her arms. "This is what my worshipers want. As if sex was all there was to me. But I'm not just love, sex, and fertility. I'm also art, beauty, song, poetry ... and storytelling." She flashed a genuine smile at me that might have struck me unconscious if it wasn't for the fact that the display of her body had already overloaded every male response this body had, leaving me numb and a little shaken.

"You know how long it has been since someone has offered me an epic like that? Extemporaneously? The only way it might have been better is if you could have improvised in meter."

"I-I'm glad you liked it."

"Like it? I *loved* it." She walked back up to me and touched the side of my face, then—before my legs gave out from the sensation of her skin touching my own—she bent down and placed a chaste kiss on my forehead. "Thank you," she whispered.

I think I blacked out for a moment.

When I blinked my eyes open, I was flat on my back in the temple, the girls bending over me, and there was no sign of the Goddess Lysea.

I blinked again and realized that the girls were no longer wearing filthy sewer-encrusted rags, or the associated sewage for that matter. They wore long tunics embroidered with gold thread, held together with copper-studded leather belts. Their hair was all styled with braids woven with flowers reminiscent of the garland the Goddess had been wearing.

"What? How long was I out?"

"A few minutes," Mary said.

"How? Your clothes—"

"She said if we're going to stay here," Grace answered me, "we need to look the part."

I sat up slowly, feeling the aftereffects of an erotic hangover. I wanted to be anywhere but lying prone, surrounded by a half-dozen teenage girls who'd been freshly cleaned, perfumed, and dressed like acolytes in a divine whorehouse.

"Are you all right?" Krys asked me.

I nodded. I wasn't, but I wasn't about to admit what was the matter, even if everyone could probably guess. I looked around and noticed who was missing. "Where's Sir Forsythe?"

"He stepped outside once the Goddess disappeared," Grace said.

Great, the unstable bastard probably ran off.

I got to my feet, happy for the excuse to step outside myself. I headed toward the brass doors and Grace said, "Wait a minute."

"What?"

"You just got kissed by a Goddess, and you have nothing to say?"

I shrugged. "These things happen?"

"Who are you, Frank Blackthorne?"

"I'll get back to you on that one." I slipped out the door before any more awkward questions came my way.

Who was I? I didn't have an answer for that anymore. As for physical displays of affection from the Goddess Lysea . . . What was there to say about it? It certainly wasn't the weirdest thing that had happened to me by any measure.

Sir Forsythe sat on the broken steps to the temple, staring out at the first glimmers of dawn light touching the gray winter sky. "Are you unhurt, My Liege?" he asked without looking at me.

"I'm fine," I said. "You're the one who doesn't look so great."

"I was not expecting Her."

"Neither was I," I said. "But didn't you say it was Her garden?"

"It was abandoned long ago, when I was a child. I never expected to see Her again."

I looked at the broken tombs. "Well I guess just looking at how torn up—" I stopped short and turned to look at Sir Forsythe. *"Again?"*

He nodded.

"When did you see her before?"

He gestured at the old destruction before us. "Shortly after this happened. My father, the tenth Lord Forsythe, was one of the men who drove her acolytes from Grünwald. He led a small group of royals and nobles to the glory of the Dark Lord. He gave the first sacrament to the woman who would become our first Dark Queen."

"What happened?"

"The Goddess came to all of us, every child of the first acolytes of Nâtlac."

I was speechless for a moment as the pieces of what she had said began tumbling into a complete picture. I sat down next to him on the steps and said, "She said she already had her revenge."

Sir Forsythe nodded.

"What did she do to you?"

He stared at the sky and shook his head. "She kissed us, showed us love and beauty and honor, and before we could pledge ourselves to Her for all time, She cursed us to serve the faith of our fathers."

For the first time Sir Forsythe appeared broken, as if all the implications of what he had said weighed him down at once.

"We served the Dark Lord, fully and without reservation, because the curse allowed nothing else. And because of the Goddess's kiss, we understood what we did."

For a goddess of love and beauty, I was starting to think she was kind of a bitch.

"My generation didn't last," Sir Forsythe said. "Too easy for most to give up, lose themselves in battle, in drink, to the altar, even their own hand." He turned to face me. "Do you remember, My Liege, when you asked me about the contradiction between being a hero and my service to Nâtlac?"

" 'I don't let that define me,' you said."

He nodded. "And do you know who named me Sir Forsythe the Good?"

"No."

"Prince—King—Dudley, as a mockery."

"I'm sorry."

"The irony is that buffoon Dudley owes his position to the Goddess. Both of his older brothers—older *legitimate* brothers—bore the same curse. Neither bore it well. He was born just too late to suffer from it."

"Prince Bartholomew?"

"Saved by being a bastard. The king's bloodline did not participate in the worship of Nâtlac, and didn't raise a hand against Her temple."

I found this new side of Sir Forsythe unnerving. Even if I now knew why he was so eager to pledge himself to me after Queen Fiona's death, and why he'd been slow to criticize the new Dark Queen for her lax observation of the rituals of the Dark Lord.

"Well, I need my knight back, Sir Forsythe."

"My Liege, I am a fraud. All I am is because of a curse laid upon me by the Goddess. Without that, I would just be another blind acolyte of Nâtlac, serving King Dudley, looking to roast your flesh and that of those children for the glory of the Dark Lord."

I stood and said, "You are not a fraud."

"You heard—"

"Quiet!" It still surprised me when I managed to get a tone of command into my voice, even if I recently was able to argue a dragon to tears.

Sir Forsythe, invested in the hierarchy of nobility as he was, shut up. I didn't like abusing his misapprehensions of who I was, but I didn't want him continuing down the path he had begun down.

"You are no fraud, Sir Forsythe. Of all the people touched by the Goddess and given this 'curse,' how many are left?"

"Only me."

"Why do you think that is?"

He shook his head. To be fair, before this moment I would have answered the question for him; as I mentioned earlier, he was crazy as a rabid goblin. But, besides not being a helpful answer, it was also the lesser answer.

"I'll tell you why," I continued. "Because I have no doubt that your peers decided to suppress the Goddess's gift. They buried it inside themselves to fit in, to earn favor, to be part of the new aristocracy of Grünwald. Am I wrong?"

"No."

"That's what killed them. That was their contradiction. They denied who they were and it destroyed them. You took what the Goddess gave you, and you embraced it. You decided to become Sir Forsythe the Good despite mockery, despite derision."

He shook his head. "It wasn't my decision."

"It's *always* your decision!"

He drew himself back from my outburst, and I suddenly felt a sense of déjà vu as I spoke the words before I understood fully what I was saying. I was facing Lucille again, and I was about to say something irrevocable.

But it wasn't my relationship to Sir Forsythe that would change with my words.

"You had no choice in what the Goddess gave you," I said, "just as you had no choice who gave you birth . . . but you decided how you'd react, you decided what person you'd make yourself into. You decided if what She gave you became a curse or a blessing. You did something no one else She touched was able to do, take what She gave you to make yourself a hero. And despite everything, you've become one."

His eyes widened. Then he lowered himself to one knee before me, lowering his head. "Thank you, My Liege."

As he repledged himself to my service, my own words echoed through my skull like a church bell ringing in a cathedral of my own stupidity.

You had no choice . . . just as you had no choice who gave you birth . . . but you decided how you'd react, you decided what person you'd make yourself into. You decided . . . curse or a blessing.

"Who are you, Frank Blackthorne?"

What person had I made myself into?

CHAPTER 18

I don't know if I asked the next question to absolve some of the guilt I was feeling, or to punish myself. It had fully sunk in how much of a bastard I had been, disappearing in a fit of pique the way I did. One of the last things I had said to Lucille—other than a grunt or a monosyllable—was that she was an ungrateful bitch.

"How is Lucille? Is she all right?"

Sir Forsythe shook his head. "The Dragon Prince is angry."

Of course she was. "I guess I can't blame her."

"The whole of the Lendowyn court, your husband especially, are convinced that your disappearance was at the hands of agents of Grünwald and King Dudley. That was why I was sent, My Liege. I was to gather proof of this, and retrieve you if I could."

Given my past interactions with Grünwald and the Grünwald court, that had been a pretty logical conclusion. Wrong, but logical. "Mission accomplished, I guess."

"You sound troubled."

"Where's Prince Bartholomew? He woke up in the princess's skin and he just left?"

"You disappeared, My Liege."

I nodded. Talking with him further, it seemed that Princess Snake had vanished the morning I'd made the bad decision to wear the Dark Lord's wedding gift. He would have had to make a run for it almost immediately. I couldn't quite reconcile that with what I had found out about this guy. I couldn't see him not taking advantage of the position he found himself in.

But he *had* disappeared, and I thought about what Sir Forsythe had said. *"The Dragon Prince is angry."*

The burned Grünwald village was even more disturbing now. Lucille hadn't waited for Sir Forsythe to return with evidence before attacking. Perhaps she took his capture to *be* that confirmation. Had she destroyed that town in retaliation for something that never happened? My heart sank.

What had I done to her?

We had to get me back to the Lendowyn court before this escalated any further.

I led Sir Forsythe in out of the cold. Inside the temple, the girls had sat down in a circle and turned their heads to face us as if they were in the middle of some sort of debate. It was still disconcerting to see them dressed as acolytes of the goddess of beauty and love. Now that I was less distracted by the aftereffects of contact with the Goddess, I noticed Lysea had gone beyond clothes and hairstyling. Most of them had elaborate makeup applied, including painted lips and nails. All except Krys.

I also noticed that Krys's clothing was different than everyone else's; her tunic had longer sleeves and a looser cut with a round neck hole rather than a vee.

Also, while the other girls had jeweled accessories, necklaces, and bracelets, Krys had a pair of solid bracers on her wrists covered in elaborate knotwork.

In other words, she looked like the boy counterpart to the acolyte dress of the other girls. She also appeared more at home in her ensemble than the others did in theirs.

The fact that most of them still had salvaged swords and other weapons made the scene all the more surreal.

"He's still here," Grace said, looking at Sir Forsythe.

"So am I," I said. "What did we interrupt?"

Mary glared at me. "You *lied* to us."

I glanced at Laya. "To be fair, you *were* holding a crossbow on me."

"You dragged us miles away from—" Mary rose to her feet.

"Mary," Grace said.

"—and nearly get us killed by these Grünwald—"

"Mary!" Grace snapped again, grabbing Mary's arm.

Mary stopped and sat back down.

"She's still right," Laya whispered.

Grace stood up. "We're not holding a crossbow on you now. Does that mean we part ways now?"

Sir Forsythe stepped forward and said, "We will never abandon a distressed maiden to her fate. You need not worry, I will—"

I held up an arm to hold him back. "Quiet," I told him. "Let the maiden tell you if she needs rescuing."

"My Liege?"

I asked Grace, "Do you want to part ways now?"

"There is no treasure in Lendowyn, is there?"

I shook my head. "There's barely a treasury." I patted Sir Forsythe's chest and dropped my arm. "The crown pays this guy with food, board, and the opportunity for extreme acts of self-sacrifice."

"I do not serve for crass material gain," Sir Forsythe said.

"Point made," I said.

"Then why bring us at all?" Krys said. "After you slipped into that assassins' camp, you didn't have to stop for us. You could have ridden the carriage on your own through Grünwald. Why bring us?"

"I didn't want to abandon you."

"What?" Grace sounded insulted.

I hooked a thumb at Sir Forsythe. "This guy is a bad influence."

"You thought we needed saving?"

"I didn't know what I thought. I was improvising. Sometimes it works out—"

Grace glared at me. "Sometimes it doesn't."

"Sometimes it doesn't," I agreed.

"We didn't need no saving until we got involved with you," Mary snapped.

"I'm sorry," I said. "I messed up. Happens a lot lately."

Six pairs of eyes stared at me and I felt more uncomfortable in my skin than I had since before I'd ever come to Lendowyn. I wanted to shout that this wasn't *me*.

Maybe that was why I clung to Snake's identity with them long after I had decided the guy was reprehensible, trying to disown my stupid decisions by being someone else.

"So in Lendowyn," Grace asked, "do they round up people for sacrificial offerings?"

"Uh, no."

"And there's less of Grünwald between us and Lendowyn than there is between us and anywhere else?"

"Yes."

Grace nodded. "Fine."

"Fine, what?"

"If you want to make things up to us, lead us across the border to Lendowyn. We can ply our trade anywhere, but I'd prefer somewhere that doesn't have a history of human sacrifice."

"But I want to go home," Thea said.

I saw Mary roll her eyes. "The farther from White Rock, the better."

"But—" Thea started to blubber. Krys reached out and pulled Thea to her. She rocked back and forth with her, whispering, "Shush, your home's with us."

"If that's what you want," I said.

"My Liege?"

"What?"

"May I make a suggestion?"

"Still trying to rescue us?" Laya asked.

I sighed and shook my head. I doubted Sir Forsythe could make things worse. "Go ahead," I told him.

"You have the right to declare your own retainers."

"What do ..." I trailed off.

"I'm sorry," Grace said. "What is he talking about?"

"He means that I should offer you all an opportunity for something other than an outlaw life in the woods living off of what you can steal."

"And if that's what we want?"

I shrugged. "Then that's what you want. Unlike Sir Forsythe, I'm not into non-consensual rescue. But he's right. I'm the new face at the court, and most of the people around me have other loyalties. The more people I hand pick, the better."

"So," Mary said, "servants?"

"Handmaids that can do some serious damage if needed," I said.

Sir Forsythe bowed and addressed them all: "My Ladies, just over the border I left a camp of the princess's most loyal followers. They only wait for me to return with her, or news of her. You can join the court immediately."

Grace shook her head with a half-smile. "And you'd pay us as much as this guy?"

"At least as well," I agreed.

"You're not thinking—" Mary began, but Grace held up a hand.

"What about martial training?" Grace said.

"I'm sure Sir Forsythe here could teach you a thing or two."

Grace said to the others, "Let's think about it."

"Uh huh," Mary said. "There's one problem here."

Only one?

"What?" I asked.

"You're not a princess right now."

There was that.

Sir Forsythe had overlooked the main flaw in his idea, that the same Lendowyn laws that had made me the princess in the first place meant that, by law, Snake was the actual princess of Lendowyn right now. And he'd remain the princess until someone else inhabited Lucille's body.

"Damn," I said, "it seemed such an elegant solution too."

Sir Forsythe rubbed his chin, smoothing his goatee. "I only know the basic lore, but the effects of the Tear are supposed to be temporary."

"Tear?" I repeated.

"The Tear of Nâtlac," he responded.

"What, in the name of all that's unholy, is the Tear of Nâtlac?"

"That is the jewel the Dark Lord gave you, My Liege. Didn't you know?"

Apparently I had missed some orientation when I fell into the role of nominal priestess of Nâtlac.

According to Sir Forsythe, every time the Dark Lord gives up possession of a soul, he sheds a single crystal tear. Of course, the crystal has some magical properties having to do with soul-swapping. Anyone who puts on the jewel will have their soul exchanged with someone whom the Tear deems compatible, a body where the soul is most comfortable.

"So he takes it off, we swap back, right?"

"No," Sir Forsythe said. "It doesn't work like that."

Of course not. "How does it work, then? You said it was supposed to be temporary."

Well, it *was* temporary, he told me. The traditional length of the enchantment was a year and a day.

I may have said something unkind.

"Is there any other way to reverse the effect?"

"The stories say that the death of the physical body will reverse the process."

"The death of—"

Mary stood and placed a hand on the hilt of her salvaged sword. "Want my help?"

"No!"

A year and a day. I cursed my own stupidity, especially now that I knew one of my own retainers had all this information about the thing. "What if . . . What if he's taken it off, and one of us puts it back on again?"

"That is not part of the lore. But I suspect that if Prince Bartholomew would re-don the jewel, his soul would be drawn back to his original body—but if *you* wore it? I don't even think the Dark Lord Himself could predict where you might find yourself."

Great. We just had to find Snake, and the jewel, and force him to put it on again. Simple . . .

Something was wrong.

Snake was a member of the Grünwald court, an exiled bastard member, but still, a member. That group was steeped in the lore of Nâtlac. King Dudley certainly assumed that his bastard half-brother knew enough of their evil little rituals to have planned a coup around sacrificing a bunch of teenage girls rather than, say, raising an army.

All that meant that, unlike me, Snake was probably quite aware of what happened as soon as he woke up in the wrong body. He'd only had to look at the necklace for confirmation.

So if that was the case, why would he run off? He'd know that by removing and replacing the necklace he'd return to his own body. If Sir Forsythe was right, slitting the princess's throat would do the same thing.

Probably, since I swapped him out while Weasel's goons were roughing him up, he hesitated returning right after it happened. But he'd know that his body was still around as long as he stayed put . . .

But still, he could have taken some sort of advantage from being the princess. Why did he disappear?

I was obviously missing something.

CHAPTER 19

It was a long day.

While I really, really wanted to get out of Grünwald as quickly as possible, discretion made us wait. We were almost on top of the capital, and trying to escape with eight not particularly inconspicuous people was going to be dangerous enough without trying to do so in broad daylight. And after last night, everyone needed some rest, including me. So we camped out in the Goddess' temple until nightfall.

I took my rest on the far side of the octagonal room from the girls, leaning against one of the pillars to catch what sleep I could. What I remembered from my dreams was fragmentary, but I think they involved a couple of rude situations with the Goddess, though she spoke with Lucille's voice and stared at me with the eyes of a dragon.

The dream was interrupted by someone touching my shoulder. "You awake?"

I yawned and blinked my eyes. "I am now."

The temple was deep in shadow. The braziers had long ago burned down to glowing coals. I could only see the outline of the person next to me, but I recognized the voice. "Krys?"

"Yeah." She quietly slid down, her back to the pillar next to me.

"What do you want?"

She quietly laughed and said, "Things I can't have, usually."

"I know—"

"—the feeling. You've said that before."

"I did?"

"And I thought you were just . . ."

"Just what?"

"You *do* know." She was quiet for a long time before she said. "You're going to find it, aren't you?"

"What?"

"That magic thing you and the knight were talking about."

"The Tear of Nâtlac?"

"Yeah, that."

"I'm going to try."

"To become the princess again."

"Yeah."

"Why?"

"It may be the only thing that can help me fix all the things I've screwed up."

She was quiet again, long enough that I almost thought she had fallen asleep. Then she said, very quietly, "But you were trapped, weren't you? It wasn't your body. It could never feel right."

"This doesn't feel right."

"It doesn't?"

I sighed. "Krys, Snake's body may be closer to how I see myself, how I used to see myself, but it still isn't me. And now it actually feels a lot less me than it was when I was in the princess's body."

"But ..."

"You were going to ask to use it, weren't you?"

"I—"

"It's all right. Someone has a magic widget that looks like it could fix all the problems in the world. Why wouldn't you want to use it? See, I know that feeling too."

"I guess you do."

"But it's not a good idea."

"Why not?"

"Using an artifact from one of the nastier Dark Lords of the Underworld? You'd have to be desperate, drunk *and* stupid to ever think that's a good idea."

"But you used it."

"Making my point."

"But you didn't know how it worked. We could be more careful this time, watch my body as I—"

"Krys?"

"What?"

"It isn't just about you. Do you want to force some random innocent guy to live through what you're living through?"

"Uh?"

"And if he *wasn't* an innocent guy, if he's a manipulative homicidal bastard like Snake here, you'll be unleashing him on your friends—the friends you would be abandoning."

"I'd come back."

"If you're lucky, you might. But that jewel has its

own logic. I ended up three kingdoms away. Who's to say it won't put an ocean between you and those you care about? And you won't just have a new body to deal with, but a new past. What if this guy is married? Has children? You'd take away someone's husband? Their father?"

She sucked in a shuddering breath and said, "T-That's not fair."

"Life isn't fair."

"But you—"

"I did something thoughtless and stupid, and hurt one of the few people I care about in this world. What's the point of that if I can't be an object lesson on what not to do?"

"So you won't let me use it."

"You still want to?"

"Yes . . . No . . . I don't know." She drew her knees up and rested her head on them. "I feel so trapped."

"Well, if you're going to look for divine intervention, I suggest that looking for it from the Goddess Lysea is less apt to end in horrifying consequences than looking for help from a Dark Lord of the Underworld."

I think I might have heard a weak chuckle. "She seems more pleasant company."

"Krys, I know my word doesn't seem like much right now. But I promise that once I undo this mess I caused, there will be a place for you if you want it."

"Your word as a princess?"

"As Princess Frank of Lendowyn."

I heard her chuckle again.

"What?" I asked.

"I bet you make a very interesting princess, Frank."
"Wait until you meet my husband."

It was a long march to the border under cover of
darkness. We were lucky that it was overcast with very
little wind, since none of us were really dressed for the
weather. I was probably best off, even though my
clothes were still crusted with the sewage we had escaped through. The girls all had the ceremonial robes
from the Goddess, which meant they were covered
and had sandals at least, but the temple garb wasn't
intended for processions through the snow.

Sir Forsythe was worst off, though he refused to
show any discomfort. Not only was he still half covered in dried sewage, but his clothing amounted to a
dirty shirt and a pair of boots that must have come
from one of the fallen guardsmen in the dungeon.

We moved without stopping, and I could tell when
we crossed the border into Lendowyn because I could
feel the weight lift off of my shoulders.

That should have been a warning.

If history had taught me anything, it should have
been the fact that *any* time things seem to improve—
especially when things improved this quickly and this
easily—it was only because I was operating on inac-
curate information. My assumptions always seemed
to come back to maul me when I wasn't looking.

I had even less excuse for my oblivious optimism
than usual, because Sir Forsythe had already spelled
it all out to me.

Instead, the first sign I recognized anything going
wrong came just as dawn began to light the sky. Rab-

bit stopped us with a series of urgent grunts as she ran forward, ahead of Sir Forsythe. She dashed up the forest path, toward a rise, crouching as she approached the top.

"My Lady, please—"

I held up a hand as I walked up next to Sir Forsythe. "Wait."

I had seen her react like this before, and I could already feel the shreds of my relief blowing away in a sudden wind. I took a deep breath of the morning air.

Damn it!

"How close are we to your camp?"

"Just over that ridge, My Liege." Sir Forsythe pointed at where Rabbit crouched. "Less than a mile. What is she doing?"

"What do you smell?"

"Smell?"

I ran up to join Rabbit. The smell I referred to was faint at this distance, muted by the cold still air, but still unmistakable. I knew what I was going to see before I cleared the top of the ridge, something I didn't want to see for too many reasons.

"No, damn it!" I said as I stood looking down across a rolling field that spread from the edge of the woods. I could see the campsite, as Sir Forsythe had said, on a hill less than a mile away.

What remained of the campsite.

A half-dozen black streaks had been seared into the ground, around the site, all intersecting in a circle about fifty yards across. A few tent poles still pointed up at odd angles, but the rest of the campsite had been rendered into piles of unidentifiable ash.

"Why?" I whispered, finding it hard to find my voice. "Lucille? Why?"

I felt something touch my hand, and I looked down to see Rabbit staring up at me with a concerned look. I just shook my head, unable to find any more words to express myself. This wasn't some snap of rage venting against an enemy, however imagined. This was systematic obliteration of her own people, six methodical passes searing the ground and ending at the former campsite.

Somehow I had pushed her too far, and she had given in to the monstrous instincts of her new body.

I had lost her.

The others caught up with me and we advanced on the wreckage like a funeral procession. The fires had cleared the thin cover of snow for hundreds of yards around the campsite, and no new snow had come in the meantime to cover the scars. Our feet crunched in a frost-covered mixture of soot and mud. It was the only sound marking our approach aside from Sir Forsythe's occasional mutter. "This makes no sense. The Prince Dragon ordered us . . . Handpicked the people who would save the princess."

Even with Sir Forsythe spelling out exactly what had happened here, however inadvertently, I still avoided putting together the last few pieces of the puzzle.

As we reached the remains of Sir Forsythe's camp, Rabbit spun around and urgently held up her hands, halting all of us. Once we all stopped moving, I still heard the sound of feet crunching in the icy, sooty mud.

Someone else was here.

The clearing where Sir Forsythe's team had made camp was made of several rolling hills, and they had chosen the tallest to make camp. From this site, they had a good view all around to the tree line. It also meant that when anyone approached the site from any direction, at least part of the clearing was blocked from view by the hill it sat on.

Someone approached from the other side, and was about to crest the hill themselves.

I barely had time to register all of that before the unseen party stepped into view, less than twenty yards from us.

Two people cleared the top of the hill, and the one in the lead was intimately familiar to me; the short stature, the curves, the blonde hair ...

... the growing expression of shock that mirrored what I imagine was showing on my own borrowed face.

I couldn't help thinking how strangely surreal it was to see the body of Princess Lucille walking around without me. Sir Forsythe took one look at her and began drawing his sword. "Prince Bartholomew?"

Then all hell broke loose.

CHAPTER 20

While Sir Forsythe was never one to show restraint when confronted by an enemy, the fact that said enemy wore the body of an attractive young woman—not to mention the body that I had worn when he had pledged his fealty to me—gave enough pause for him to hesitate, sword drawn. I shared his momentary paralysis as I stared into her eyes.

Unfortunately for the person wearing Lucille's body, we were accompanied by a half-dozen girls who didn't share our hesitation.

Mary's voice echoed Sir Forsythe: "Prince Bartholomew?"

That was immediately followed by Grace in full Fearless Leader mode. "Get her!"

I barely had a chance to yell at them not to kill anyone before they tackled Lucille's body to the ground. As she fell under an avalanche of feral teenagers, Sir Forsythe moved. Not against the person in Lucille's skin, but to block the advance of a mountain of a man who had been accompanying her up the hill. Sir Forsythe had his sword to bear between the huge man and the girls, and he froze again as he and the man-mountain faced each other with expressions of dull surprise.

From under the girl pile I heard a familiar voice cursing. "Brock! Someone! Get these brats off of me."

"Brock?" I have no idea why I was surprised. Brock, like Sir Forsythe, was pledged to the princess. It made perfect sense that he was with Lucille's body, though he should be smart enough to figure out that someone else had taken up residence.

Unless . . .

Brock looked at Sir Forsythe, and then at me. "Who are you?"

"Address your liege properly, barbarian." I'm sure Sir Forsythe thought he was helping.

From beneath the girls I heard a shaky voice say, "Frank?"

With that one word, I finally put together all the elements I'd been missing.

"Get off of her!" I yelled at the girls.

Grace looked up at me from the pile with an incredulous expression. "What? If *this* is Snake—"

"No. It's the princess!"

"But you're the princess?" Krys's muffled voice came from near the middle of the pile.

"Not right now. She's the original."

"How do you know?" Grace asked.

"Frank!" Lucille gasped.

"Just get off of her!"

It was all so glaringly obvious in retrospect.

It never made sense that Snake would disappear from Lendowyn in the princess's body. He'd known about the cursed jewel I had used. It would be simple for him to put it on again to send his soul back home.

If he didn't, it meant he had figured out how to leverage where he had found himself.

Not only leverage his identity as the princess, but leverage the rift I'd put between me and Lucille.

From her perspective it had been out of the blue, and Lucille still didn't quite understand what had happened. "Princess Frank" had come to her the day after my drunken use of the artifact—meaning "Princess Snake" had actually come to her—to give her a gift. At this point, I don't think anyone listening to her story—aside from Brock—needed to be told what the gift had been.

"I was so happy," she said to me. "I thought you had forgiven me."

I didn't think I could feel worse about what had happened. I was wrong.

"And ever since I became a dragon, I'd never worn jewelry. That was the only thing I really missed, dressing up. Making myself pretty. And somewhere you had even found a chain long enough to fit my wrist. So tiny, but it was beautiful."

I barely listened as she explained what happened next. She placed Snake's gift on her wrist, and the next thing she knew, she was standing in her own body staring up at a laughing dragon. Before she had gotten a grip on what had happened, before she had recovered from the disorienting perception shift, a squad of guards appeared to take her prisoner.

Even *that* made sense in retrospect. A good proportion of the palace guard were former Grünwald soldiers who had pledged their service after I had defeated Queen Fiona. But they had pledged themselves to me as Princess Frank, not Lucille or Lendowyn. If Snake had come to them with a plot for a coup, especially one that hinged on an artifact from the Dark Lord himself, I doubt they'd express any reluctance.

I asked Sir Forsythe why Snake hadn't tried to recruit him.

"There was a faction in Grünwald that supported the bastard prince. I was never among them."

And neither were the rest of the men that Snake sent with you to save a princess that he'd taken prisoner himself.

Snake's plans were horrifying in their efficiency. If his interest was Grünwald, not Lendowyn, how better to exploit his new position in the Lendowyn court than by pointing Lendowyn itself at its rival, Grünwald. What better way to do that than disappear the princess and blame Grünwald for it? Then send a core group of potentially disloyal royal guard, led by Sir Forsythe, off to rescue the missing princess. Then, when they're disappeared as well . . . just blame Grünwald again.

There was no denying that Snake was way more a thief than I ever could hope to be. He had managed to steal an entire kingdom.

It was Lendowyn, but still . . .

And doing so from inside the skin of a murderous fifty-foot, fire-breathing lizard was just a bonus.

It fit together so well that I spent most of the description of Brock's rescue of Lucille mentally berating myself for not seeing it sooner. Both dragon attacks, Grünwald and Lendowyn, *had* to be Snake. It never made sense from Lucille's point of view, but from Snake's it made nothing but. He wanted war between the two kingdoms. The only thing I couldn't figure was how he intended to win given the state of Lendowyn's treasury.

I didn't realize that I had almost answered my own question, because I forced myself back into listening to Lucille.

After Brock pulled her out of the dungeon, they both made their escape from Lendowyn Castle. There was no telling who served the legitimate crown, and who served the usurper dragon. They had come here because Brock knew that most of those who would be loyal to the real princess had been sent here with Sir Forsythe to save her.

"Wait," Grace asked. "I'm confused now. Loyal to what princess? You or Frank?"

"Yeah," Mary added. "Didn't those guards think Frank was taking over?"

Lucille turned from them to me and Sir Forsythe. "Who are these girls?"

"That's Grace, that's Mary, Laya, Krys, Rabbit, and Thea."

"You've taken to abducting acolytes from Lysean temples now?"

"We're not Lysean virgins," Krys snapped.

"The abduction was mutual," I said.

"I don't understand what's happening," Lucille said. "We came here and I saw—" She waved toward the burned campsite around us. "I thought y-you did . . . but if you're not . . . Who's in my castle?"

"The Bastard Prince Bartholomew of Grünwald,

whose body I'm wearing." The explanation poured out of me in remarkably coherent fashion considering how much of Snake's thought processes I had to extrapolate. But still, the more I thought about it, the more sense it made. He knew the Tear of Nâtlac and what it did. The weird status of the Lendowyn court was public knowledge, so he knew exactly what he was doing when he gave her the jewel. Even more diabolical, he wasn't even stuck as the dragon as long as he held on to the Tear, if he put it on he'd reclaim his own body.

"So it wasn't ever you?"

"No."

She stepped up and backhanded me across the face.

"Ow! I'm sorry. I screwed up—"

She backhanded me on the other cheek.

"Ow!"

"You did this! You ran off and left my kingdom to this monster!"

She lifted her arm to strike me again, and Sir Forsythe grabbed her wrist. "That is enough, Your Majesty."

Brock put his hand on the hilt of his sword. "Let the princess go."

"I cannot permit this attack on my liege."

"Let me go."

"Brock will not let you harm the princess."

"Stop it!" I yelled. "She's right!"

Everyone stopped the bickering to face me.

"It is *all* my fault! I got drunk on self-pity and used an artifact from the Dark Lord Nâtlac when I had no real clue what would happen. It was terminally stupid, and she'd be better off slitting my throat where I stand if it wasn't for the fact we don't know what it would do to the effects of the Dark Lord's little toy."

"Frank?" she said.

"It was bad enough when I thought you were so upset at losing track of me that you burned a town to the ground—"

"What town?" she asked, weakly.

"—but it's because I gave him access to that artifact, and to *you*. I can't forgive myself. I certainly can't ask that of anyone else." Everyone stared at me, and I turned around so I couldn't see their eyes anymore. "Ever since I realized what I had done, what I'd *really* done . . . I had some hope I could fix it. I can't."

I walked away from everyone, not knowing or caring where I was going.

I didn't go far. Just to the edge of the woods where a tree had fallen, giving me a place to sit down and feel sorry for myself. I'd never felt more helpless than I did at that moment. Even if I could connive some way to undo what had happened, what really mattered was the damage already done. I had not only betrayed Lucille, I had betrayed the position in Lendowyn I had inherited from her. I hated the idea of aristocracy, and I felt unclean just becoming part of it, but it was what they had in Lendowyn. Backing away from it didn't undo the idea that some people were fit to rule others; it just left a hole to be filled by someone infinitely worse.

I sat there for a long time before I heard a familiar voice say, "Why?"

I looked up and saw Lucille. Oddly enough, it almost didn't seem right looking at her in her own body. There was something about her posture, and the tilt of her head that I could recognize from the dragon. How much had I taken from her?

I shook my head and laughed into my hands; it only sounded like sobbing.

"Frank?" She sounded alarmed, and probably with good reason. The sounds coming from me probably edged a little too close to the gibbering that followed the Dark Lord Nâtlac around.

"Five months ago," I said, catching my breath. "This would have been perfect, wouldn't it? You back in your original body, like I promised. And I get something close to mine . . ." I looked back up to her and I had to blink a few times because she was unaccountably blurry. "I am *so* sorry."

"Just tell me why, Frank."

"Because I'm an idiot, that's why."

"You're no idiot. Tell me why. What did you *think* would happen?"

I was about to glibly beat myself up again, but I could see something in her eyes that went deeper than the anger, something I recognized because I felt it myself. Grief. A sense of something that might be irrevocably lost, and no sense of how it could be saved.

She deserved better than me. *From* me. It pained me to put away the self-pity, having barely tapped my supply, but I decided to try being honest for once. "I thought I could just go back to being a guy for a while. I thought if the necklace was really a problem, I could just take it off again." I shook my head. "But really, I

was drunk, and angry, and in retrospect I wasn't thinking at all. After what happened the last time we
brushed against this sort of magic, I should have
known better. Even drunk I should have had the
sense to tell myself to wait until I sobered—"

"I wasn't thinking either."

"—up and could think cle—what?"

"I took you for granted. What you did for me, my
kingdom. Our kingdom."

"Yeah, I certainly screwed all that up," I mumbled.

"I didn't really understand what it was like for you.
Not until you told me off." I heard her sniff, and I realized she was crying. "Damn it, Frank. I thought I lost
you!"

"I thought you didn't know it was Prince Bartholomew?"

"You're not an idiot, but sometimes you act like
one."

"What?"

"I thought you were gone long before that!"

I stared at her, unsure how to react. I stood up and
reached for her. "Lucille—"

She batted my hand away.

"Do you understand yet? When that usurper came
to me in my—your—*this* body. I thought it was *you*. I
thought you might have forgiven me, and when you
didn't, when the dragon laughed at me and your
guardsmen dragged me away, I *still* thought it was you.
I thought it was you because I thought I *deserved* it!"

I shook my head. "No, I would never—"

She laughed, and the sound was sad and bitter.
"But you did, didn't you?"

"But not—I didn't want to hurt you."

She shook her head. "Don't lie to me, Frank."

I sighed and turned away. "It's one of the few things I do well," I whispered. After a moment of uncomfortable silence, I added, "I am really sorry this happened. I'm sorry I left and let that bastard take my place. And I'm sorry I said those things to you."

She sighed. "You have more than enough to be guilty for. Don't be guilty for yelling at me."

I turned around. "But—"

"But what? That, at least, I deserved after pushing you into this stupid royal play-acting. I couldn't stand the role Father put me in, the pretty little thing decorating the court while the serious men did their serious business. If you saved me from anything, you saved me from *that*. And I thanked you by letting Father put you in the same position."

"Yeah, I probably still could have handled it better."

"Me too," she said. "I was so wrapped up in suddenly being a functional part of my own kingdom that I completely forgot about you. That was shabby of me, and completely worthy of your horrid opinion of nobility."

"No, Lucille, you were never *that* bad."

She covered her face and shook her head. After a moment I realized she was laughing.

"What?"

"No," she said. "You aren't an idiot, but sometimes you act like one. Everything you said about so-called 'noble blood' is *right*. You're right, you screwed up, but you know what it is you did?"

"I think so?" I said tentatively.

"At first I thought we'd pushed you so far into the royal role that you made up your mind to embrace the part—with all the backstabbing, betrayal, and lust for power that entails. Now I find out that people are dead, not because *you* decided to play royal, but because you were inadvertently replaced by someone with actual noble blood in their veins—"

She looked at me, then at her own hands. "Metaphorical blood, anyway. Someone who believes his ancestry alone legitimizes any atrocity he commits."

I wasn't able to respond to that.

"But you said you didn't know what the jewel would do before you wore it."

"I just wanted to be a man again."

"So that, *thing*, chose Prince Bartholomew."

"As far as I know."

She sighed and looked at the ground.

"Lucille—"

"Why come back?"

"What?"

"I drove you away. This was never your kingdom. What do you care what happens here now? Why come back at all?"

"I do care." *I care what happened to you.*

She started crying again and when I reached for her this time she didn't push me away. She sobbed into my chest.

"I'm still angry at you," she whispered.

"I know."

CHAPTER 21

So here I was, with the woman I cared most about in the world in my arms pressing against me. As an added bonus, we were alone in the woods, and for the first time since we'd been declared husband and wife, our bodies reflected the common understanding of the institution.

I know exactly where the story is supposed to go from this point. I've heard enough heroic ballads.

Have I mentioned that I'm not a hero?

I have a long history of less than reputable pursuits, resulting in the allegedly more reputable pursuing me. I've always moved around a lot, and the few women who've had the bad sense to get close to me did so as a prelude to having their heart broken.

I stared into her eyes as she searched for me in Snake Bartholomew's face, and all I could see was her inevitable disappointment. After all of this, it was remarkable that I didn't see it already.

Our faces were inches apart, and I felt her breath on my cheek.

I felt the panic build, and did what I always do when I see an angry troll lumbering down an alley at me.

I dodged.

"I think I have an idea how to fix this." I took her wrists and started back toward the others by the burned camp.

"What?"

The others had been busy salvaging things from the wreckage. The girls seemed to have perfected the knack of adapting savaged armor to smaller sizes. By the time I'd returned with Lucille, they looked a lot more like they had when I had first run into them, except for the jewelry and hairstyles, which made an unnerving contrast with the sooty armor of debatable origin.

Even Sir Forsythe had managed to find his own armor. Apparently he had worn something a bit more subdued into Grünwald.

Everyone converged on us as I reached the top of the rise.

"We need to go to Fell Green," I said.

"What's Fell Green?" Grace asked.

"A wizard town," Sir Forsythe said. "A vile congregation of all manner of dark artisans and unsavory cultists."

"Hey," Laya said, "aren't you an acolyte of the Dark Lord What's-His-Name?"

"Hardly representative," Sir Forsythe muttered.

"We need someone who knows what they're doing to solve this whole evil cursed artifact thing," I said. "Without an actual wizard, we're just guessing."

I heard Lucille mutter behind me, "So *now* you think of asking a wizard about this thing?"

I couldn't argue with her there.

"Brock has heard of this place," Brock said, "and Brock doesn't like what Brock's heard."

"Fell Green has another advantage, besides being a place where a blind drunk goblin could trip over a wizard before leaving the tavern."

"And that is what?" Grace asked.

"No one claims jurisdiction over it. Dermonica is after us—"

"After Snake," Mary added.

"—Grünwald is after us—"

"Snake again," Mary reiterated.

"—and now that Prince Bartholomew has taken over, Lendowyn is going to be after us as well. Fell Green is the only place reasonably close by that avoids all of them."

"We'll need the toll," Lucille said.

"Toll?" Grace asked.

"You can't get in without a toll," I said.

"So you can't sneak us in, mister master thief?" Mary asked.

"No," I said. "You *can't* get in without paying."

"Like I said—" Mary started.

Lucille sighed and said, "He means, if you don't pay the toll, the city isn't there."

"What do you mean, 'isn't there'?"

"It isn't fully in this world," I said. "It's a wizard town. What do you expect?"

Of course this all led to a bunch of questions about how I knew about the place. Fortunately, Lucille volunteered to relate our adventures this time. Even if I came across as more of an ass in her version, I was all storied out. That, and the girls were fascinated about her life as a dragon.

I shut it out because I was guilty enough about what had happened. So she regaled the girls as I led the way to Fell Green. We trudged along a slushy road that followed the perimeter of the Lendowyn border. Traveling by foot, we were probably two or three days away from the bridge on the Fell River that led to our destination—and that was only if the rumors that the town actually moved around were hyperbole.

That was probably a good thing, since I needed to figure out how we were going to pay the toll. There were ten of us now, and nine-tenths of us were recent escapees who were lucky to have boots, much less a purse. Of us all, only Brock had any money, and since he worked for the Lendowyn court now, he only had two gold crowns and an assortment of copper that might be enough for three of us to enter.

Not to mention that, despite salvaging bits of armor, the girls were not dressed for the weather, and were starting to show it. Also, we had all been moving since nightfall the prior day, and the pause by Sir Forsythe's burned camp was barely enough for the girls to catch a second wind. We needed to find rest and shelter soon.

It was clear that I was going to have to indulge in some old professional skills if we were going to have a chance of just getting to Fell Green.

We could hijack some merchant caravan, if we were lucky enough to come across one. The problem was, unless we were a little more bloodthirsty than I was comfortable with, it would probably draw the wrong kind of attention. Merchants, if left alive, would likely report such a theft to the nearest city guard, and the makeup of our party was strange enough that news would probably reach as far as the royal court and Prince Bartholomew . . .

If we were really lucky, we'd run across a merchant dealing in contraband, like Lucille and I had accidentally stumbled upon before our prior trip to the wizard town. Someone already on the wrong side of the law was probably not going to go running to the nearest city watch.

And that gave me an idea.

"Sir Forsythe?"

"Yes, My Liege?"

"Does this area look at all familiar to you?"

"Perhaps, but I have traveled widely in your kingdom."

"Her kingdom." I gestured at Lucille, who had just gotten to the part of the story where the elves showed up. "But when you first met me in her body, you were just coming across from Grünwald, weren't you?"

"Yes?"

"So this road?"

"There are several, but yes, I think this road might be it."

"Good. That means that the inn is just a few miles farther down."

"Inn?" Grace heard me. Her breath came out in a fog and I had the sense that she was forcefully resisting the impulse to hug herself for warmth.

"The Headless Earl," I said.

"I thought we didn't even have the money for the damned toll. How're we going to afford an inn?"

"I wasn't planning on buying anything."

"You weren't . . . oh." I saw a light begin to shine in her eyes. Slowly, she smiled. *"Oh."*

Lucille stopped her storytelling. "What are you planning?"

I've said before that my specialty when it came to liberating objects outside my possession has always been stealth and the liberal use of nimble fingers, and if need be, nimble tongue. However, the last five months of my life had taught me nothing if it hadn't taught me to be adaptable. There was a time for stealth, and then there was a time for cracking skulls.

The Headless Earl was an instance of the latter. It was a literal den of thieves, and one that—after my last stay here—I felt I owed no particular professional courtesy. Everyone there, innkeep on down, was an outlaw of some stripe—mostly of the bash you on the head and steal your boots variety. We came up on the place in the early afternoon, and I had everyone hang back in the woods as we watched people enter and leave. We heard the voices and the sounds of the midday meal in full swing.

"Frank?" Lucille crouched next to me, about thirty yards from the rear of the inn by the stables, peering through the underbrush at my target. "There have to be thirty people in there, maybe more."

I nodded.

"This is insane."

I nodded again.

"You have some sort of plan?"

This time I didn't nod.

"Frank?"

"You know me," I said.

"Improvising?"

I nodded.

"Damn it!"

I shrugged.

"You do realize you don't have a dragon backing you up this time?"

"I've got Sir Forsythe."

"He's not a dragon."

"Lucille, I want to rob the place, not burn it to the ground."

"All by yourself?"

"Hey, you said yourself that I'm not an idiot."

"Are you trying to prove me wrong?"

"Shh." I turned and waved Grace over.

She crouched down on the side of me opposite Lucille. "You going to tell us how we get in there?"

"First things first, we pare down the opposition." I pointed at the inn. "See that door, back by the stables? That's to the kitchen."

"Yeah, and the two guys sharing a bottle next to it."

"Well, little miss outlaw, you think you and yours can remove those guys quietly without unnecessary bloodshed?"

"What about necessary bloodshed?"

"If it's quiet."

"I thought you'd never ask." Grace slipped away.

Lucille grabbed my arm and yanked, glaring at me. "You're sending a bunch of children in there?"

"They know what they're doing."

"But—"

"If you're going to worry, worry about those two guys."

She gaped at me.

If I had any sense left, I probably would have shared her concern. After all, my assessment of the girls' aptitude with the wrong skills was based mostly on circumstantial evidence.

Behind me, the six girls slipped silently into the woods. After a tense five or ten minutes, I caught sight of Rabbit slipping out from the tree line to sneak into the stables on the far side from the two men. The horses barely made a sound to acknowledge her presence.

I saw a small bit of snow dust the ground from above, and glanced up to see Laya flatten herself against the stable roof. After another minute or so, Grace stepped out from the woods. She had stripped off her salvaged armor and weapons, and stood now in the robes of a virgin acolyte of Lysea. She stood there for nearly a minute before the guys with the bottle noticed her.

"What is she doing?"

I held up my finger. "Shh."

There was the predictable banter and shoving when they noticed her. None loud enough for me to make out at this distance. The two men started heading toward Grace, all drunken swagger and ill intent. The larger one said something, and Grace responded with a come-hither smile and a hooked finger as she slipped back into the woods.

The big one broke into a loping run, reaching for his belt, while his smaller companion said something that sounded like it might have been, "Wait up!" By the time the second man was just reaching the end of the stables, the larger man was just about at the woods, and paying no attention to his companion.

That was why he didn't see Laya rise up, twirling an improvised sling to send a rock sailing down on the top of his companion's head. His companion's response was to fall down face first into the slush, at which point Rabbit jumped out from between the last two horses to land on his back to restrain him with what appeared to be three repurposed bridles.

I turned to watch the first guy just in time to see him slip into the woods, and three shadows drop from the trees on top of him. I saw nothing of the impact but some shaking foliage, but after a brief moment Mary and Krys ran out of the woods to where Rabbit had finished tying up the second guy. They reached him as Laya dropped down from the roof, and the four of them each grabbed an arm or a leg and ran off to the woods, carrying the man between them.

I turned to Lucille and I reached up and lifted her chin, just so a bug wouldn't fly in her mouth.

CHAPTER 22

I glanced in the back window, into the kitchen. The cook fires were burning, and I saw three people working. More precisely, two people working, and one balding guy standing by the inside doorway yelling orders. I glanced behind me at the girls, and they had all fallen back against the side of the inn on the stable side of the door. Even in the weak afternoon sun, the shadows were deep enough so no one would see them from the front of the building.

In front of all of them was Lucille. I had tried to object, but five months as a dragon had made her much more assertive.

I wiped my palms on my new clothes, freshly liberated from the larger of the two guys who were now tied and gagged in the woods. For once, the stolen clothing fit.

That was probably the last time that would ever happen.

I waited, giving Brock and Sir Forsythe time to get into position. Then I pulled the door open and stepped into the kitchen. The balding guy, who I remembered as the innkeep, was busy shouting orders at the two women dishing out the remains of a roasted animal of some sort—not enough left on the spit to clearly identify it—along with a thin barley stew and some nearly black bread. The woman placing bowls on a tray glanced up briefly, saw me, and didn't seem to consider me worth the attention as she went back to work.

The bald guy turned toward me. "Karl, are you and Jonah finally done watering the hors—you're not Karl."

I smiled and shook my head. "Sorry, I'm not."

"That lazy bastard—look, no guests back here. Go out front and I'll show you a room. Food's included." He hooked a thumb back out the door he stood by and turned his attention back to the two serving women.

I walked up next to him and said quietly, "Don't you know who I am?"

"Should I care?" He didn't turn to look at me.

"The name's Bartholomew," I whispered to him. "Lately they call me Snake."

"Never heard of you."

Well, how about that?

He finally turned to face me. "So what do you want, Mr. Bartholomew Snake?"

"This."

I slammed my fist into his face.

His head snapped back and hit the doorframe with a hollow thud. He sputtered and blinked at me and I grabbed his shirt, pulling him into the crook of my arm so I could squeeze his neck and help him complete the job of passing out. I heard dishes crash and turned to see both women staring at me.

"I suggest you run," I told them.

Instead, one of them grabbed a knife from a hook on the wall and leveled it at me. "I suggest you let him go."

"Wrong choice," I said as a rock sailed from the doorway and slammed into the side of her head. The knife fell from her hand, to stick upright in the floor as she grabbed her bleeding temple and cursed.

The other woman grabbed for something, another weapon probably. I didn't see what it was, because suddenly the kitchen was filled with bloodthirsty teenage girls. There was a shout or two before the two serving women were subdued, but the noise from the common room was more than enough to cover the sounds.

As the three defenders were trussed up, I closed the door to the kitchen and moved a heavy bench up to lean against it and bar it shut.

When I turned around, all seven faced me. Grace was grinning ear-to-ear, Rabbit had grabbed a hunk of whatever roast beast they'd been serving and was quietly munching on it, Mary and Krys were looking at a few shiny bits of jewelry they must have taken from the women, Laya was squeezing Thea's shoulder with one hand while hefting a rock with the other.

Lucille folded her arms and asked, "Still improvising?"

"Only the details," I said as I pulled a couple of fist-size bundles from the pouch at my belt. The bundles were Brock's contribution; two pouches made from precisely folded leaves and packed with mosses, mushrooms, herbs, and other things that he'd scavenged from the woods.

Brock had never been a good fighter, and before his home village sent him on a quest to get rid of him, he had spent a lot of time with the old women of the tribe learning things like herbal lore.

Sometimes that knowledge came in handy.

I gestured with one hand toward a wooden door a few paces from the one I'd braced shut. "That's the pantry; in the back should be a ladder that will take you up to a secret passage running over all the rooms on the second floor. You should be able to drop down into any of them. If you have to deal with someone, be quiet about it."

"Got it." Grace walked over to the door and pulled it open. In the back of the pantry I could see the ladder just as I remembered it.

"Don't come down till the smoke clears," I said.

Grace nodded, and started waving the girls through and up the ladder. Lucille stayed behind. "And what are you planning to do?"

I hefted a tightly packed leaf. "I'm going to brighten everyone's day." I tossed Lucille the packages. "Hold those for a moment."

I bent down to move the bench I had blocking the door out to the common area.

"You're not planning to go out there, are you?" she asked.

"Of course I am," I said, plucking Brock's packages out of her hands.

"There's thirty armed men out there."

"None of whom know who I am or what I'm doing. I'm just another outlaw taking my respite from my unlawful deeds."

She bit her lip.

"I've faced worse odds than this. If you don't trust me, trust Brock."

"I don't know why, but I do trust you."

"Good. Now hold your breath when you see smoke, and get ready to barricade that door again once I come running through."

Lucille nodded and I strode out into the common room.

Lucille had overstated the case. There were probably only twenty guys in the common room. Maybe twenty-five. Several looked over in my direction when I came out, but after a tense moment they resumed chatting with their neighbors and I realized that those were the people who had yet to have a plate in front of them.

Sorry guys, I thought, *you're going to have a long wait.*

By all rights I shouldn't have been nearly as nervous as I was. This *was* my element after all. I should have felt more at home here than I ever could at the Lendowyn court. I could look out over this rowdy congregation of leather, scars, and facial hair and see the lower third of every thieves' guild I had ever been part of.

Instead, I felt even more on edge. The unease brought uncomfortable flashbacks of the last time I was here, when I was in Lucille's body. Back then the discomfort had been because of the implicit threat of being near this crowd in a woman's body . . .

It was as if I still felt that now.

Or maybe I had gained enough distance from my prior peers to see them more clearly than I wanted to.

While a nearby table broke into a rude ballad about a young woman of unnatural flexibility, I walked over to the large stone fireplace as if to warm myself. I bent over in front of it and took a few deep breaths as I stared into the flames. Then I tossed Brock's packages below the burning logs to land on the pile of coals that glowed on the floor of the hearth beneath the fire.

I held my breath and prepared to run, just as the "Ballad of Bendy Brigit" cut itself short in the midst of some acrobatic maneuver.

"You!"

I turned to make my escape, still holding my breath, but chairs crashed and a large gray-haired man with a heavily scarred face stepped into my path, brandishing a dagger. "Look who we got here, fellas."

A shorter man with a goatee and a ponytail stepped up next to him. "I don't believe it. Snake?"

"Believe it. Just look at him."

From behind me, I heard someone else say, "What you think the reward is?"

"Reward?" someone else said. "The guild wants his liver."

"*Your* guild."

"Why you ain't saying nothing?" said the first man.

I was getting dizzy from holding my breath.

How long before—

My thought was cut short by two men grabbing me from behind. I gasped in surprise just as Brock's packages erupted into clouds of white herb-scented smoke. The men holding me let go as they started coughing, and I fell forward toward the floor.

And I kept falling.

After a long time I put my hands out to break my fall, and the floor felt so far away . . . as if I was trying to reach out and touch the moon.

I tasted licorice on the air and realized I was supposed to be holding my breath . . .

"What What did did you you do do do do do?"

I looked up from the floor I didn't remember hitting and shook my head, trying to make sense of the chaos I saw. The common room had become huge, cavernous, a universe all to itself filled with colors brighter than anything I ever remembered seeing. Burning colors. Some I didn't have a name for. The gray-haired man with the knife ran at me from a mile or two away. His voice echoed off the mountainsides that had once been serving tables.

"What what what did did did did you you you you do do do do do?"

On top of a neighboring cliff, a monstrous scorpion with a human face screamed down at the man, "Where's my ale? I want my ale!"

The gray-haired man turned in the direction of the scorpion, who pounced.

"Give me my damn ale!" it screamed as the two tumbled and fell down a ravine between me and the kitchen.

I got unsteadily to my feet and someone grabbed for me. I stepped aside and a man tumbled to the ground in front of me. At least I think it was a man. When I looked closer at him his face got all amphibian on me.

The giant toad he had become started croaking, "The rats. You see the rats? Do you see the rats?"

I stepped away from the toad and stumbled into a forest that had grown up between a pair of mountains ahead of me. As I did, a raven flew right at my face, pecking at my eyes and cawing, "Don't eat the verbs! Don't eat the verbs!"

I managed to bat it away from my face and ran into the relative calm of the woods, jumping over a python that redundantly hissed "Sssssnake . . ." at me.

It felt like I ran for hours, the forest creatures shouting nonsense at me when they weren't trying to kill each other. I finally broke through to a sunlit clearing, all meadow grass and flowers whose colors burned.

"Wait," I said. "It's winter . . . isn't it?"

"Of course it is. You're hallucinating."

I spun around to find the speaker and saw nothing. "What?"

"This way," the voice came from above me.

I looked up, and a woman stepped out of the sun to stand before me. She was shorter than before, and wore a white dress that was so sheer that she might as well have still been nude.

"Hello again, Frank."

"Lysea?"

"Who did you expect? How many gods do you serve?"

"Serve . . . What?"

She reached out and touched my cheek. "You weren't looking for that bad boy who wrecked my temple, were you?"

"I wasn't looking . . ."

"Of course you were. That's why you're here, and not down there."

I looked down and saw we floated far above the forest floor of The Headless Earl. The woods themselves seemed engulfed in a war between nonsense-babbling forest creatures. I swallowed, remembering my dislike of heights, and tried to will my stomach to stop rolling.

"This is an accident," I said. "I wasn't supposed to inhale."

"My dear," Lysea said, lifting my chin. "No one goes on a vision quest by accident."

"But—" She placed a finger on my lips, silencing me.

"Unexpected does not mean accidental." She gazed into my eyes, smiling as if enjoying some private joke at my expense. "Also, fate is the sum total of the paths we choose to take."

"What?"

"I am the goddess of love and storytelling," she said. She bent over to kiss me lightly on the lips, sending a shudder through my body that felt as if it broke apart the world around me. "That makes you particularly fascinating to me."

I blinked and looked down again, and we were floating above Lendowyn Castle. More immediately, I was back in Lucille's body, wearing the dress that I'd worn when I had married her. "What?" I said, realizing that being intoxicated by Brock's herbs allowed the return of my singular drunken eloquence.

She traced her fingers down the side of my face and my throat. "There's something of greatness in you."

"I don't think so."

"No, you don't." Her fingers lightly touched my breast and I shuddered. "But when it is offered, you choose the higher fate."

I shook my head.

"Look down there," she said.

I did. Swarming the castle were the forest animals, still fighting, wrecking the castle below while still spouting their nonsense.

"Those men below, given the choice, embraced the animal." She turned my face back toward her. "You chose to embrace the divine."

She kissed me again, and this time it was no light peck on the lips. The world melted around me again. When she let me go I stumbled back against the door to her temple, back in the midst of the abandoned memorials. Lysea stood before me as the gigantic nude she had been when we had summoned her. For a moment I thought I had never left her temple, and that everything since had been an extended dream. But I saw myself and realized I was still hallucinating. I was no longer Lucille, I was back in my original body, just as I had been when I saw the Dark Lord Nâtlac.

"What is—"

She rested her fingers on my lips again. "Quiet, my love."

Around us the war of the animals still raged through the city, even though we were in Grünwald now, not Lendowyn. And above the babbling of ravens and foxes and wolves and mice and badgers I heard something roar. A shadow crossed the sun. A familiar fifty-foot lizard descended from the skies, screeching. I tried to back away, but Lysea held me in place.

Fortunately, the dragon was not dropping to attack me.

Not exactly.

It didn't drop toward the temple where I stood, but as I watched, I saw another version of myself, just as I had emerged from the catacombs, covered in sewage, stumbling between the abandoned tombs of Lysea's garden. The dragon fell down on that version of me, and I shut my eyes to avoid watching the carnage.

I had seen my body die once before. This was too much.

"Seen enough?" Lysea whispered in my ear. "Time to go home."

CHAPTER 23

"What? Wait!" I opened my eyes and I was lying on the forest floor. I stared up into the eyes of a huge dragon. It spoke to me in Lucille's voice. "Frank? Are you awake? Frank?"

I blinked and the colors of my vision drained away into a pool of rainbow shimmers as the leathery skin melted off the dragon's face to reveal a human Princess Lucille looking down at me.

I blinked a couple more times before my brain rejoined the waking world. "The girls!" I sat bolt upright, sending my consciousness sloshing around my skull in a very vertigo-inducing manner. "Ulp," I said as I covered my mouth.

"Everyone's fine," Lucille said.

I shook my head slowly. "How long—"

"How long were you out?"

"Yes," I said. I resisted the urge to nod because shaking my head had sent the whole world spinning on a second axis, and I didn't want to add a third.

"About three hours."

"Three hour . . ." I tried to get up, and the universe tilted on that last axis and I just tumbled sideways in front of Lucille in a rather embarrassing manner. She

took my shoulders and rolled me back onto the bed-
roll I'd been resting on.

"I said it's all right. Stay put. Brock says that it
takes a while for the smoke to wear off."

"Yeah." I rubbed my temples and watched as rainbow auras shot across my vision. The one around Lucille was shaped like a dragon. "I think I need to talk
to Brock about that."

"Then talk to Brock." Brock stepped into view,
eclipsing the evening sky and most of the forest. The
shimmering rainbows around him outlined a bearish
silhouette. He held a battered tin cup that seemed tiny
in his hands. He knelt next to Lucille and offered the
cup to me. Steam wafted up from the dark liquid in it.
"Brock made this for you," he said.

I took the cup. The contents smelled like boiled
moss. "What is it?"

"Boiled moss," Brock said. "To help the spirit find
the rest of the way home."

"My spirit has been homeless for a long time," I
muttered before I drank.

All I can say is that I've tasted worse. After I was
done, it felt as if the moss was growing on my tongue,
but the world had stopped spinning, and the rainbow
auras had faded.

"Thank you," I said.

"Brock told you to hold your breath," he said, taking the cup back.

Now that the world had stabilized, I could sit up
without vertigo. "I seem to remember you hanging
out with the village shaman, right?"

"Brock was shown many visions."

"Did those visions happen to involve a packed leaf full of herbs tossed into a fire?"

"Yes."

I sighed. "Did we just give an inn full of thieves prophetic visions?"

"No. Without a shaman to lead Brock, Brock would only see his totem animal."

"Okay," I said. "That explains all the woodland creatures spouting gibberish."

"Brock doesn't understand."

"That makes two of us." I got unsteadily to my feet. Lucille placed a steadying hand on my arm. "So you saw a totem animal?" She asked.

"Maybe everyone else's. Mine? No. Not unless the Goddess Lysea counts."

"Goddess . . ." Brock said.

"Goddess?" Lucille repeated.

"Yeah, Goddess. I sort of inadvertently made an offering to her after we escaped from the dungeons—long story." I shook my head and laughed, still feeling a bit light-headed. "Long story, that's a good one. The offering's a long story." The chuckling got worse.

"A goddess came to you?" Brock asked.

"It was a pretty elaborate hallucination."

"What did you see?"

"All sorts of things," I said. Brock stared at me with an uncomfortable intensity—especially uncomfortable on a man the size of a middling-large bear. "Is there a problem?"

He shook his head. "No. Brock shouldn't pry. Vision is between you and the Goddess."

"Wait a minute. Vision? Go ahead, pry."

Brock shook his head. "Every shaman sees their own world when the spirit walks. Brock could not tell you what it meant."

"Shaman? What shaman?"

"You, Frank."

"Me, what? I'm no shaman."

"Most see their animal when the spirit walks. A shaman sees gods."

"No, I'm no shaman." I turned to Lucille for support, and she was grinning as if she was enjoying this. "I'm not?"

"Why?" Lucille asked. "You're already the Dark Queen, High Priestess of Nâtlac."

"That's different."

"How?"

"It . . . it just is."

Brock placed a hand on my shoulder. "The Goddess touched you, spoke to you, and only you can say what she meant."

"Great," I whispered. "It was bad enough as a hallucination. As a prophetic vision it's worse."

"What did you see, Frank?" Lucille asked.

"I saw Lendowyn Castle fall," I said, "and I saw a dragon kill me."

We left that subject to lie there, but it tracked us like a pack of wolves, just out of sight, waiting for someone to separate from the group.

Sometimes my own metaphors make me uncomfortable.

The good news was that our raid on The Headless Earl was an unqualified success aside from my unscheduled detour into a love goddess's apocalyptic visions. Brock's shaman weed packets had completely incapacitated the majority of the inn's inhabitants. The few who tried to escape from their spirit-walking companions had run into the waiting arms of Brock and Sir Forsythe and were very quickly subdued. Now we had horses, camping gear, weapons, and the girls had fully equipped themselves for the weather. Most important, we had liberated enough gold to pay the toll into Fell Green, pay for lodging there, and have enough left to afford some wizard who knew what they were doing to help straighten out the mess we found ourselves in.

Our group had only stopped briefly, just long enough for Brock to revive me and everyone to sort out the new horses and equipment. Within the hour, we were moving again, toward the Fell River. However well things had gone, we had added a group of twenty-some thieves and highwaymen to the list of people who were probably after us. With any luck they were several hours behind. More if they hadn't been able to retrieve the horses that we hadn't taken; Rabbit had stripped all their tack and sent them off into the woods. By the time our new horses needed to rest, twilight had turned full dark and we had reached the point where the Fell River met the Lendowyn border. We found a place to camp in a clearing in sight of the river. It gave us a wide space both for the horses to graze on what spots of grass poked through the snow, and for us to see any unwanted approach.

Just like Sir Forsythe's men, right before they were barbecued.

I took the first opportunity to walk off by myself

and sit on a rock to watch the river. The cloudy, dark, moonless sky perfectly matched my mood. Below me, the river boiled, too violent to ice over.

Yeah, things went perfectly.

I couldn't even blame the knots in my stomach on Brock's moss drink. It had worn off hours ago. It had been bad enough when I was contemplating what my mistakes had already done. Thinking of what they might lead to wasn't pleasant. Snake had outmaneuvered me even before I'd known who he was. Even the most drastic solution that Sir Forsythe had mentioned, death breaking the enchantment, now seemed out of reach. Death of one body causing a swap back was straightforward enough when it was just us two. But Snake had moved on.

What did that mean? Would it cause a swap with the dragon? A swap with Lucille? Nothing?

This is why we're going to hire a wizard.

That didn't make me feel much better. The logic was inescapable—which was why we were headed there—but that didn't mean I liked it. I'd never been too fond of those in the wizarding profession even before one had banished me from my original body so he could steal it. I also couldn't say that Fell Green was anywhere near the top of my list of fine tourist destinations.

"Hey, want something to eat?"

I turned at the voice briefly expecting—*hoping*—for Lucille.

It was Mary. I couldn't help think about the last time she had tried to bring me dinner . . .

"Sure," I said. I turned back to the river. She set

down a tin plate on the rock next to me. On it steamed a couple of sausages that must have come from the pantry of The Headless Earl. "Thank you," I said, uncertain about what else to say.

She didn't go away. I wasn't surprised. Whatever frustration or anger the girls had with me, half of it seemed focused through her. I could feel the swelling of an epic tirade behind me, and I braced myself for it. But when it finally came, nothing really could have prepared me for the gut-punch.

"Do you love her?" she asked.

I spun around and gaped at her.

She waited a moment, then asked, "Frank?"

"What?"

"Do you love her?"

"Who?"

"Who you think?"

"I know. I'm stalling."

She walked around and crouched in front of my rock and shook her head. Now that she had donned stolen leather and a furred cloak, she looked more herself. Less lost child, more young warrior goddess. Her face was too shadowed in the nighttime darkness to reveal her expression.

"Why don't you answer the question?" she asked.

"It's complicated."

"Is it?"

"Why are you asking?"

"Why you stalling?"

I sighed. "You heard my story, didn't you?"

"The true one or the bushel of lies you introduced yourself with?"

"That's just my point."

"You have a point?"

"My point is—you had the right idea about me all along. I'm not a hero. I'm not even a particularly good thief. I'm reckless, impulsive, and the people around me get hurt even when I'm not being a self-serving bastard. One of my best skills is lying to people, right after lying to myself. I only even know Lucille because of a series of accidents that were either out of my control, or a result of my own bad decisions. Every woman who's had the bad sense to get attached to me has had her heart broken . . ." I couldn't help thinking of Evelyn. It may not have been a real romance, but she had come all the way from Grünwald only to be frightened to death by an angry dragon—

An angry dragon.

"Oh crap," I whispered. I rubbed my forehead as I began realizing the *real* reason Lucille had been so angry. Of course she was. If she had felt anything remotely like what I . . .

And she found me with someone else . . .

"Frank?"

"Sometimes I don't realize the full stupidity of my actions until long after the fact. But I've already hurt her, a lot—"

"Frank?"

"What?"

"You're not answering the question."

"I told you—"

"Everything but whether or not you love her."

"I—"

"But I think I know." She stood up and started walking away.

"Wait."

She stopped.

"Why are you asking?" I asked her.

"Because there's one thing I never saw those dangerous smooth-talking men ever do," she said without turning around. She walked away before I could ask her anything more.

CHAPTER 24

It was nearly a full day's ride before we reached the bridge across the Fell River. Because we followed the river, we rode through a more heavily populated area than the border with Grünwald. It made for a few tense moments, but every group that seemed like it might have made trouble for us had less than half our number, and when you're facing armed riders in leather armor, it matters more that there are ten of them than the fact that most are teenage girls. Everyone gave us a wide berth.

We reached the bridge around sunset. I dismounted and led my horse to the front of the bridge and waited. Behind me I heard Grace say, "Where is this place? Across the river?"

"Just wait," I called back.

At the moment, the stone bridge arced over the boiling waters, the setting sun glinting off the icy stones in an unbroken arch from the Lendowyn shore across to Dermonica. Despite being the only crossing for miles in either direction, the immediate surroundings were the emptiest stretch of the river coastline we'd come across. For a few moments the only sound was the rushing of the river and the distant cawing of a raven somewhere.

Behind me, Grace spoke up again. "What are we waiting—Where'd he come from?"

A familiar bald man with ancient clouded eyes staggered down the bridge toward us, leaning heavily on his staff and holding out a wooden bowl. "Alms—" he began. Then he stopped short about ten feet away from me. His posture got straighter and his blind expression turned into an annoyed frown. "You again?"

"Uh, not exactly . . ."

"And you have the dragon with you."

"Again, not exactly."

The man gave an exasperated sigh and held out the bowl. I threw in a gold crown for each of us. Behind me, I heard Grace say, "And where did *that* come from?"

Once the toll was paid, the bridge became much shorter, and the river itself much wider, as a dagger-shaped island came into existence between the two shorelines. The space where the bridge had been became a broad avenue that cut across the island roughly in the middle. On one side was a forest that was a little too lush, too green, too dense—especially for this time of year.

On the other side was a walled city that filled that whole half of the island. Towers reached up from within the walls to pierce a sky that felt as wrong as the forest.

"Come on," I told everyone as I led my horse up across the bridge.

Lucille rode up next to me. "This looks so different."

"I imagine it does."

"Things shouldn't feel this wrong," she whispered.

"Things *are* wrong," I said.

"This is the body I was born in." Her voice was barely audible. She looked behind us, at the rest of our party, then looked down at me. "How did that man know you?"

I shook my head. "He may look blind, but I suspect that being gatekeeper for this town requires types of sight most people don't have."

"He could *see* who you were?"

"I guess so."

"He said you still had the dragon with you."

I smiled at her. "I do."

She shook her head.

"I should tell you something."

"What?" she asked.

"When I was waking up from Brock's herbs, I was still—I—uh—saw something."

"Yes?"

"Auras I think, outlines of your soul or spirit or something."

"My soul?"

"Maybe. But what I saw, it was the shape of a dragon."

"It . . . you're mocking me."

"No I'm—"

"Just stop it! I know how you feel about me. You're right, but you don't need to be so cruel about it."

"Lucille, I didn't—" I had to jump back because she spun her horse around and rode away. For a moment I was afraid she was going to abandon us and gallop back into Lendowyn, but she just rode back to the rear of our group, next to Brock.

What did I say?

I hate it when I screw up without even knowing what I had done.

We unloaded ourselves into an inn called The Talking Eye. It might have served customers as sketchy as those of The Headless Earl, but at least it was a completely different flavor of sketchy—much more hooded robes and arcane symbols than leather and battle scars. The innkeep didn't look twice at my party of teenage Amazon warriors, and gladly took our ill-gotten gold for a pair of neighboring rooms.

Lucille didn't look at me as I let the girls into their room, though I think I saw her smile weakly as she watched Rabbit run and throw herself on the bed with a joyful grunt. The other girls walked in, looking around the room as if they'd just walked into the elf-king's palace. There was a small iron stove in the corner, with a fire already burning inside. Laya and Krys walked over and crouched next to it, shedding their gauntlets and rubbing their hands.

Behind me, Sir Forsythe said, "The young master should stay with us."

Everyone turned to face him. "What 'young master'?" Lucille asked.

"The young boy by the stove," he said. "It would be improper for him to stay—why are they laughing?"

Krys wasn't laughing. She stood up and appeared a little embarrassed. "I'm afraid I'm a girl too, Sir Knight."

"But—"

I patted Sir Forsythe on the arm and said, "It's

okay. You've been with me long enough I can understand how you'd be confused. Let them get settled."

He stepped back and said, "Yes, My Liege."

At first it seemed unfair that Lucille was wedged into a room with a half-dozen people, but once Brock, Sir Forsythe, and I entered the neighboring room, I envied her. I think just by mass alone, Brock counted as a half-dozen people, and through sheer height and length of limb, Sir Forsythe took up the remaining space.

The less said about the snoring, the better.

The next day I greased several palms to find someone who was expert in the lore surrounding the Dark Lord Nâtlac.

The Wizard Crumley resided in one of the least pleasant areas of Fell Green, and that's saying something. It wasn't winter here, and apparently never was. It felt too warm and too humid, uncomfortably midsummer. Every flat surface seemed to grow sickly moss, and even in midday the alleys and doorways were cloaked in impenetrable shadow. Just standing on the street gave you a feeling that your skin was in danger of being infected by some damp rot. The small patches of open ground resembled swamp, complete with a menagerie of buzzing insects.

Crumley resided at the end of a crooked lane that aimed generally toward the city wall, descending as it did so, until I was certain that we had traveled below the level of the Fell River. The door to Crumley's lair was black oak streaked with green, held together by rusty iron bands. When I used the heavy iron knocker, the sound was muffled by the dampness of the wood.

"Are you sure this is the right place?" Lucille asked me.

"The dwarf was rather specific."

"Before or after you paid him?"

Behind me, Mary said, "Seems rather soggy for a mage."

"Brock's socks are wet."

"I told you," I said. "This is our best chance for a local expert. Most of the people who study the Dark Lord aren't very approachable."

I reached up and tried the knocker again.

"Maybe he isn't home?" I think I heard a hopeful note in Laya's voice. "Maybe you can come back and try later?"

Lucille leaned over and whispered to me, "Why don't you send the girls back to the inn with Brock? Do they need to be here?"

I shook my head. "They can handle themselves fine, and I don't want us to split up."

"Why not?"

"What happened the last time we split up in this town?"

"Oh—"

She was interrupted by the screech of rusty hinges as the door opened inward into a dim passage.

"What?" called a raspy voice. It took a moment before I identified the source. I peered into the darkness and a voice called up from somewhere around the level of my belt, "You just going to stand there, or you going to say something?"

I looked down and saw a stooped old man shorter than Lucille. He had long white hair and beard, both stained with streaks of green. "We're looking for Wizard Crumley."

"Why else would you come down here?" He peered at me through narrow eyes and leaned forward to start sniffing me. The man smelled so strongly of fish and seaweed I had no idea how he could smell anything else. "What do you want?"

"Advice on an enchantment," I said. "Help undoing it."

The man waddled over to Lucille, leaning on a bone-white cane that seemed made of driftwood. He smelled her as well, causing her to back up a step. He licked his lips and turned toward me. "Enchantment, eh? No help for the lovelorn?"

"Huh? No?"

He shrugged. "You're dripping with the Goddess's touch, boy. But your choice." He leaned forward and said in a fish-scented stage whisper, "But watch out for this one, lots of fire there, if you get my drift."

"Are *you* the wizard?" Lucille interrupted.

"See?" The old man winked at me. He spun around and bowed at all of us. "Of course, I am Wizard Crumley the Boundless, the Exceptional, the Knowledgeable—"

"The long-winded," I heard Mary mutter from behind me.

"Can you help us with the Dark Lord Nâtlac?" I asked.

Wizard Crumley sighed and brought his staff down on the stones with a weak crack. "Of course it would be him. Are you sure it isn't the Goddess? She's much more fun."

"We were told you know about the Dark Lord," Lucille said.

"Such knowledge costs, Madam Dragon."

"What—" Lucille gaped at him.

"We brought payment," I said, hefting our pouch of ill-gotten gold.

"Of course you did." He sounded almost disappointed at the prospect. "Come on in then."

"Wait," Lucille said, "why did you say 'Madam Dragon'?"

"Really?" Wizard Crumley waved his hand at her dismissively. "You stink of the lizard, almost as badly as the tall one stinks of the Dark Lord himself. You come for my expertise and you think I cannot sense these things? Maybe you should go elsewhere."

I hefted my purse. "Now you don't want our gold?"

"And be insulted?"

I leaned forward. "If I hadn't heard otherwise about your expertise in the lore of the Dark One, I'd almost suspect you're trying to avoid being hired."

"Are you questioning my expertise?"

"Of course not," I said. "But anyone who had no idea of the vast store of knowledge hoarded by the Wizard Crumley might come to the wrong conclusion, wouldn't they?"

"Don't test me."

"Why would I, when I can hire you?" I held out the pouch. "I can hire you, can't I?"

He glanced from me, to Lucille, to the rest of our party behind us. He reached up and snatched the purse from my hand and said, "Come in, wipe your feet, and don't touch anything."

CHAPTER 25

Crumley led us through several corridors piled with threadbare and mildew-spotted carpeting. We passed overfilled bookshelves where volumes seemed to have been shoved to be forgotten as they slowly crumbled away. The air was damp and heavy, and the halls were dark aside from the occasional candelabra. As we walked, Krys reached out to run her fingers along the spine of one of the books. Without turning, Crumley stopped and grumbled.

"No touching!" he shouted back. Krys yanked her hand away.

He grabbed a torch from a wall sconce and led us down a narrow stone stair that descended through arched vaults where the walls were thick with white mineral deposits. Parts of the walls glistened from the moisture. The steps themselves were stained green and black from mildew, mold, and algae.

Someday I was going to find a wizard who enjoyed working in the open air and sunshine.

Crumley's workshop was deep underground. So deep that I suspected it was not only beneath the surface level of the Fell River, but possibly beneath the floor of the riverbed—if any of that mattered in a town that was only half in our world at best.

Crumley's workshop was a vast space where the torchlight didn't quite reach the far wall. The immediate area was dominated by several long tables piled high with all manner of artifacts; jars of liquid, powders, dried leaves; large mineral specimens; skulls from various creatures; arcane volumes open to arcane passages describing arcane rituals in arcane languages. One space near the foot of the stairs held a half circle of tall black candles as thick as my forearm. They flickered around one of the few clear spaces on any of the tables. Inside the arc of the candles a ceramic crock steamed above a small brazier filled with glowing coals. Crumley held up a hand as we reached the foot of the stairs. "You interrupted me, now please wait."

He hobbled over to the steaming crock, climbed on a small stepstool that stood before it, and strained to lean over it. He inhaled deeply and smiled. "Good. Perfect."

He reached over to a glass vial filled with white crystals and carefully poured a small amount into the crock. He grabbed a wooden spoon and stirred the mixture. After a moment he grabbed a small china cup from the mess on the table, squinted to look inside, and shook it out over the floor. He set it down next to the brazier and started pouring the contents of the crock out into it. A small spider jumped out of the cup and scurried over the side and away before it drowned.

Crumley glanced back at us and asked, "Anyone care for some tea?"

Several voices behind me said, "No thank you," simultaneously.

Crumley took his china cup and took a sip. He smiled and stepped off of the stool. "This is about you and the dragon, isn't it?"

I looked over at Lucille and said, "Yes."

He picked up his driftwood staff with his free hand and gestured to a couple of chairs deeper in the room. "You two sit over there."

He pointed it at the girls, Brock, and Sir Forsythe. "You all stay out of the way." Then he spoke to me and Lucille. "What are you waiting for? You're paying for this."

We walked over to the chairs and sat as directed. Crumley walked in front of us and stood, staring, as he sipped his tea. After five minutes or so of uncomfortable silence, Grace asked, "What are you doing?"

"Quiet!" Crumley slammed his staff down on a nearby table without looking around. "No talking!"

He peered at us for several more minutes, occasionally grunting to himself. Then he finally set down his tea and pulled a pair of spectacles out from the piles on one of the long tables. He perched them on his nose then fished out a bundle of herbs from another table.

He lit the top of the bundle on fire from one of the black candles. He let it flame for a moment before blowing the fire out. He walked up to us and started weaving the smoking bundle around us in a set of intricate patterns. The smoke wrapped us in a white fog that reminded me a little too much of Brock's little packages at The Headless Earl. My eyes watered and I started coughing.

"Well, well, well . . ."

"What?" I gasped. I was dizzy and light-headed from the smoke. I glanced at Lucille to see how she was doing, and I wasn't that surprised that the shadow I saw through the dissipating smoke was more dragon-shaped than Lucille-shaped.

"Both of you have been touched by the Tear of Nâtlac."

"We could have told you that," I said.

"Oh really," Crumley said. "You came all the way here just to impress *me* with your expertise?"

Lucille punched me in the arm. "Please go on," she said.

Crumley paced around. "The Dark Lord's influence has woven itself into your souls, even before the effect of the artifact, I see. This is not the first time your spirits have been uprooted. In you especially—" He pointed at Lucille.

"Me?"

"Clearly your soul was birthed in that body, but it no longer fits, does it?"

"Uh—"

Crumley pivoted to me. "And you, it fits too well."

I shook my head. "What are you talking about?"

He chuckled. "Just that someone who hates their body doesn't want clothes that fit too closely."

"Snake is nothing like me."

Crumley shook his head and held up a finger. "The Tear chooses first the soul's own birth body." He pointed to Lucille. "If your spirit is already displaced, the Tear of Nâtlac will send it home even if it wasn't the Tear that displaced you."

He held up two fingers. "But if it can't do that, it *will* find the best fit."

"My soul doesn't fit in this bastard!"

Crumley strode up and placed his face less than an inch from my own. "A life centered on being something you are not. A liar, a thief. An outlaw tied to royalty and to the Dark Lord himself. A disregard for consequences. Dissatisfaction with where you find yourself in your current life. A deep-seated desire to see King Dudley of Grünwald rotating slowly over an open flame—shall I go on?"

"B-But—" Lucille shook her head, and I think she might have been crying. "I don't understand."

To my relief Crumley and his breath retreated from me. "Understand what?"

"You said my soul doesn't fit. *This is my body!*"

Crumley shook his head. "Not anymore, my dear. The soul is not static. It grows, changes, and becomes what we are. You've moved beyond where you began. Unlike your wife over there." He gestured at me and chuckled.

"Enough," I said. "How do we fix this? Short of waiting a year and a day?"

"Oh, I'm afraid even that won't work now."

"What?" Lucille and I said simultaneously.

Sir Forsythe had been more or less right about the Tear of Nâtlac and what it did, as far as he went with it. Wearing the jewel swapped the wearer with the inhabitant of closest "compatible" body somewhere, for the jewel's own measure of compatible, and the soul's birth body took precedence over other considerations—Lucille's current discomfort to the contrary. Normally the passage of a year and a day would reverse the effects.

Unfortunately, "normally" in this instance meant that the souls in question stayed where the jewel had put them. By accident or design—and I leaned toward design—Snake's maneuver to get Lucille to wear the jewel had mucked everything up. It was bad enough that the Tear of Nâtlac swapped Lucille with someone already affected by the same jewel, but it also swapped her back into her own body.

The expiration of the effect on me meant my soul would want to return to the body I had vacated—but Snake was no longer there to swap back. Worse, when the second transfer expired, Snake's soul would "want" to transfer back to Lucille's body, where it had been. But Lucille was now resident in her own body, and the mere expiration of an enchantment would not have the strength to displace it again. Lucille was not going to move again unless someone invoked a new enchantment.

Snake had effectively made this all permanent.

"Impressive how he exploited the loopholes—"

"Damn it. I want to know how to undo what he did."

"What if someone gets killed?" asked Mary.

"Umm . . . Normally killing someone would knock their soul free and abort the effects of the enchantment—" Crumley leaned over and peered at Lucille.

"You're still a bottleneck, though." He stroked his beard. "But it's possible that killing this body might clear the obstruction."

"That's not a solution," I said.

"Brock wonders if someone destroyed the arti-fact—"

Crumley snorted. "That's treating an arrow wound by burning the bow. Not that you could manage it anyway."

In the end, the wizard was not very helpful. We came away from Crumley with only three pieces of good news.

First, even if she represented a threat to his claim to the throne of Lendowyn, killing Lucille was going to be last on Snake's to-do list since that was one thing that could prematurely de-dragon him.

Second, killing me was probably just as low on the list, since it seemed likely that his coup in Lendowyn was only a prelude to a claim on Grünwald's throne, a claim that he probably wanted to stake wearing his own skin.

The third point flowed from the second. He was not going to destroy or lose the Tear of Nâtlac anytime soon, since that was his only sure ticket back into that skin.

That meant we did have a solution to the Snake issue: All we needed to do was locate wherever he had the artifact stashed, steal it, and—somehow—get a few tons of dragon to wear the thing so he gets deposited back into his own body.

Simple.

I suppose it could have gone worse. My past interactions with wizards had not been what one would call pleasant. I couldn't help feeling a little cheated, though. Somehow I had half convinced myself that hiring one decent magic user would fix everything. In the end, we had spent a lot of gold for someone to tell us he couldn't do much of anything for us. The only concrete thing we were left with after parting from the waterlogged wizard was a small iron token on a metal chain. According to Crumley, like a compass, it would find itself magnetically attracted to concentrations of the Dark Lord's power.

In theory it should make finding the Tear of Nâtlac a bit easier.

I just wished it didn't look so evil. The twisted abstraction of the pendant appeared way more like an icon of unimaginable evil than any of the actual evil magical artifacts that I'd ever seen. I stashed it under my shirt, and it felt as if the unclean metal shape was trying to burrow under my skin.

As we returned to the inn, I allowed myself to think that we had earned a moment or two to breathe, relax, and figure out what our next move would be.

It's never what I expect.

CHAPTER 26

As we entered The Talking Eye, I knew instantly that something was wrong. Having the professional thief's appreciation for quiet and subtlety made me aware of the normal sounds that populated the world around me as well as an appreciation of the fact that there were actually very few circumstances where complete and utter silence was a good thing.

This inn at dusk, time for the evening meal, was not one of those circumstances.

Sir Forsythe picked up on it as quickly as I did. "My Liege—"

"I know." I held up a hand. "I think it may be a good idea to leave, right now."

"What's the matter?" asked Grace. She hadn't picked up on it yet, but I didn't hold it against her. She plied her trade in the woods, and probably didn't have the kind of instincts about people and groups I did—and frankly, I didn't have them when I was her age.

I turned around to usher everyone back out the door. "I'll explain once we're safely outside..." I trailed off because everyone was looking *past* me, not at me. I sighed. "It's behind me, isn't it?"

"Yes, Prince Bartholomew."

"We are behind you."

"Or do you prefer Francis Blackthorne?"

Past our group, through the still-open door, I saw at least a score of sword-wielding guardsmen quick-march into position on the street in front of The Talking Eye, cutting off any retreat.

I turned around slowly to face the speakers. "Call me Frank," I said. "I hate Francis."

Three tall figures stood in front of us, dominating the common room of the inn. They wore long robes that were primarily colored in shades of black, white, and gray, though the fabric shimmered in the evening light, subtly reflecting every color I could name. The hoods they wore hid most of their faces in shadow, except for the mouth and chin, which barely moved as each figure spoke in turn.

"Then we will address you as Frank."

"Your presence here has caused us problems."

"Problems that must be addressed."

"What is the meaning of this?" Lucille spoke up from behind me. "I am the Princess Lucille of Lendowyn, and in the name of the king I demand to know who is addressing us."

"Uh—" the trio responded before I could compose a coherent objection to her throwing her royal weight around.

"The Princess Lucille, indeed."

"The source of other problems."

"Perhaps you know you are missed?"

"Who are you?" I asked.

"We are the Triumvirate."

"You are within our demesne."

"And you are under our authority."

Sir Forsythe stepped in front of both of us, his own sword drawn. "I am Sir Forsythe the Good, and I accept no authority aside from that I have pledged fealty to. You shall allow My Liege to pass unhindered!"

"Do not test us."

"Do not threaten us."

"Force shall not be tolerated."

All three gestured in unison and Sir Forsythe's sword glowed red and the air filled with the tang of heated metal. Sir Forsythe's gauntlets began to smoke and he dropped the sword, hopping backward in an undignified manner. The glowing sword fell to the wooden floor, and waist-high flames shot upward from where the sword burned itself into the wood. Another synchronized gesture and the flames snuffed out, leaving a long puddle of once molten metal cradled in a blackened trench in the floor.

Note to self, raising arms against a trio of powerful mages is a bad idea.

"What do you want from us?" I asked.

"We must maintain neutrality."

"We must protect our demesne."

"You must depart."

"We got what we came for," Lucille said. She turned to me. "That shouldn't be a problem, right?"

I nodded. "It shouldn't be. But given the fact these three brought an army I suspect there's a reason we might be expected to object. Right?"

"There are forces at play."

"Forces not of our concern."

"We will not be party to your wars."

"Wars?!" Lucille snapped. *"What wars?"*

"The Lendowyn king masses his army."

"He waits on his shore."

"He demands his princess."

"The Lendowyn...Father?" Lucille's voice sounded weak.

"Of course he is," I said, rubbing my temples. "He's probably still under the impression that you're me and were kidnapped by Grünwald. Snake's probably convinced him Fell Green has an alliance with them now. Not a stretch, since Dudley's been known to frequent this place."

"What a mess," Grace muttered.

"So we go back," Lucille said. "We can talk to Father and get this straightened out."

"Frank cannot go with you."

"The Prince of Dermonica masses his own army."

"And he calls for the man in Prince Bartholomew's skin."

Oh crap. "I don't believe this. I can understand King Alfred the Inconvenient, we've been riding across Lendowyn territory for days, but how in the world did Prince Oliver find us here?"

Someone behind me cleared their throat. I turned around and saw Rabbit holding up a dagger. A familiar-looking dagger.

"Where'd you get that? You were all disarmed when—" I picked up the assassin's weapon and it wasn't exactly the same one I had carried during my escape. "They were at The Headless Earl."

Rabbit nodded.

"Of course they were. Why didn't anyone mention this to me?"

"We thought you knew," Mary said. "We dragged four of them out of the same room you were in."

"Four . . ."

"𝔜𝔬𝔲 𝔥𝔞𝔳𝔢 𝔟𝔯𝔬𝔲𝔤𝔥𝔱 𝔞𝔯𝔪𝔦𝔢𝔰 𝔱𝔬 𝔬𝔲𝔯 𝔟𝔬𝔯𝔡𝔢𝔯."

"𝔗𝔥𝔦𝔰 𝔦𝔰 𝔫𝔬𝔱 𝔱𝔬𝔩𝔢𝔯𝔞𝔟𝔩𝔢."

"𝔚𝔢 𝔪𝔲𝔰𝔱 𝔯𝔢𝔱𝔲𝔯𝔫 𝔶𝔬𝔲 𝔱𝔬 𝔱𝔥𝔢𝔪."

"I get it," I snapped. There was no way to fight this. We were outnumbered by the guard outside, and even without a small army backing them up, it would require a very special kind of stupid to try and defy wizards who apparently were the major force for law and order in a town filled with other wizards.

I took Lucille's hands. "You need to go back to your father."

"And leave you to Dermonica? No, I'm not—"

"We don't have a choice."

"What about Prince Bartholomew? He's still a dragon. Even if I tell Father what's happening, even if he believes me, he's still legally the prince and my husband in that body."

I nodded. "But you'll be safe. He can't hurt you without risking his position." I reached into my collar and pulled out the iron pendant. "Take this to find the Tear. We just need him to wear it and it will send him back to his own body."

She took it from me and wrapped her hand around it. "Simple."

"Go with Brock and Sir Forsythe, they can corroborate your story." I glanced over my shoulder at the trio of mages. "The Dermonican prince, did he mention anyone else?"

"𝔥𝔢 𝔡𝔢𝔪𝔞𝔫𝔡𝔰 𝔱𝔥𝔢 𝔓𝔯𝔦𝔫𝔠𝔢 𝔅𝔞𝔯𝔱𝔥𝔬𝔩𝔬𝔪𝔢𝔴."

"The king demands the Princess Frank."

"Only you. Only her."

"Frank?" she whispered. "I don't want to lose you again."

I suddenly felt the real possibility that I might not see her again. I leaned down and gently kissed her forehead. "Don't worry," I whispered to her. "You're not going to be rid of me that easily."

I think I may have said it more for me than for her.

I turned around to face the Triumvirate again. "The girls aren't part of this, right?"

I heard Grace said, "Wait a minute."

"We have no quarrel with them."

"They may remain."

"As they wish."

Grace grabbed my arm. "Are you crazy? You're going to walk out to that prince and a bunch of assassins alone?"

"I'm not going to fight. I'm going to surrender."

Her hand dropped. "What?"

"It's not your fight. Time we parted ways."

"You're giving up?"

"This isn't something I can fight head-on *or* sneak around. I'm going to have to rely on the fact they want me alive. Besides, they don't want me, they want Snake. I just need to convince them where Snake is, and we might have an ally in this."

"That's crazy," Grace said.

"That's why I'm going alone."

I'm still trying to figure out how I managed to be so matter-of-fact in front of everyone. Even though I had faced arguably worse situations, I'd never walked into one so deliberately. Even though I likely had no choice, it still gave me way too long to contemplate what I was doing.

The guards of Fell Green escorted me through the town, and I imagined a half-dozen scenarios where I slipped away from them and back into the city. A younger Frank Blackthorne would have made the attempt. But the worst part of my experience of the last week was the loss of my blissful obliviousness to the consequences of my own actions.

I missed it.

I couldn't help but imagine what my successful escape might result in, not just for the girls, who were ready-made hostages to the powers of Fell Green, but for the city itself. I had no love for wizards and the shady merchants who dealt with them, and none for assassins or the royal house of Dermonica, but could I blithely set the two at war? It was something Snake Bartholomew would do, and something deep inside me balked at Crumley's assertion that I held such common ground with the last tenant of this body.

So they brought me to the Dermonica side of the bridge and I set out upon it, alone. I walked down the center of the cobbled span as the wizard city evaporated behind me. Ahead of me, I saw a dozen of Oliver's masked assassins. They stood on the ground where the bridge made landfall, waiting.

I glanced behind me, and with the island gone from between us, I could see the opposite shore, and the arrayed forces of Lendowyn. I could hear cheering in the distance, and while I couldn't see Lucille in the crowd on the distant shore, Brock and Sir Forsythe were easy to distinguish.

I turned back to my own welcoming party.

They still waited, hands on their weapons now.

I could run, back across the bridge.

And spark a war with Lendowyn . . .

I could jump into the river . . .

. . . the swollen, icy, violent river.

Maybe I should stick to the plan.

I sighed, because like most of my extemporaneous plans, this particular one was tissue thin and dangerous as all hell, and my new awareness of the consequences of my actions didn't stop with the options I had rejected.

This wasn't going to go well.

The assassins grabbed hold of me as I stepped off the bridge. I didn't resist. They dragged me back to their campsite where Prince Oliver stood waiting for me next to a wagon that supported a heavy-looking iron cage.

A pair of the assassins held me up before him.

"Hello, Your Highness."

Oliver scowled, strode to me and backhanded me across the face.

Not well at all.

I spat blood on the ground and said, "Can we talk a moment?"

For someone of his girth and aristocratic upbringing, he hit pretty hard. As I shook some sense back into my rattled skull he grabbed my chin and pulled my face up to look into his own. He reached up with his other hand and wiped blood off my cheek with his thumb. "Talk?" he said in a conversational tone.

I made an almost-nod against the hand gripping my chin and said, "There're things you should know."

"Are there?"

"Yes I—" What I was about to say was cut off by his fist's unwanted advances in the vicinity of my left kidney. My legs dropped from under me. I think I heard the assassins holding me groan with the sudden weight, though it may have been me.

A fist twisted itself in the hair at the back of my head and yanked my head back. Oliver smiled down at me.

At least someone was in a good mood.

"I'm listening, Bartholomew."

I struggled to get the words in the right order as they stumbled out of my rapidly swelling mouth. "I'm not who you think I am. My name's Frank Blackthorne. The man you want used an enchantment to swap bodies. He's in the Lendowyn court now."

"Really? Fascinating."

"Yes, King Alfred will need allies to fight against him. Snake's appropriated the body of a dragon, and is probably preparing now to lead forces against Grünwald."

The fist loosened in my hair. "That is an incredible story."

"I know, but it's what happened. It's why I came back here, willingly, alone."

Oliver nodded and took a step back from me. He studied me for a moment and said, "There's something *I* should tell *you*."

"What?"

"When the Pirates of Darkblood Reef descended

on Fellhaven, the lord mayor was in the first line of defenders. He fell in the first moments of the battle. But his wife, she was in the second line. And the third . . . And the last. She led the defense street by street, as the militia and the town were destroyed around her. Her final stand was with old women and men too wounded to retreat. She's the only reason that most of the people of Fellhaven made it to safety inland."

"She sounds like a good—" My sentence was abruptly punctuated by Oliver's boot burying itself in my gut.

"Her name was Madeline," he said. He kicked me again; hard enough that my vision went dark and I didn't remember my collapse to the ground. I could barely hear him now through the blood rushing in my ears.

"She was my daughter."

Yeah, I thought. *Not well at all.*

CHAPTER 27

They disarmed me, tied my arms and legs, and threw me into the cage on the wagon.

I tried to talk to Prince Oliver again, but he wasn't having any of it. Every attempt led to the butt end of a spear coming through the bars to collide with some yet-unbruised part of my anatomy. I decided to cut my losses while there were still parts of my body that didn't hurt. I doubted that I could convince Oliver of anything, not without some measure of proof.

About the only bright spot was, despite being motivated by revenge, Oliver was intent on bringing me back before the Dermonica court to face justice. That would at least give me another opportunity to tell the truth, though I suspected things would probably go as well with his father the duke as it had with Oliver.

It did mean two things. One was they weren't going to kill me right now. The second was that they probably weren't going to sacrifice me in some ritual to their dark gods.

I had to take the good where I found it.

They camped the night through an ice storm. Someone threw a sheet of canvas over my cage, but as I froze through the night I revised my theory about Oliver not wanting to kill me. Sure he would bring me to justice, but if I accidentally died of exposure along the way I doubt Oliver would fret much over it.

I didn't sleep much, and once I did, it felt as if it was only for a few minutes before they started breaking camp and the noise and movement around me made sleep impossible. Shortly after, we all started moving down the road. My cart riding in the midst of a score of paid assassins.

At least I had *thought* it was around twenty armed and mounted men. When I peeked around at what I could see around my cage, the contingent seemed lighter than I remembered from the previous evening. My wagon was still flanked by riders, but when I looked behind, a trio of riders seemed to be falling behind.

Deliberately falling behind.

It took me much longer than it should have to piece together what was about to happen. I plead lack of sleep.

But it is sort of obvious when you think about it. There's one major problem in hiring mercenaries and assassins and such; whatever the alleged principles of the group involved, they've established—by definition—a price on their services. So there's always the threat of someone coming along and offering a better deal.

The risk doesn't even have to come from someone with a deeper purse. When you hire a band of assassins, you have to pay all of them. Someone wanting to sabotage your efforts only needs to pay a few of them—for the sake of argument say three of them—better than you are paid.

And given the number of people after Snake Bartholomew's hide, it was pretty clear that at least one party was willing to make that kind of investment.

The rider to the left of my wagon noticed the stragglers a bit too late. He pulled his horse up and began turning it around as a crossbow bolt suddenly sprouted from his neck. He dropped the reins and his horse stopped in the middle of the road as the wagon kept pulling away. He fell forward and tumbled off the saddle into the road.

I can't give a truly honest account of the massacre, since I did the sane thing and flattened myself in the corner of my iron cage to present as small a target as possible. I heard the cries of men and horses, and the wagon accelerated as the team drawing it broke into a predictably short-lived gallop. When it stopped, it was sudden and accompanied by the sound of screaming horses and splintering wood as the wagon tumbled onto its side. I rolled into the bars on one side of the cage and didn't move. The canvas was frozen to the bars in places, and remained draped over two-thirds of the cage, blocking whatever view I would have had.

Around me I heard curses, shouts, the sound of stamping horses, and the clash of metal against metal.

You could cut the déjà vu with a knife.

I struggled with my bonds, but honestly, if I could have managed freeing myself from them I would have done so long before now. The sound of battle died around me, ending with the sound of a horse or two galloping off somewhere fading into silence; silence that was broken by the sound of footsteps crunching in the snow.

Even though I had braced for it, I still winced when the canvas was ripped from the cage with the sound of tearing fabric. One look at the clothing of the men told me who had won the conflict. They weighed their look much more toward highwayman than assassin.

They also appeared vaguely familiar, in the way that most muscular goons tend to look alike if you've run into enough of them. They opened the cage and dragged me out, and my sense of familiarity ran deeper.

"Now," one of them said as he lifted me by the arms. "I hate interruptions."

"Me too," said one of his companions as he cut free the ropes on my legs. He gave me a grin that had too few teeth of too varying colors. "Now where were we?"

I'd say it's never what I expect, but by all rights I should have seen this one coming from miles away.

A pair of too-familiar goons marched me through the aftermath of a battle that had ended rather poorly for Prince Oliver's assassins, and only slightly less poorly for the prince—as he still breathed. They had bound the prince's arms and had set him kneeling in the muddy slush. My goons forced me down to my knees next to him, and the prince gave me a glare that would have given the Dark Lord Nâtlac pause.

"Of course *you* survived."

"A surprising number of people want Mr. Bartholomew alive," I said.

"I hold you responsible for this!"

I shook my head. "Are you kidding? You can lay a lot at the feet of this guy, but you *knew* how many other people are after him. You're the one who had the ill judgment to employ a bunch of contract assassins instead of Dermonica military—" Something occurred to me. "The duke doesn't know what you're doing, does he?"

Given the intensity of his glare, I found it somewhat surprising that one of us didn't spontaneously burst into flame.

"And now you're a hostage. I don't think he's going to like that."

"I will—" He didn't get to finish the statement because a familiar voice called out, *"Snake!"*

I turned my head to look up at the face that had first greeted me upon my arrival in Snake's body. Weasel was grinning.

"You know," I said, "I never got your name."

Weasel kept grinning and said, "Like that matters. I take back what I had said about you putting up a fight. Setting up rivals after your head just so they can beat each other silly and you escape in the chaos. It would be genius if it wasn't completely bloody insane."

I figured I had a second chance. It was worth a try at least. "I'm not the Snake you think I am."

"Not this fairy tale again," Oliver grumbled.

"Let me hear this," Weasel said, the grin never wavering. "Go on."

"Snake, Prince Bartholomew, is in the Lendowyn court right now."

"Indeed? But you look so much like him."

"Yes, this is his body, but my name's Frank Black-thorne . . ." I was able to relate the broad strokes of my story without interruption. Unlike Oliver, Weasel didn't seem to have any emotional investment in beating me into a pulp.

I finished my latest iteration of my tale and Weasel gave me a slow clap. "Bravo. Bravo, Frank. Bravo."

I sighed. I really had no reasonable expectation that I'd be able to convince— "You called me Frank?"

Weasel stopped his applause. "That's your name, isn't it?"

"You don't actually believe this lying bastard?" Oliver choked out.

"Oh, I don't trust him a bit. I'm sure that he's regaled us with his share of lies and half-truths. But . . ." Weasel leaned conspiratorially toward Prince Oliver. "This guy isn't Snake."

"How can you say that?"

"Because if this guy is the legendary Snake, the lost Grünwald heir, why are there so many rumors of Grünwald agents slipping into various cities in various domains—places with a history with our outlaw prince—and slipping back out more heavily laden than when they arrived? Why are these agents, so obviously of Grünwald origin, going in the direction of Lendowyn rather than their own homeland? Hmm?" Weasel bent to stage-whisper in Oliver's ear. "And you've been preoccupied, but I suspect your father has noticed that poor, weak little Lendowyn has been raising quite an army."

It suddenly fell into place, the final nagging question of why Snake had been massing wealth far beyond what any one person might ever need. Snake's string of more and more spectacular thefts had a larger goal in mind. It always had.

"He was always working to finance an attack on Grünwald," I said quietly. "He wants to take the throne."

"No," Oliver said. "That doesn't make sense. We have him right here!"

Weasel clucked his tongue as he straightened up. "And that's the problem with aristocrats right there. Can't admit they're wrong." He waved one of his goons over. "Now, Mr. Frank Blackthorne, I have a proposal for you."

"What?"

"I'm an independent businessman. At the moment I am at a decision point. Now, we may agree about who you are, and who Snake is at the moment—but the prince here demonstrates exactly how convincing your tale is to those with an emotional tie to the fate of the Bastard Prince Bartholomew. So I could, with a minimal risk to my humble self, return to the White Rock Thieves' Guild with you and receive significant compensation."

"But you know I'm not who they want."

Weasel shrugged. "It matters little to me that they'll be unable to extract the information they want from you. They'll slake their thirst for vengeance at least, and I'll be able to justify the expense of tracking you down in the first place."

Prince Oliver muttered something about there being some justice in the world. If my hands weren't tied, I would have been tempted to punch him.

"But there's another possibility," Weasel said.

"What?"

"I'm a businessman. I have no particular tie to the White Rock Thieves' Guild, they simply offer the highest bounty for your particular skin. Could the Dermonica scion here offer me more, I would gladly hand you back to him."

Oliver brightened. "I can offer you—"

"No, you can't," Weasel snapped. "I know what you were paying."

"If I petition my father, I know I can—"

"Pipe down, sonny."

Oliver started to say something, and one of Weasel's goons grabbed him and placed a dagger against his throat. The prince satisfied himself with glaring at Weasel.

"Where were we?" Weasel said. "Yes. You see, I have a more risky option, but potentially a far more lucrative one. And let's just say that if I was averse to all risk, we wouldn't be talking here."

"What is it?"

"It has been pointed out to me that if our friend Snake is within the Lendowyn court, and if he is indeed massing all his ill-gotten gains to finance an attack on Grünwald, then it logically follows that the spoils from several of the most notorious thefts of the past century are now being collected in one location. The wealth of several nations, unimaginable in scope, hoarded in the only place that our bastard prince would trust."

"Where?" Oliver croaked out involuntarily, wincing at the point of the knife.

"Snake has become the Dragon Prince of Lendowyn. Those he knew would be disloyal to him, he sent on a mission to save the missing princess, only to be immolated in an attack that has almost certainly been laid at the feet of Grünwald. Those he knew would be more loyal to the king, and the king himself, have traveled to the other side of Fell Green to 'save' the actual princess. Left in the halls of Lendowyn Castle are guards loyal to the Dragon Prince, the lost prince of Grünwald—numbers that are unquestionably swelling as his agents return with his wealth. Where else would he store that wealth but within the treasury of a fortress filled with his loyal troops, guarded by a great and terrible dragon?"

Okay, that makes sense . . . "You were talking about a more risky option . . . You don't mean . . ."

Weasel laughed. "Of course I do. The people who pointed most of this out to me also pointed out to me how Frank Blackthorne is actually more valuable than the absent Snake. I have here before me someone who knows that fortress, and knows it with the access of a royal and the mind of a thief."

"You mentioned it yourself," I said. "There's a dragon."

"A dragon you have your own reason to confront. How else will you make him don the accursed jewel?"

"Damn it!" I snapped. "That's enough. How can you possibly know all this?"

From behind me I heard a familiar voice say, "We told him."

I turned around and saw Grace and the rest of the girls standing in among Weasel's goons.

Thea smiled and waved at me. "Hi, Frank."

CHAPTER 28

"What are you doing here?"

"We followed you," Thea said.

"It wasn't difficult," Grace said.

"Since we've been following the prince here since his ambush," Weasel said, "it was inevitable that we would find your distaff allies following him as well."

"*We* found *you*," Mary said.

"We can call it a mutual discovery." Weasel shook his head. "Along with a number of very interesting conversations."

I turned to Grace. "Why? You didn't need to get involved in this again."

Grace snorted. "You offered us a share of Snake's treasure when we got to Lendowyn. You're going to make good on that."

I opened my mouth, and closed it. That almost seemed reasonable.

Almost.

I was left wondering if a half-dozen teenage girls had decided on their own to pull my bacon out of the fire, and if that was the case, I was completely unable to articulate how I felt about it.

"So?" Weasel addressed me. "We have two possibilities on the table. You help us plan a theft of the Lendowyn treasury, or I introduce you to the White Rock Thieves' Guild and you can try persuading them not to disassemble your carcass joint by joint."

I sighed. "You knew what I was going to answer or you'd never ask the question."

"Perhaps, but what I've heard about Frank Blackthorne does not suggest a completely flawless capacity for decision making."

"So you're going to insult your new advisor?"

"Am I wrong?"

"No," I said. "But that is why I'm agreeing to your suicidal scheme." I asked a nearby goon, "So can you untie me now?"

Said goon reached down and sliced my bonds apart with a flourish that made me wince. I rubbed my wrists as I looked over at Oliver. "What about him?"

Weasel made a gesture and the goon holding Oliver lowered the dagger at his neck. "Hostage for Dermonica's good behavior. We'll let him go once we're safely out of his father's reach."

"If you want safety then you'll release me immediately!"

Weasel walked up and tore a necklace from Oliver's neck. He handed it to a nearby goon. "Ride to the Dermonica court and explain that Prince Oliver is our honored guest and will be escorting us during our stay in this fine country." He waved over another pair of goons. "See our guest to his accommodations."

"You'll pay for this." Oliver spat as the two goons lifted him to his feet. "Along with him!"

Weasel chuckled. "Note please, that I did not tell

my man to inform the duke of your unilateral excursions into neighboring kingdoms. Or was your bloodshed on foreign soil diplomatically sanctioned?"

Oliver continued to glare as the goons led him away.

"I thought not," Weasel said. He turned to face me and the girls, who had walked up to flank me. He looked us all up and down. "You have interesting allies, Frank Blackthorne."

"I collect them," I said. "It's a hobby of mine."

"Keep them out of trouble while we plan this thing."

"I think they can take care of themselves."

"I'm sure," he said. "But this job will require more men than I have here, and I would not be happy if the new men and your girls took care of each other."

Grace stepped forward. "What exactly do you mean by that?"

"Anything that you care to make of it," Weasel said. "You chose a rude profession." He waved dismissively. "One of my men will take you to a tent. Eat, rest, we start planning this evening."

When he said "a tent" he didn't misspeak. All seven of us were crammed into a single canvas pavilion. I counted five bedrolls and resigned myself to having a chilly night. Mary threw her pack down in one corner of the octagonal tent in obvious frustration. "I don't believe that rat-faced ass—"

"Ass-faced rat?" Thea said, sending Rabbit into a fit of rather strange-sounding laughter.

"There would be no job, nothing to plan, if we hadn't shown up."

"Calm down," Grace said. "The plan worked."

"Guess I shouldn't expect any more from someone who dealt with White Rock."

"Shouldn't expect any more from a man," Grace said.

"Um." I cleared my throat. "Man here." Rabbit had almost stopped laughing, but she took one look at me and started again.

"Speaking of which," Krys said, pointing at me. "Shouldn't someone talk to Princess Frank about the plan?"

"What plan?"

Grace smiled. "Well, you can get our rat-ass into the Lendowyn treasury, right?"

"That seems to be why I'm not tied up in a burlap sack heading back north."

"So what would it take to set things up so that we get there first?"

"What?"

"You think they're going to let us have a share?" Mary said. "The oaf can't even share credit."

"So we quietly slip in first," Grace said. "Take our share before that oaf can object. Even better, his men can be a distraction covering our escape."

"You realize this is insane," I said.

"You owe us," Grace said. "Not to mention you promised us a share of Snake's treasure in Lendowyn."

"And if he figures you're double-crossing him—" I started.

"He won't," Krys said. "He's too busy double-crossing us. A bunch of girls? I don't think the possibility would even occur to him."

I looked around at all of them. Rabbit had stopped laughing, and even Thea wasn't smiling anymore. "You're serious," I said.

"Yes," Grace said.

"What if I refused?"

"We have something you need," Laya said.

Rabbit pulled a folded cloth out of her pouch.

"What's that?" I asked.

"Rabbit isn't just a good tracker," Grace said. "She's our best pickpocket."

As Grace spoke, Rabbit unfolded the cloth to reveal an unpleasant iron talisman on a chain.

"I gave that to Lucille!" I grabbed for it, but Rabbit snatched it away and shoved it back in her pouch.

"In a room filled with cutpurses and thieves," Grace said.

"And you have some nerve being offended," Mary said.

"We want you to straighten out your personal life," Krys said. "But you're right. It's not our fight."

"But that treasure . . ." Grace said.

I nodded. "But that treasure."

"You're with us?" Laya asked.

After a moment I said, "Yes."

I didn't know if I should have been impressed or disappointed.

The next several days with Weasel and his growing army of brigands and thieves felt very strange. Weasel's immediate crew too easily made the transition from wanting to beat me with blunt objects to slapping me on the back and offering me draughts of ale.

Then there were the trio of assassins who had turned on Prince Oliver. When they lowered their masks I recognized at least one of them from my hallucinatory visit to The Headless Earl; he was easy to pick out because of the strange looks he gave me. Not hostile looks, more the kind of looks a stray dog might give you if you fed it a piece of cheese from your pouch; attentive, head cocked, trying desperately to figure out where the cheese is coming from.

Then there were the others, the recruits who came into Weasel's encampment as we planned the largest theft in recorded history. Many of them I recognized, some from my last visit to The Headless Earl, some from my first one. A few I knew from back during my days when I had thieving as a profession . . .

That, in the end, was what made things strange — thinking of myself in the past tense. These men all had been my peers at one point, for better or worse. Now, for better or worse, I really no longer counted among their number. I was key to their plans, not because I was ever a particularly good thief, but because I was a royal insider.

With these new men came news of the situation deteriorating around us.

The armies of Lendowyn and Grünwald prepared to face each other. Apparently the return of the princess had not defused matters and it appeared Lucille's father was pressing forward with an army whose size belied the state of the Lendowyn treasury when I had been princess. That increased everyone's urgency.

Not that Weasel or his allies cared much about the

potential for open war. They were more distressed at the obvious drain on Snake Bartholomew's assets.

No one mentioned the Dragon Prince being anywhere near the front lines. To me that sounded like Snake. I doubted he would put himself in harm's way, even if he had a dragon's body. Best to sit behind the walls of a castle and let someone else's army do the dirty work.

A fortnight after my "rescue" we exploited the one positive aspect of the massed armies on the Grünwald border. The concentration of Lendowyn's army allowed Weasel's much smaller force of outlaws and assassins to outflank them and cross the Fell River far behind the main body of troops.

True to his word, once the last boat ferried the last group of outlaws into Lendowyn, Prince Oliver had been left on the opposite shore, fuming but unharmed.

Moving over the next three nights, we reached sight of the castle without being detected. Of course, remaining undetected at this point became a significant issue, given the large city surrounding the castle. If we had planned this expedition with mercenaries rather than an army of thieves, this would be problematic.

As it was, Weasel's army of nearly fifty brigands, cutpurses, thieves, and outlaws was able to slip into the city largely unnoticed in groups of twos and threes over the span of two days. This was a good thing, as any large body of men would probably be noticed by the large lizard periodically circling the castle.

The girls had stayed out of trouble, despite the

presence of a few late arrivals from the White Rock
Thieves' Guild. This wasn't due to any deference to
Weasel, but due to the fact that Mary—the one most
likely to feed those men a sensitive part of their own
anatomy—had left to enter the city a full day ahead
of everyone else. No one noticed the lanky redhead
missing before the thief army started melting into the
city, and I was able to slip the rest of the girls in, in
three groups, mixed with male escorts.

The fact that the first group I sent was weighted
two-to-one in favor of my girls didn't register on anyone. And since that didn't register, no one realized
that by the time I sent Rabbit and two men into town,
the odds would be three to one.

After that, the girls were on their own, and I had a
break-in to supervise. I was in the last group to slip
into town, along with Weasel and one of his goons.

Four hours past midnight, and I stood with Weasel in
a stable in the shadow of Lendowyn Castle. It was
cloudy and the moon had set, and the night was broken only by a few flickers of torchlight from high on
the castle walls. My breath fogged, but the air in the
stable was warmed, not just from the snorting horses
in their stalls, but from the press of black-clad bodies
that had been filing in over the course of the night.

We had been waiting for close to half an hour for
the trio of Oliver's turncoat assassins to complete
their job.

"Mr. Blackthorne," Weasel said as we waited. "Do
you have a backup plan?"

"Those are your people."

"It was your plan."

"I never guaranteed this would work. Snake could have changed the guard rotation or where men are stationed—"

"Perhaps. But do you want to explain that to the men in here?"

I glanced back into the shadows, to see the vague outlines of more than two score ruffians. I couldn't help but wish for one of Brock's herb packets and a fire to toss it into.

"If we need to, I'll think of something."

"Good man."

Fortunately for everyone, I was not required to indulge in my talents for improvisation. After another quarter hour, a tiny bright flame flared twice in the small doorway beside the main drawbridge.

"That's the signal," Weasel said. "Get the boats."

"Boat" was a generous term for the three misshapen objects we hauled the quarter mile to the moat's edge. They were, at best, improvised half-breed rafts made from rope, canvas, planks, and logs covered with a generous coating of still-tacky tar until the thing was blacker than the sky above us. They were wobbly, leaky, and just enough to ferry us across the twenty yards to the raised underside of the drawbridge where three ropes waited for us.

It took three trips for the entire group to make it across, the last half-dozen men swimming as one of the "boats" inevitably sank into the moat. Luckily for those men, the Lendowyn crown never could afford to stock the moat with anything more threatening than leeches or the occasional frog.

Weasel's thief army slipped into the main courtyard, squishy and non-squishy alike. They hugged the walls and the deepest shadows as they filed in. Even with my eyes well adjusted to the dark, a quick glance at the space didn't reveal anything out of place, though the last time this many people filled this courtyard was my wedding.

I led them to an oak door at the base of the keep. In a siege it could be barred and sealed against invasion, but now it was just overseen by a conveniently deceased guard. I paused by the body, wondering if I had known the guy. He was almost certainly one of Snake's loyalists. Snake wouldn't give guard duty to anyone questionable. But still, the corpse lay there wrapped in the colors of the Lendowyn crown, and everything felt deeply wrong.

Not that anything had been right for a long time.

From behind me I heard Weasel's voice. "What's the holdup, Frank?"

I didn't have much choice, did I?

I pushed the oak door open, revealing a dark stone corridor. I waved Weasel in.

"Here."

The thieves filed in after me, and after the last of them slipped in, I led them through a maze of corridors and down to the treasury. No one questioned the absence of the guards and the fact that the doors hung open. The glint of gold and jewels in the dim torchlight was enough to capture their attention. Even Weasel, the practical one, stood in the doorway staring in at the piles of treasure that disappeared into the darkness out of the torches' reach.

That momentary distraction was enough for me to slip away. They'd notice me missing in a few moments, but I was betting that the unimaginable riches laid out before them would take priority. Weasel would probably be relieved that he didn't owe me a share.

I was just happy that the girls had been here and already gone with whatever they could carry. Good for them. I had other priorities.

I scrambled up the levels of the castle, up past the great hall and the royal chambers. The Tear of Nâtlac had to be here. I had already narrowed down the possible locations by a process of elimination. Snake would not have wanted to destroy the jewel, as it was the only way back into his own skin. It followed from that that it would be unlikely he would risk flying off with such a crucial element of his plans. For that matter he wouldn't hand it off to a subordinate, however trusted.

Of course, that left a limited number of places it could be, as the castle itself was not constructed to accommodate a dragon. It had to be in the upper reaches, close to where Princess Snake had handed Lucille his "gift."

I slipped out of a door and into the night air. I shivered a little as I looked out over the shadowed towers of the castle, silhouetted by the faintest hint of dawn, still hours away. My breath came out in a fog, and I felt my heart thud in my throat.

It wasn't fear. I had been in more dangerous situations before.

It was memory.

I stood here, in the upper reaches of the castle

where I had spent time talking to Lucille, my dragon husband, before her duties had taken her away, and before my own depression and self-pity had taken me.

Did I *miss* that?

What sense did that make? I didn't belong here. The old fishy wizard was right. I fit much better in the role of Snake the thief . . .

I faced the night sky and whispered, "If that's the case, I best get to some stealing."

CHAPTER 29

"Okay, let's see if this thing was worth it."

I pulled the ugly iron talisman from around my neck and held it up so it dangled, slowly twisting on its chain. I didn't know exactly what I'd do if this didn't work. Even if my reasoning had been perfect and the artifact was up here somewhere, there were still innumerable hiding places, and without some further direction I could spend days searching buttresses and parapets for something not much larger than the talisman I held out in front of me.

I stared at the thing, wondering if there was some sort of invocation needed for it to work, or if I'd be able to tell if it *was* working.

I needed to stop thinking of ways this could go wrong.

Looking at the twisted knot of iron made my brain ache with a sense of wrongness—especially when I realized that I saw the thing quite clearly in near darkness. It didn't help that it appeared to be slowly twisting in on itself, despite hanging straight down from its chain.

A glow pulsed within it. Something about it made me sick to my stomach, but I couldn't help but stare deep into the pale emerald light. As I did, the twisted iron moved apart, like an eye opening, an eye that didn't belong in this universe.

The green glow faded until I was looking through the open iron framework at the silhouette of a parapet near the top of the tallest tower. As the otherworldly eye closed again, I saw a dim reflection of the sick green light wink at me from the top of the parapet.

I put the talisman away.

I can take a hint.

The unused tower was one of several places around the castle that, over the years, had been closed off due to lack of funds. It was easy enough to get inside from the roof and begin ascending. However, about halfway up, I ran out of stairs.

And floors.

I climbed out onto a pile of broken stone and timbers, looking up at the hollow interior.

It's never easy.

I pulled myself up on the pile of rubble near one of the walls. Then I pulled myself up and started to scale the inside wall toward the top of the tower.

I've had worse climbs in my career. The remains of the stairway left more than enough purchase for me to make my way upward. It just took a while in the dark. I lost any sense of time, and when I squeezed out of one of the upper windows to climb up the last dozen feet to the parapet, the sky had turned much lighter.

But I saw the Tear of Nâtlac, its chain wrapped around the neck of a gargoyle. I couldn't believe my luck, having something finally going right.

I was right not to.

I climbed out of the tower, back onto the roof, and the sky's rosy dawn glow was already fading. If all had gone as planned, Weasel's men were long gone and I was the only invader left in the castle. My strategy, as it was, was to hide myself somewhere and stake out an opportunity to try and ambush the dragon.

When a shadow passed between me and the sky, I realized that the "ambush" part of that plan wasn't going to work.

Something thudded onto the castle roof behind me.

"Frank Blackthorne."

That impossibly deep voice was very familiar to me, but it had been months since I'd found it actually frightening.

"You're not going to kill me," I whispered. Unfortunately, my certainty was tempered by the memory of what had happened to the late Wizard Elhared when he said pretty much the same thing to me. You don't tend to forget plunging a dagger into your own neck, regardless of who happened to be wearing it at the time.

"No one said anything about killing you."

Unfortunately, that was not at all reassuring.

I slowly turned around toward the speaker. The dragon faced me, early morning light shining almost iridescent against the black scales, the serpentine neck twisting so that the massive head hovered above me, looking down, giving a bowel-draining view of a set of jaws that could easily snap me in half.

For months I had grown used to Lucille in this skin, to the point where I had forgotten the atavistic fear of standing this close to something that could crush me like a bug while setting me on fire. Forgotten it, but I hadn't lost it. I just could see Lucille inside the dragon's skin.

The dragon now—the posture was different, the look in the eyes, the cock of the head. Everything screamed to me that this was someone else, and the thought was so wrong that everything inside me dissolved into quivering spineless jelly.

It was a miracle I didn't collapse into a blubbering puddle.

"Your reputation precedes you."

"I could say the same."

"Perhaps, then, you might rethink what you are doing."

I held up the Tear of Nâtlac so it glittered between us. "Perhaps you might rethink what you're doing."

"Believe me, I have thought quite deeply about this."

"Put it on," I said. "End this."

The dragon laughed. It was unnerving when Lucille had chuckled in that form, but with Snake behind it, the laugh felt as if a crack in the world had suddenly started leaking all the sanity out.

The dragon shook its head. **"That is why you should join me, Frank. Our goals coincide, the only issue you have with me is the timing."**

"Hardly the *only* issue."

"Beyond possession of this body, what is there?"

"Really? You think I haven't noticed you starting a war with Grünwald?"

"Please. You tell me that war with Grünwald is anything other than inevitable? You stood in front of the queen herself and prevented an invasion."

"And you're trying to provoke one!"

"First rule of war. Advantage goes to the party that chooses the time and place of battle. And if you care for Lendowyn, you should welcome my hand in this."

"By all the Dark Lords of the Underworld, *why?*"

The dragon lowered its head until its eyes were nearly even with my own, the fang-filled mouth barely a foot from me. If it hadn't been a dragon speaking, it might have been a conspiratorial whisper. As it was, the words vibrated the teeth in the rear of my mouth.

"Because, Frank, Lendowyn is not going to win any other way."

The dragon withdrew and cocked its head. When Lucille looked at me like that it was inquisitive. When Snake did, it was just condescending.

"Return that token, and I promise I will relinquish this body—but only when the throne of Grünwald is empty of my pretender brother."

"No. I've seen what you did to Sir Forsythe's men."

"Your posturing is becoming tiresome. Those men were threats to the crown."

"You, maybe. Not the crown."

"You know Lendowyn law. While I wear this body I *am* the prince."

"I'm not going to let you do this."

The dragon laughed and lifted a taloned hand to reach for me. I backed up a step and dropped the jewel to the flagstones at my feet. I rested my heel on it and said, "Stop."

The dragon stopped reaching for me and said, **"You aren't going to destroy that."**

If you were certain, you wouldn't have stopped reaching. "Back off, Bartholomew. You must have some idea why I put this on. I could happily live the rest of my life in your skin. But I think *you* want it back, or you would have smashed this yourself."

I started to think of demands. I had negotiated with the elf-king himself, I was certain I could leverage this momentary advantage into an overall solution. Even if Snake just took the dragon and flew off to bother Grünwald without any soul-shifting—there were worse fates than consoling a permanently human Lucille. There would be legal ramifications but—

The dragon was laughing at me again.

"Don't try anything!"

The dragon shook its head and said, **"Look down to the courtyard."**

"Why?"

"Humility."

I glanced over the edge of the parapet beside me, down to the courtyard in front of the keep. I saw a mass of armed men wearing black Grünwald armor. It was obvious even though they wore tabards with the Lendowyn colors, as the spikes and embossed skulls were something of a giveaway.

Unfortunately, they weren't the only ones down there. A group of ragged and bloody men had been

herded into a small area surrounded by Grünwald
troops three deep. I recognized them as part of Weasel's army. There were maybe a dozen of them. I
wanted to believe that meant the majority of them
had made their escape, but Weasel stared upward with
an expression that told me that optimism was a suck-
er's game.

**"Did you really think I'd allow a group of petty
thieves to take away the work of years?"**

"To be honest, that wasn't my idea."

**"Of course, you used them to distract me. Slightly
more competent of you, but just as futile. Return that
bauble, Frank."**

"Why should I give up my one bargaining chip?"

"You should look down there again."

I did.

Oh crap.

Lucille and King Alfred were both imprisoned with
the thieves and outlaws. Normally I'd be all for cutting
the royalty down a peg, but nothing about this was
normal.

**"Tell me that there isn't someone down there you
would prefer to continue living?"**

I shook my head. "You're bluffing. You can't kill her."

"I don't bluff, Frank." He called down to the courtyard, **"Captain, kill someone trivial."**

One of the larger Grünwald goons pulled someone
out of the crowd of prisoners. "Wait, don't—" The
sword came out and down before those two words
were out of my mouth. I didn't know the man who
crumpled at the Grünwald captain's feet, but I now
saw at least three of my girls in with the prisoners.

No this is going so wrong—

The dragon turned its head toward me. **"Only one person down there matters to me."**

"Stop this—"

"Captain!"

"Stop!" I kicked the jewel away, between us.

A set of talons the size of my forearm came to slam point-down on the flagstones between me and the jewel. **"Now,"** the dragon said, **"you're showing some good sense."**

He dragged the jewel back toward him, slowly, talons screeching on the flagstones. **"While we wait for the guard to come up here, maybe you could enlighten me on how you were planning to make me wear this token before I was ready?"**

I shrugged. "I like to improvise."

CHAPTER 30

There wasn't anything I could do with everyone held hostage by Snake's men. At least nothing that came to mind before a pair of Grünwald-armored thugs came to escort me down to the rest of the prisoners.

Like the bridge at Fell Green, my escape was blocked off not by physical restraints, but by the potential consequences of my attempt. Snake had too many hostages and I couldn't endanger them like that. Especially since I was already feeling the guilt over the three girls I hadn't seen with the prisoners. I couldn't help but blame myself for the whole catastrophic sequence of events.

Another unwanted similarity between me and Snake: the death and destruction we left in our wakes.

I suppose the smart thing to do at this point was to let Snake follow through on his plan and trust his word that he didn't care about Lendowyn and would return the reins of the kingdom once he attained his own throne.

For some strange reason, I didn't find his promise reassuring. I had never known an aristocrat to willingly relinquish power once acquired. Aside from that, there was the question of how much of Lendowyn would actually remain once Snake had successfully stomped King Dudley's army.

At this point, Fate would have had to go through some severe contortions to make things worse.

Fate was up to the challenge.

A pair of Grünwald thugs marched me down through the castle, down toward the courtyard and the prisoners. I guessed from the fresh armor that these guys were new men, brought in via Snake's attempt to beef up the anemic Lendowyn army. The men who had followed me, in my role as the new Dark Queen, tended to have more worn and battle-scarred armor.

Not that they were any more battle-hardened than these guys, but new armor costs money. I also strongly suspected that most of those men had followed Sir Forsythe in the doomed mission to Grünwald.

It's funny how I had managed to live my whole life up to now without truly hating anyone. Even the damn Wizard Elhared who had so screwed up the lives around him, thrusting me into the princess's body in the first place . . . I don't think I truly *hated* the man. He had pissed me off beyond all reason, caused me and Lucille no end of grief, but what I felt about him was barely a flicker compared to the bonfire of loathing I felt for Snake Bartholomew.

If I could get my hands on Dracheslayer . . .

Then I could what?

Yes, there was a magic dragon-slaying sword in the armory, and I would dearly enjoy plunging the thing through Snake's neck. But I wasn't Sir Forsythe, and I doubted that I'd ever get close enough to land a killing blow. It might protect against dragon fire, but not from a rock dropped from a sufficient height, or from a castle full of the dragon's allies.

Get the sword and get it to Sir Forsythe.

Really, that possibility—even if my momentary escape didn't trigger a wholesale execution of hostages—had the same faults as wielding the thing myself, though he'd probably kill a lot more of the dragon's allies before a rock got dropped on his head.

As we moved through one of the corridors in the upper reaches of the keep, one of my escorts drew his sword and held it up in front of me, blocking his partner with the flat of the blade. "Hold up, Leo. Something's up."

"What?" his companion asked.

"Ahead. Right."

We both stared ahead of us to see what he was talking about. We stood in the middle of a long corridor hung with threadbare tapestries. Forward and to our right, one of the tapestries bulged from the wall at the base. The bottom, where it touched the floor, showed a spreading dark stain.

The man with the sword walked up to the tapestry and used the point of the sword to pull it the rest of the way from the wall, revealing a corpse hastily hidden behind it. The tapestry rippled and fell down at his prodding, dropping down over the body. Almost simultaneously, the other guard released my arm. I turned to my side, as he dropped to the ground next to me.

The man with the sword turned to face us. "We have to raise—" When he saw his comrade on the floor by my feet, the sword came up to point at my throat. "Don't move!"

I raised my hands in a hopefully inoffensive manner. "I didn't—"

"What did you—" He was interrupted by something round and shiny suddenly appearing across the bridge of his nose with a solid wet thud. His head snapped back and he dropped like a bag of wet barley through the hands of a drunk brewer.

I spun around and saw Laya step out of the shadows behind us, a leather sling dangling from her hand.

"You're all right!" I said.

"So are you," she said, smiling a bit as she bent down to retrieve a shiny yellow object from next to the first guard's head. Mary and Krys ran ahead and stationed themselves at the end of the corridor, past the body and the tapestry.

"You're all all right!" I said, feeling a relief completely aside from the fact I was suddenly free to think of some way to fight Snake, or at least free the hostages.

"We can take care of ourselves," Mary said.

"The others?" Krys asked, looking over her shoulder at me.

"Grace, Rabbit, Thea—they're in the courtyard with a bunch of hostages and more of Snake's troops."

Laya ran up and grabbed the other shiny blob from the remains of the swordsman's face. She shook some of his face from the object and I could see that it was a heavy gold nugget. She saw me looking and Laya sighed. "I only have three of these. It was a mess down in the treasury, I had to improvise some ammo." She faced the tapestry. "So why'd you kill this guy and not the ones holding you?"

"Why'd I?" I ran up to the tapestry. "I thought *you* had."

"We were coming from the other direction," Mary said. "Hurry up. We're exposed out here."

I pulled the tapestry away from the body.

The body on the floor sported a dagger in the throat, and it was a dagger I recognized.

Yep, it's gotten worse.

Snake was right. I had been using Weasel's thieving expedition as a distraction to take the attention off of myself as I tried to recover the Tear of Nâtlac. The girls had tried to use it as a distraction to cover their own escape.

It was such a good idea, why wouldn't someone else decide to appropriate it?

What if, just for the sake of argument here, the three turncoat assassins Weasel had used to open up the way to the treasury weren't really turncoats? What if, upon being recruited by Weasel and company, those assassins reported back to their employer exactly what he was planning? What if Prince Oliver wasn't as obtuse as both Weasel and I had been assuming? What if, knowing what Weasel had known about the movement of Snake's assets, Prince Oliver had come to the same conclusion Weasel had, that Snake had taken over Lendowyn in a secret coup? And what if, despite his protests to the contrary, Oliver had believed what I had told him about Snake vacating this body in favor of that of the Dragon Prince?

What if *all* of this was Dermonica's feint before the *real* attack?

All of which would be a somewhat weak chain of reasoning based on the presence of one misplaced assassin's dagger, if it wasn't accompanied by the sudden sounds of battle outside the keep.

We were still high enough in the keep proper for us to find an arrow slit to look down on the outside of the castle walls.

It was bad.

"Prince Oliver," I said, "why'd you have to be smarter than Prince Bartholomew?"

"What's going on out there?" Mary asked.

I stepped aside and said, "Look for yourself."

Mary peeked out and whistled.

"Those aren't just assassins and mercenary thugs," I said. "That's the entire Dermonica army." And what I had seen was a military force larger than anything I think Lendowyn could have managed, even with Snake's financing.

"How did they get here unopposed?" Mary said.

"Between massing on the Grünwald border and preparing for a fifty-thief invasion here, I think our friend Snake left the entire Dermonica border undefended."

"Wait," Krys said, "that doesn't make sense. Prince Oliver didn't believe you, and his father didn't even know . . . Oh."

"He fed everyone a bucket of goblin crap," Mary said.

"We were all played for fools," Laya said.

"Well," I told her, "I'm sure Snake feels worse."

*   *   *

If I had any good sense—which I obviously didn't, given the situation I found myself in—I would have found a way to slip outside and run for my life.

Instead, while the mass of the Dermonica army worked to breach the outer wall, I led our way down to the courtyard. We met no other living guardsmen inside the keep. The trio of non-turncoat assassins had been keeping themselves busy eliminating most of the defenders inside the building. The only ones left to defend the wall were the men Snake had massed in the courtyard for my benefit.

In the interests of keeping myself calm in the face of adversity, I did not attempt to calculate the ratio of attackers to defenders. After five-to-one, did it really matter?

Down in the courtyard, the prisoners had been clustered into a group behind a single thin line of guards who faced outward at the new threat across a now nearly empty courtyard. Attackers poured over the wall, engaging the bulk of Snake's men who had rushed up to defend against the breaches that appeared to come from all sides simultaneously.

Lucky for everyone, I and a trio of girls sneaked out of the keep to their undefended rear instead of one of the assassins who must be still at large.

The four of us were able to slip into the rear of the crowd of prisoners and start cutting bonds. I worked my way to the edge of the group and slit the rope binding the wrists of Sir Forsythe.

Without warning, someone grabbed my collar and pulled me away from him. I landed on my ass at the feet of a huge Grünwald mercenary. He raised his sword, and I brandished my recovered assassin's dagger as if it could provide an adequate defense.

The man started a lethal swing, then halted himself, sword in mid-stroke, eyes widening. I saw him curse in frustration, right before Sir Forsythe tackled him.

Of course, Snake wants this body intact. Everyone would have orders not to kill me.

"What does he think he's doing?" I heard a familiar voice yelling. I turned away from Sir Forsythe's pounding of the unfortunate guardsman to see Princess Lucille stepping out from the mass of prisoners, rubbing her wrists. She stared up at Snake the Dragon doing lazy circles in the sky above us. The guardsmen turned, raising swords uncertainly at her. Snake had obviously given similar orders in regard to the princess as he had me.

"Look at him up there," Lucille said. "Why doesn't he strafe the enemy?" She yelled up at him, *"Don't you know how to be a bloody dragon?"*

"He can't hear you," I said.

She turned around and saw me. "Frank?"

Just then, the guards around her lost their indecision. They whipped around and ran off toward a column of Dermonica troops that had broken the defensive line and were storming down one of the staircases to the courtyard.

I remembered my vision of Lendowyn Castle being overrun.

"I think we may be in trouble," I said.

CHAPTER 31

The girls finished freeing the prisoners and we stood in the center of a slowly contracting circle of calm. There were no guards left as such, as all had run to defend against the Dermonica troops pushing down from the walls. The dragon flew above us, doing nothing.

We moved toward the only defensible position left, the keep itself. But as we moved, a group of a half-dozen Dermonica troops broke from the surrounding melee to rush to meet us. Sir Forsythe raised his captured sword and yelled, "For Honor!" as he ran ahead to meet the attackers.

Snake finally acted. He swooped down, flew over Sir Forsythe, and immolated the attackers less than a dozen feet from him. The flame shot out in a cone, washing over the six Dermonica attackers to splash against the base of the wall near the keep, catching a few of his own mercenaries.

The fighting around us seemed to pause for a moment as everyone suddenly realized a dragon was part of this fight. For a few seconds all I heard was the crackle of flames and the screams of the poor bastards who hadn't been killed instantly.

Two things occurred to me then.

First, Snake did not have a particularly precise weapon.

Second, he didn't engage the enemy like Lucille wanted because he was preoccupied with keeping us alive. To hell with the keep, or the people defending it, he couldn't let me or Lucille die.

Some think courage is the absence of fear.

Some think courage is acting in spite of fear.

I think courage is just not having the time or inclination to fully contemplate how stupid or dangerous what you're doing actually is.

Sir Forsythe stumbled back from the dead Dermonica attackers missing a substantial amount of his once-grand facial hair. As he did, I stepped forward and grabbed his sword. He looked at me with wide eyes and said, "My Liege?" before breaking out in a fit of coughing.

I don't blame him. Burned hair smells awful.

Sword in hand, I ran toward the thickest part of the melee. I heard Lucille and several of the girls call out to me, and I supposed from their perspective I was engaged in a stupid suicidal gesture.

But that was beside the point.

As I placed myself shoulder-to-shoulder with the Grünwald defenders, swinging a too-heavy sword in a particularly ineffective manner, I wasn't expecting to add much to the sum of Lendowyn's defenses.

That was Snake's job.

I barely got three swings in before a shadow passed above us and a wall of fire fell down just behind the line of Dermonica troops we were fighting. In moments, my section of the defensive line—no thanks to my efforts—began pushing back the attackers.

I couldn't help grinning even as my blade hit helmets and shields with uselessly bone-jarring force. I might not be a factor in the defense of the castle, but I could damn well encourage Snake to participate to keep his own borrowed skin intact. The dragon laid waste to dozens of Dermonica attackers almost before we reached them, and we waded through charred carnage all the way to the top of the wall.

That's when the flaws in my plan became apparent.

Despite the endless supply of attackers, we had run out of them. The Dermonica command wasn't stupid. They had seen quite clearly that the dragon had focused its attacks on one section of the wall, so—quite logically—they had dropped the attack in front of me to concentrate on the unburned flanks.

There was also a second flaw in my plan.

Dermonica troops now filled the courtyard, and the prisoners and about a dozen Grünwald mercenaries were pinned down at the base of the keep, cut off from any way inside.

I watched Snake fly down to carve flaming swaths through the enemy in the courtyard, but while Dermonica seemed to have an endless supply of fresh reserves, we had only the one dragon. I saw the flame was weaker now, and as Snake flew low enough to do damage, a wall of arrows flew up toward him, fired from the walls to either side of me.

I saw one draconic eye turn in my direction, glaring.

He coughed out a ball of flame to slam into the archers on top of one wall. As he pulled upward I heard a vile curse on the air, followed by one word.

"Enough!"

The dragon flew up and perched unsteadily on top of one of the highest towers in the keep. He was obviously near exhaustion, sides glistening with the blood from dozens of wounds and pulsing with his labored breathing. The dragon lifted one bloody clawed hand, and I saw something glitter in its grasp.

"Oh no, you're not—"

He was.

"Crap!" I bellowed as my brain slammed into a point dizzyingly high above the courtyard. My vision blurred and the colors went all wrong. My mouth—my huge, huge mouth—filled with the taste of blood and sulfur. Every part of me was too big and too far away, and my head swayed in an impossible way above my body as my stomach began to rebel at my precarious location and my head throbbed with the multiple hammer blows of having my consciousness ripped from my body *again*.

I blinked with one eyelid too many and my vision cleared enough to see a tiny version of Snake lying on top of a soot-scarred castle wall, still far from any enemy troops. As I watched, he got unsteadily to his feet and started a wobbly run toward the outer parapets.

"No, you bastard!" I yelled as he climbed over the outside wall. The pain from speech caused my vision to blur. Disoriented, I reached out with a long muscular forearm to swipe at him with a taloned hand. My arms might have been way too long, but they weren't *that* long. I leaned forward too far and I felt the huge mass of wings and tail fly out unconsciously to pull against my back to keep me from toppling forward with the swipe.

It surprised me and I made the mistake of looking behind me. My head whipped around on its impossible neck until I was staring straight down at my own scaled backside, massive tail, and a hundred feet of nothing between me and the top of the castle. The vertigo hit me full force, and everything around me began toppling. I grabbed the tiny bauble that hung around my neck and tried to grip my perch even tighter with my feet, tearing away chunks of the tower in my panic.

I spread my wings as the tower gave way with my balance, but the castle decided to wrap me in a cloud of rubble and the realization that a single dragon is not the be- or end-all of military supremacy.

I managed to cling to my consciousness and the tiny bauble in my hand as the castle came up and hit me. After a stunned moment, I began clawing my way out of the wreckage. I was strong, almost intoxicatingly so, but every stone I threw away ignited fiery pains all along my body. The pain didn't go away. It got worse. As the throbbing mess inside my skull faded from my awareness, it only made way so I could feel the physical injuries full force.

I pushed the last of the rubble aside with a trembling taloned hand and stared at the smears of blood I left across the surface. In the distance I heard voices calling out, "Dragon! Get the dragon!"

Something finally connected in the front part of my mind.

I'm the dragon now.

Flying must be an instinctual aspect of dragonkind, because as that particular thought struck me I was already rocketing upward, shedding blood, ashes, and small parts of castle. I clutched my fist tighter around the Tear of Nâtlac, my thoughts tumbling in a worse chaos than the clouds around me.

Dragon.

Snake's back in his body . . .

They think I'm still him . . .

Hurts.

My stomach suddenly realized where I was and rebelled. I looked down across my massive body and couldn't see ground. Through my pain-blurred vision I couldn't even tell up from down. I screwed my eyes shut to try and calm the welling sickness inside me.

That must have been when I passed out.

For a moment I woke enough to realize I had landed, painfully, somewhere in the woods. I had just enough energy to unclench my taloned hand to see I still clutched the tiny evil jewel. Then I groaned and passed out again.

I slowly became aware of myself and my surroundings some time later. I didn't even have the small blessing of a moment or two to forget what had happened to me. Unlike my first few weeks as the princess, the sensations from this body were too radically different to allow me that small comfort. As soon as I was aware enough to realize I was conscious, I knew something horrible had happened to my body.

Lucille had been okay with this?

I blinked a bloody haze from my lizard eyes and saw a small clearing scattered with the broken remnants of small trees. Actually, the clearing was ringed by small trees. The forest was *filled* with small trees.

Not small trees.

I sighed, and white brimstone-flavored steam curled from my nostrils. I stared at it, then down at my nose. I didn't have to move anything but my eyes, and I could see the black-scaled ridges that formed the upper half of the dragon's snout dominating the lower part of my field of vision.

I had to admit the central flaw in my original plan. I had no idea what to do after convincing Snake to abdicate his coup of Lendowyn by returning to his own body. I certainly hadn't planned for it to happen so . . . inconveniently.

Even when I win, I lose . . .

It was tempting to just use the jewel still clutched in my hand to run away from my problems again. It would serve Snake right to come back to a half-broken dragon. Fortunately, I wasn't drunk, so it only occurred in passing as I mentally itemized all the parts of me that hurt, a list that included parts of me where I'd never had parts before.

One pain proved hard to locate. Somehow I felt a burning sensation that seemed to float outside my body. As it came closer, and became more intense, I turned my head in the direction it seemed to come from.

"Oh you're kidding me," I groaned.

About a hundred yards away, jumping over downed

trees, I saw Grace leading the rest of the girls. They had managed to arm themselves again and, most importantly, Mary carried the unmistakable glowing red-runed blade, *Dracheslayer*.

I held up a bloody taloned hand and said, **"Hold up there!"**

They pulled up to a halt outside my reach, and the others formed a tight group behind Mary and the dragon-slaying sword. Except for Grace, who took a few steps in front. "You know what that blade is?"

"What do you think you're doing?"

"There's a price on your head, Snake," Grace said. "So I see two options. We take that head, or you start telling us where the rest of your treasure is."

I lowered my forearm. It hurt to hold it up for too long anyway. I sighed and dropped my head to the ground.

The universe really loves me.

"Two problems with that ultimatum, Grace."

"I know you must have left something in reserve. You couldn't be sure this would have worked."

"First, you're actually assuming that a complete rat like Snake Bartholomew would honestly tell you where he hid something? It's not like you can take several tons of lizard prisoner and have him lead you there."

"Head then."

"Second, you're assuming that Snake hasn't moved on with his plans."

"What?"

"I'm Frank, Grace. How do you think I know your name?"

"No. He ran off. Left us . . ."

"Flew off." I pulled my other hand out from under my body and unclenched it. The Tear of Nâtlac glittered in my palm. **"He always planned to take his body back. That's why his soldiers wouldn't kill me, and why he flew down to defend me when I charged the wall."**

"You're trying to trick us," Grace said.

"Look at me. I'm half-dead here. He abandoned this body after it took too much damage to be useful. Snake is probably headed right for his army on the Grünwald border, that's what he cares about. Not the dragon, not Dermonica, not the chaos he left at Lendowyn Castle."

"Damn it!" Grace snapped.

Mary sighed and lowered *Dracheslayer* and stabbed it point-first into the ground. "Great, so we went back after this thing for nothing?"

CHAPTER 32

It hadn't been a bad plan as such things went. I had been out of it for most of the day. In the meantime, the Dermonica troops had spent a large amount of time and effort securing the castle and the surrounding town, enough time and effort to give Grace and company the time to slip into the keep and find the armory. They had known of *Dracheslayer* because they had overheard Lucille lamenting the fact that she hadn't retrieved it and inserted it into a select part of the dragon's anatomy back when she had the chance.

After slipping away from the castle, Grace's plan had been something along the lines of, get information, slay dragon, be hero, and escape to retrieve gold and riches at leisure.

I almost felt guilty for screwing that up.

But we all had something else to worry about. In my unconscious flight, I had flown in the wrong direction. I had landed somewhere between the castle and the Fell River, putting the mass of the Dermonica army between us, Snake, and Grünwald.

And the mass of that army, once the castle was secure, would be moving in the direction of the nominal reason for their invasion . . .

Me.

Dragon or not, I was in no shape to face an army.

"You need to fly out of here," Krys said. "They can't be more than an hour or two behind us."

I stretched, causing the girls to backpedal from a wall of black-scaled muscle. The movement fired off dozens of flares of pain across the whole of my body. When I tried to spread my wings, a spasm ran fifty feet down the length of my spine and back, slamming the back of my skull with white-hot pain that elicited a groan that set off a small bonfire in front of me.

The girls, remarkably tiny, had managed to put a hundred feet between me and them. They all stared at me and the fire.

"Sorry." I shook my head. **"I don't know if I'm in condition to fly."**

"So what?" Grace said. "You give up? We leave you for them?"

Mary leaned against *Dracheslayer*. "I don't think they'll give you time to explain who you are."

"We could go back," Laya said.

"We'll explain what happened," Thea said, excitedly. "We could fix everything!"

"No one's going to listen to us," Grace said. "A bunch of girls playing dress-up? They're going to take us seriously?"

"Grace?" Thea said.

"Grow up!" Grace snapped.

"This isn't her fault," Mary said.

"You don't need to tell me whose fault it is," Grace said. "I know!"

"She wasn't saying—" Krys began to say.

"Shut up! I know what she was saying!"

"P-Please," Thea said. "Don't be angry."

"Why not?" Grace shouted at her. "Why shouldn't I be angry! Do you have any idea how bad things are? How they're getting worse?"

Thea cowered from Grace's outburst, shaking her head. "P-Please stop."

"What? You think a whole army's going to stop when they catch up with us? You think some tears are going to make anything bett—"

Grace's tirade was cut short by a sharp slap. She turned to face Rabbit, who stood next to her now, glaring bloody murder. Grace rubbed the side of her face and said, "Rabbit?"

Rabbit hauled back and hit her with an open hand slap on the other side of her face. The sound echoed through woods that were suddenly silent. Grace took a shaky step back, staring at the mute girl in open-mouthed shock. "But . . ."

Rabbit turned away from her and started walking away.

Grace seemed to deflate, to look her age. "I'm sorry."

Rabbit stopped walking away.

"I keep trying. But it just . . ." She shook her head.

"Don't let that stop you."

She looked up at me, startled, as if she had forgotten I was there.

"What?"

"Failure. It happens. It keeps happening. But if you let it stop you, it's all you're left with."

"So do you have a suggestion on what to do now? You can't move."

"No. What I said was I couldn't *fly*."

Our best option was to continue to draw the Dermonica forces away from the castle. That meant a straight line toward the Dermonica border. And while I was too injured to fly, I could still move at a respectable pace overland.

However, there was only one way to do that without leaving the girls behind.

I think I was the one most hesitant about the girls climbing on my back. Given the size differential now, they all seemed too fragile to me. Feeling them climb up and perch themselves between my wings made me almost afraid to move, as if the lightest breeze might carry them away.

"What you waiting for?" I heard Mary's voice and turned my neck in what felt like impossible ways to look down at my own back. All six of them had taken hold of part of a wing.

"Hang on," I said.

They hung on.

I don't know how fast I moved, but I think I may have outpaced a good horse for a few stretches. I was frightened when I heard someone screaming, but when I turned my head to check on them, Rabbit, of all people, had risen to her knees, hooking one hand under the base of my wing and waving the other above her head, making a guttural sound, looking like a war goddess riding into battle.

"Really?" I said.

She gave me a sheepish smile and crouched back down with the others. We came up to the Fell River as the last of daylight faded. I could hear the rushing water as we closed on it. Before we came in sight of it, I felt tugging at the base of my wing. I slowed to a stop and turned my head to see Rabbit on her knees again. This time, however, she wasn't playing. She faced the evening sky, wrinkling her nose with an expression I'd seen too many times before.

I took a deep breath and I smelled it too. Wood fire.

"Get down." I didn't quite manage a whisper.

"What?" Grace said.

"Something's ahead of us."

They all scrambled off my back and I gestured for them to get back. I may have done it more aggressively than I intended, because they fell over each other backing away from me.

Once they were a safe distance away, I grabbed the trunk of the tallest, straightest tree in reach and pulled myself up on my hind legs. It ignited pains over the length of my body, but I managed to stand, breaking branches aside, shedding an avalanche of snow. I grabbed the tree with my other hand and pulled myself up. The tree groaned with my weight as my feet left the ground to dig their talons into the base of the trunk.

I only had to climb up a short distance—relative to my own size—before I could extend my head above the tree canopy to see the surrounding terrain. I craned my neck as the tree creaked and swayed with my weight. I tried to spread my wings to stabilize things, but they only caught the wind and made things worse. I heard something snap inside the trunk and immediately folded them back as tightly as I could manage.

The good news was there wasn't another burned–out town awaiting us.

The bad news was I had made an error in assuming we had left the bulk of the Dermonica army *behind* us.

From my vantage above the trees, I saw across the Fell River to an encampment of troops maybe five times the force that had taken Lendowyn Castle. I saw tents, horses, and a large pavilion flying a recognizable royal banner.

Then the tree shuddered with another snap and I suddenly tilted away from the river as my head fell below the trees.

"Watch out!" I called down as the tree and I crashed back through the forest canopy. I fell on my back with a thud that shook the snow from every tree around me. I groaned as the remains of the splintered tree rolled off of me to crunch against another tree that echoed my groan.

The girls ran up to me, Krys yelling, "Are you all right?"

"Yes." I stared up at the sky through the large hole my descent had torn in the canopy. **"That was not stealthy."**

"What?" someone said. Probably Grace.

I groaned again as I struggled to right myself. **"This dragon thing,"** I said. **"It doesn't play to my strengths."**

"What did you see?"

**"We have a problem. And we better move down-
stream before we have more of one."**

Amazingly, my draconic pratfall did not draw a battal-
ion of Dermonica soldiers to finish us off. I suppose
that being a mile upstream and having the river between us made it less obvious. That, and anyone looking for a dragon would probably be looking up.

"You sure that it's the duke?" Grace asked once
we'd stopped again.

**"I know the banners. They wouldn't be flying over
another commander."**

"Don't that make that pavilion a target?" Mary
asked.

I snorted. **"It is a wonderful thing to be able to sus-
pend the rules of logic and strategy by decree and divine right. Staying on the Dermonica side is probably
the only concession the duke's made to his generals."**

"You should counterattack," Grace said. "They're
obviously not expecting it."

"What?"

"You have their ruler, they have yours," Grace said.
"You could work out some sort of deal with that,
couldn't you?"

**"If I *had* that. But we're on the wrong side of the
river and an army."**

"We have to cross the river anyway," Mary said, "or
we'll have to deal with the soldiers already on this side
of the river."

"Don't remind me."

"Can you fly yet?" Thea asked.

I shook my head and looked up at the sky. **"Even if**

I could, there's no cloud cover and a nearly full moon. The archers would shred me before I got anywhere near the pavilion. They'll be expecting an attack from the air."

"We can't stay here," Grace said. "We'll be pinned between them."

"Think of something," Krys said. "I heard your stories, I know you can come up with something."

I sighed and lowered my head. **"I'm not a miracle worker. You can't defeat a whole army with six girls, a half-dead dragon, and a magic sword . . ."** I raised my head and faced the sky again. No cloud cover at all. **"A magic *dragon-slaying* sword."**

"You thought of something!" Krys said.

"We'll probably regret it, but yes."

CHAPTER 33

Stealth and misdirection were some of my primary strengths, and, as I'd told the girls, being a dragon really didn't play to them. However, that also meant that those tactics would be the least expected by those who anticipated the possibility of going toe-to-toe with a dragon.

Searching back upstream toward the main encampment Rabbit was able to scout out the small navy's worth of barges that Dermonica had used to ferry the ground troops across the frigid waters of the Fell River. There was a light contingent of a dozen guards or so, all of whom came to the quick conclusion that protecting a fleet of glorified rafts was not that important once I came crashing through the tree line belching fire. In less than a minute, the guards had run off and half the rafts were burning.

As I turned to add the tops of the winter-naked trees to the conflagration, a bubble of clear, unheated air moved from the woods, through the fire, toward the rafts. At the center of the bubble moved Mary, holding *Dracheslayer* aloft. The enchanted sword kept the flames and heat at bay enough so that the tightly grouped girls could move freely through the firestorm to cut the ropes on the burning rafts, setting them free to float into the river. While they worked to free the rafts, I made sure to stand upright and spread my wings while dramatically backlit by the burning woods. I bellowed a roar that would have terrified me if I wasn't the creature making it.

It would have been perfect if I hadn't broken into a coughing fit at the end.

Coughing aside, for those across the river, it was an unmistakable announcement. The dragon was coming. And as the barges and the woods burned, black smoke roiled up and crossed the river, hiding the stars and moon.

I now had my cloud cover, and the defenders would have a nerve-wracking time staring at a featureless sky, trying to discern a winged shadow in a cauldron of smoke, ash, and floating embers.

"Good luck with that."

Behind the ranks of burning barges, we had left one intact. Mary led the girls climbing up on it. They flattened themselves in the center of the raft as I slid into the water under the cover of the floating conflagration.

The frigid water was a shock, shoving icicles into every bruise and wound all over my oversize body. The river rushed over my back and tail as I pushed the barge against the current, straight across the river, toward the shore just a half mile downstream from the Dermonica encampment.

As my back end sank as the river deepened, I realized a flaw in my plan. I didn't know if dragons could swim. The way my legs and tail sank argued against it.

Fortunately, my legs found the muddy bottom before the rest of me followed suit.

Above us, the sky had turned into an orange maelstrom, and I could hear the chaos of shouts as the troops by the encampment scrambled into a defensive formation facing the river. With the forest fire and the burning barges, no one seemed to notice the lone barge floating back across the river.

I stayed as submerged as possible, even though parts of me were going numb. As the dozens of aches and pains that had been beaten into this lizard body faded from my awareness, I worried about this body's sensitivity to the temperature. Dragons weren't cold-blooded, but this was really pushing it.

We approached the opposite shore and my feet dug into the mud of the rising riverbank. Only a few dozen yards away from shore, I was still submerged, belly in the mud and river rushing over my back. The woods rustled and suddenly a dozen men broke through aiming bows at the single barge.

Damn.

They didn't notice me yet. The bulk of the barge, which was meant for two or three times the company that faced us, blocked their view of the part of me that was still above water. The lead man drew his sword and pointed at the raft. "You there! Drop your weapons and surrender now to the Dermonica crown!"

The girls stood up, one by one, and in the glow from the fires behind us, I could see his expression change from grim determination to confusion.

"A bunch of . . . girls?" The tip of his sword faltered. Grace stepped out in front of the girls, who all stood within ten feet of Mary, with *Dracheslayer* hidden behind her back.

What are you doing? If you're not by the sword I can't blast them safely.

"Sir, I have to suggest that you are the ones who should surrender."

"What?"

"Drop your weapons, and call forward all your men still in the woods."

Oh.

Grace was thinking a few steps ahead of me now. The point of the whole conflagration on the opposite shore was to get me in close without alerting the enemy, which would be pointless if a bunch of troops burst into flame the moment we hit shore.

There was an extended silence broken by a few laughs here and there. The leader raised his sword back to point at the girls. "What gives a brat like you the nerve to issue ultimatums?"

"If you don't," Grace said, "you're going to die." She took a step back to join Mary and the others within the safe radius of *Dracheslayer*.

"That's it," their leader said. "If they don't come forward in five seconds—" He stopped as a wave of frigid water washed across his boots. He looked slowly up as I pushed myself out of the water.

"Do as she says," I said as quietly as I could manage.

The sword splashed into the water as he let it go.

We managed landfall without having to set one guy on fire. I oversaw things as the girls liberated the men of their weapons, marched them into the barge, and tied them hand and foot with their own bowstrings. I leaned over them as I pushed the barge back into the river. **"Relax. By the time you get out of this, things should be over."** I watched them as the barge followed the current down the Fell River.

Once we were clear of the patrol, we headed inland, making a wide circle around the Dermonica encampment. Once away from shore, we appeared to be away from any other patrols.

We came up to the encampment from behind, and while the rear faced a wide clearing, recently trampled, only a few guards faced the muddy field. Most of them seemed to pay more attention to the smoke-shrouded sky than the rear approach to their camp, so they didn't notice immediately as Laya dropped them one by one with a crossbow.

It wasn't until number five that the others noticed what was happening. Before they could react, I broke out our last distraction.

I erupted from the cover to the rear of the encampment, roared, and launched myself unsteadily into the sky. A couple of wild arrows flew my way, but went wide. I did a circuit of the field, strafing a line of fire along the rear of the encampment. That did two things. It kept everyone's attention on me, and it gave the girls cover as they ran across the field.

Mary and *Dracheslayer* carved a temporary path through the wall of fire, letting them into the camp proper as more archers were brought to bear on yours truly. When a longbow shaft bounced off my tail, I took it as a clue to shoot up above the smoke. My stomach churned at the altitude, and my wings felt as if they were about to tear free from my back.

I sucked in a frigid breath of clean air and looked down at a carpet of smoke lit by the moon. Small tears in the carpet showed tents and tiny people moving below me. It was frightening how easily now I could rain destruction down on them.

I'm not Snake.

I watched where my shadow fell on the smoke below and saw arrows and bolts ineffectively piercing the smoke. I flew higher, even though it made me feel dizzy and more sick to my stomach. I let the shadow move farther away from my target as I rose, drawing their fire and attention away.

Then I dropped.

I fell fast, and my shadow moved faster, faster than the enemy should be able to track me. I broke through the layer of smoke and saw the pavilion with the royal banners as I felt an arrow or three plunge into my backside.

I twisted and landed on my feet with an earth-shaking thud and swept my talons across the roof of the pavilion, tearing yards of canvas away, tossing it at the archers who had plunged two more arrows into my neck. Below me, in the pavilion, an old man in rich robes stood in the center of a ring of guards who had just started looking up.

One of them pointed a crossbow up toward my face, but a bolt erupted from his neck before he could fire. Below me, Grace's girls broke from the shadows to engage the distracted guards. While they were engaging, I reached down and snatched the old man from their midst.

I felt more arrows hit me and I held up the man in my taloned hand and called out, **"If you value your ruler, cease fire now!"**

I tensed, since I've tried similar threats before, and sometimes people just didn't care for their sovereigns all that much. But the arrows ceased flying, and the fight stopped in the pavilion below me.

I opened my hand and looked at the duke in my palm.

"We have to talk," I said.

"Do we?"

I stared at the man in my hand. My first thought was that being able to charbroil your opposite number should make negotiations run a bit smoother. At least a little fear would have been nice.

"You realize I'm a dragon?"

"I've noticed."

"I could set you on fire, bite you in half—"

"Yes, yes, you can kill me. So can every single man I've ever spoken to. Killing someone is easy."

"Huh?"

"And you aren't going to kill me."

"What are you talking about?"

"You want something from me and I'm the only one who can give it to you."

"I want you to withdraw from Lendowyn and release the royal court, then I'll let you go unharmed."

"You are suffering from the illusion of false equivalence."

"You understand I have you hostage?"

"You assume that I have a king, you have a duke, and as such, a trade has equal value to both parties and is inevitable. You've miscalculated. Yes, you have hold of the ruler of Dermonica, I have the ruler of Lendowyn. But I also have the court, the castle, and an occupying army. I have a host of allies all poised to assist me in the deposing of Prince Bartholomew. I have a son ready to take command in my absence. I have recovered your ill-gotten gains. You're asking Dermonica to trade all of that for the life of one old man."

"You're bluffing."

"You are bluffing. Taking my life now would be suicide for you and your new kingdom. Acceding to your demand would require a craven cowardice of me that would be more appropriate to your own family."

"I can still . . . My family?"

"The truth stings, doesn't it, Prince?"

I buried my face in my free hand. **"I'm not Prince Bartholomew."**

"What?"

I sighed and lowered my hand, setting my prisoner on the ground in the midst of the royal pavilion. The girls had taken care of the royal guard and made their own ring around the duke. He stared up at me as I reached up and started pulling arrows out of my neck.

"What do you mean you're not Prince Bartholomew?"

"I'm Frank Blackthorne. The prince you want is back in his own body."

"You're lying . . ."

"Then tell me why I'm here bargaining for Lendowyn, rather than leading an army into Grünwald."

"You ..." It was his turn to put a hand to his head. Slowly he said, "Yes. You're right. We need to talk."

Things were a bit more complicated than they first appeared.

Then, again, what else is new?

It probably should have been obvious that Dermonica had fielded a much larger force than should have been possible for a place just slightly larger than Lendowyn, and one that had recently lost a major part of its income thanks to Snake. I guess I'd been too busy trying to stay alive to notice. But the ruler of Dermonica had leveraged a seemingly endless list of Snake's enemies into a large alliance of forces under the Dermonica banner. All of whom went to battle on the strength of two promises: the repatriation of Snake's treasure to the participants, and the capture, trial, and public execution of Prince Bartholomew ... trial optional.

Given that these foreign forces were now occupying Lendowyn *and* Dermonica, failure to make good on either of these points would be a bad thing for both.

"Still an impasse."

"You're still trying to broker a deal?"

"What happens to Dermonica if you and I die, and Snake still takes the throne of Grünwald?"

"You have a point."

"What if Lendowyn joins your alliance?"

"You have no army."

"We have a dragon."

*   *   *

Even rushed diplomacy is slow. I didn't mind so much as it gave me some time to recover from my injuries. Fortunately, by Lendowyn law, I was clearly the prince now I wore the dragon's skin, and there weren't any arguments about my legitimacy to negotiate. Especially since King Alfred had issued a proclamation giving the prince authority to negotiate with Dermonica back when I was still the princess on a diplomatic mission, and that order had never been rescinded.

Over the next two days or so, several couriers were sent to the Fell River bearing orders from the Dermonica duke, changing status from occupation to alliance. I know that, for one, Prince Oliver—who was commanding troops in the field—was not pleased with this development. The duke read his son's first response at one of our meetings, and after hearing the most profanity-laden official document I'd ever heard tell of, the duke waved the parchment and said, "Now you see what *I* have to deal with."

Grace and the girls, who had by default become my royal honor guard, weren't pleased either, though they expressed it in a less profane manner. Grace spoke for everyone when she said, "So no treasure for us."

"What did you expect?"

"*Something* in return for everything we've gone through."

"Believe me," I told her. **"The world doesn't work that way."**

CHAPTER 34

I returned to the damaged Lendowyn Castle, half-healed, treaty in one taloned hand and the rest of the combined army of seven kingdoms in tow. I didn't receive a hero's welcome, but given I was no hero I didn't mind. The remains of the Lendowyn court met me in the rubble-strewn courtyard. King Alfred appeared shell-shocked as he received me, Lucille just looked annoyed. They were flanked by Sir Forsythe and Brock, who seemed to be the only members of the royal guard to have survived. There were another dozen troops wearing the colors of Lendowyn, but they seemed to be mostly the remnants of Weasel's thief army.

It sank in that the girls and I now probably represented half of Lendowyn's military force—more than half once I finished healing.

I presented the treaty to King Alfred. He read it with a shaking hand, then said, "What have you done to us, Frank?"

"I'm sorry, Your Highness."

"Look around you. My castle is in ruins, my kingdom is overrun by foreign armies. I treated you like my daughter, and look at the destruction you brought down on the house that took you in." He crumpled the treaty in his hand. "And you have the gall to sign a peace in my name? To commit me to action with the men who breached my walls and killed my men?"

My heart sank, more so because every word he spoke rang true. I had unleashed this on Lendowyn. I lowered my head and swallowed a ball of brimstone that had caught in my throat.

King Alfred threw the treaty on the ground and leveled a finger at me. "This will not stand. It is my kingdom, you quit any claim to it when you abandoned it in favor of that Grünwald pretender. You are no longer my daughter, or my son, or my dragon!"

"Father—" Lucille said.

"I banish you from this land, quit this kingdom and never return."

"Father, stop it!"

"This is a matter of State, please hold your tongue, daughter."

The courtyard reverberated with the sound of Lucille's slap. It snapped the king's head so hard that his crown went askew.

"L-Lucille! How dare you!"

Lucille placed herself between me and the king and said, "How dare you! Suddenly I'm a useless appendage to the throne again?"

"No, that's not—"

"Hold my tongue? *Hold my tongue?!*" She grabbed the edges of the king's robe and pulled him down so he was facing her. "You are about to banish my wife—husband—spouse. I'm supposed to hold my tongue? You're about to trample a treaty out of pride when it's the only thing that will allow this kingdom to continue to exist? I'm supposed to hold my tongue?"

"Daughter, please—"

"I don't breathe fire anymore, but that does *not* mean I'm the same damsel in distress you pimped out in payment for her own rescue. I will *not* hold my tongue. Especially since you are to blame for this mess as much as Frank is."

"W-What?"

"What?"

"As much as *I* am." She let the king go and reached down to pick up the treaty. "You think Frank wanted this? You think he risked his life coming back here because this was his intent? All he did was leave, and he left because we treated him the way *you* used to treat *me*. The way you just treated me. The blood and death and destruction? That's the fault of one bastard aristocrat who thinks his privileged blood justifies *anything*. If Frank is culpable for Prince Bartholomew's actions, so are we for driving Frank away in the first place."

"Lucille—"

She spun around and leveled a finger at me. "You hold your tongue!"

I shut up.

She faced her father and slapped him in the chest with the crumpled treaty. "Now, if you want our kingdom to go down in flames tear up the treaty, banish Frank. You know as well as I that it will be your last official act."

King Alfred reached up and took the parchment.

"If you want to be a king," Lucille said, "forgive him."

He watched as Lucille stepped away from between us. "You've changed," he said.

"No," Lucille said, "I just haven't changed *back*."

King Alfred sighed at the parchment. "My daughter, much as it pains me to admit it, has a point."

When the combined forces of eight kingdoms marched across the frontier into Grünwald, I had a bird's-eye view of the destruction that one bastard aristocrat had left in his wake. It was enough to make me forget how heights made me sick to my stomach.

Seeing the damage, it was hard to imagine that he thought of Grünwald as *his* kingdom in the same way that Alfred or Lucille thought of Lendowyn.

We reached the capital of Brightwood, and it was that much worse. A third of the city was in ruins. I flew over rubble and pillars of smoke as my stomach tied itself in a knot. The sick feeling was less for the ground whipping by so far below, and more for the fact that I was looking at the efforts of one man who thought himself entitled to the Grünwald crown.

Someone, in Lucille's words, "whose privileged blood justifies *anything*." I felt a surge of shame for having once placed Lucille in the same category.

Snake was in a class by himself.

Then, below me, I saw the shell that used to be a tavern named The Three-Legged Boar.

I didn't know if Evelyn had ever returned from our aborted tryst in Dermonica, and in some part of my mind I *did* know that it was unlikely that the serving staff would remain in a tavern as a hostile army descended on the city.

But that thought didn't prevent me from screeching a sky-splitting roar and falling on Snake's army in a brimstone-spewing fury. I introduced the allied army's attack by tearing a smoking trench through the forces massed at the castle walls. As I swooped by, a pair of burning siege towers collapsed in an eruption of smoke, flame, and glowing embers.

Before Snake's army could reorient itself to concentrate return fire on me, the allied army broke upon their flanks. As the men laying siege were trapped between Dermonica and its allies, and the castle walls, I flew down their line and rained hell down on them.

For a time, I think I went a little crazy. It wasn't the troops I attacked, it was Snake. Below me, every enemy solider was Prince Bartholomew by proxy. Every one of them carried the responsibility for Snake's evil and bore the weight in dragon fire.

Blind fury and dragons are two things that really shouldn't be mixed together.

In retrospect, despite my less-than-tactical thought process at the time, I managed—by contrast with the debacle at Lendowyn Castle—to prove that a dragon was much more effective militarily when supporting a large attacking ground force.

Fortunately for my state of mind, the dragon's body was still recovering from the last two battles, and my ability to breathe fire was exhausted after a few passes over the enemy. Once the ability to literally vent my anger had dissipated, I had a chance to come halfway back to my senses.

I *wasn't* attacking Snake. I knew better than that. The bastard prince was here somewhere, directing the action against King Dudley, but probably not from the smoldering forces below me. I swooped up to get a good view of the surrounding area.

The southern side of the castle was a mess. Dermonica's allies were wrapping a crescent-shaped front against Snake's forces, pinning more than half the defenders between their swords and the castle walls. Smoke still rose from the trenches I had burned through their ranks.

I told myself that the sick feeling in the pit of my stomach was the height again.

This felt wrong. Snake had planned this attack for years, and it amounted to throwing a large army at the castle walls and hoping for the best? That seemed very conventional for someone who managed a coup in a neighboring country on the spur of the moment.

Ever since I traded places with him, I've been looking at the wrong thing, making the wrong assumptions.

So look away from the battle.

I banked away from the south side of the castle to orbit above, looking at the ground to see anything we were missing. Anything *I* was missing.

I'm supposed to be like Snake, I thought. The jewel and the wizard said so. If that was the case, however much I might loathe the idea, I should be able to think like him.

So if I had years to plan this, with a thief's tactics, no scruples, and unlimited funds, how would I pull this off?

I'd want to breach the wall before Dudley knew there was a war.

I'd be inside already.

Oh crap . . .

With my view up on high, I was able to find what I looked for in just a few moments. To the north, one small section of town had been thoroughly devastated, covering just a block or two that happened to be completely removed from all the other damage. Snake's army had come from the south to lay siege to the castle, so there was no reason for any fighting past the castle. But there were the smoking ruins, still crawling with Snake's men, nearly half a mile north of the main battle.

And in the center of the misplaced rubble, a blacksmith's shop stood, completely undamaged.

As I swooped by, I also saw a column of Snake's army, in full retreat from the collapsing siege. They marched double-time into the occupied area around the blacksmith's shop, and, as I watched, they disappeared into it.

Forty or fifty men vanished into the shop, and none came out.

Time, funds, a thief's sensibilities, and no scruples . . .

The first three and a few guys with shovels gave you a route into the castle. The last gives you an army of paid cannon fodder to soak up enemy damage just to distract the defenders.

"No! This isn't going to happen!" That got everyone's attention. Arrows started flying in my direction, but I was too high up. The few arrows that hit me had lost so much momentum that they bounced off of my scales.

I still had no fire, so I swooped down to the edge of

the field of wreckage they occupied, grabbing a large chunk of still-intact stone wall. It started crumbling in my arms almost immediately, but I held on until I was a few hundred feet above the blacksmith's shop. Then I let it go.

It crashed through the roof in a cloud of stone-dust and mortar. The floor caved in so that when the dust cleared below me, I saw a deep crater ringed by splintered wood and four sagging walls.

Everyone below me now knew their secret was out, and an implausible number of arrows and quarrels sprouted from the ground toward me. Several found their mark as I kept flying upward, out of range.

I'm not going to manage that again.

Fortunately, I wasn't in this alone.

I sucked in a breath and bellowed toward the castle. **"The siege is a fraud! They've already tunneled inside! The entrance is here!"** I bellowed it again, out over the battlefield, yelling my long throat raw.

My voice carried.

Only a few minutes of calling attention to myself— something the dragon was good at—and I saw a cluster of the allied forces break from the east flank of the battle to head north, toward me.

The thing about mercenary armies is that their loyalty can be bought, but only to a point. Once it becomes unclear if their employer will survive to pay them, they become a bit more independent. They start considering things like the strength of the opposing force, the dragon flying above them, and the fact that a good part of their number was about to be trapped in a confined space underground, caught between two armies.

Below me, Snake's men scattered.

I flew south, over the allied forces and over the castle walls. I continued yelling down, **"Dudley! Your brother's already tunneled inside! Forget the siege, send your forces down and you can trap him now! Do you hear me? Bartholomew's inside your walls!"**

I yelled down as the Dermonica forces overran the remains of the tunnel entrance, until my voice went the way of my fire. But it proved the most effective military use of a dragon's ability I had seen to date. The siege collapsed below me as I swooped above the castle, smiling inside at the end of the largest part of the fighting.

I got you, you bastard.

Then the thought gripped me.

Snake would be the last person to bravely go down with his troops. He'd probably look for an escape the moment he saw how bad things were going. And there was at least one escape route I knew of that Dudley didn't.

He could be slipping away right now . . .

"No, you're not escaping this." My voice was hoarse, dry and barely comprehensible. But even as I said it, I remembered something, and I think my lizard face managed a grin. **"This ends. Now!"**

I swooped down toward the western edges of Brightwood that had so far escaped the battle.

CHAPTER 35

For all I knew, there were dozens of secret passages out of Grünwald Castle. However, I had only seen one of them in a prophetic vision.

I had assumed that I had seen the Dragon Snake putting an end to me. It hadn't quite registered that I was making some unwarranted assumptions about who was wearing the dragon's body, and who was wearing Snake's.

I swooped down onto the ruins of Lysea's garden burning with rage and filled with an unnatural certainty. As my shadow flew across the nearly unbroken snow between the broken monuments, I saw a lone figure trudging away from the woods where Sir Forsythe had led us out of the catacombs. Snake was tiny, easily missed if not for the contrast between his sewage-encrusted clothes and the pristine snow.

He didn't realize he was in trouble until my shadow caught up with him. He looked back up over his shoulder and I think he might have screamed. I screamed back; a draconic roar bearing enough fury that, had I not exhausted my fire during the battle, would have left the legendary Snake little more than a sooty stain between the mausoleums.

The great Snake blubbered and dashed in a frantic, stumbling run toward Lysea's temple. I finally saw the family resemblance between him and Dudley.

As panicked as he was, no man on foot is going to outrun a dragon, even a clumsy, wounded one.

I fell on him just like the dragon in my vision. Almost. My vision had been slightly less clumsy. The real me stumbled a bit on landing and added a bit to the cemetery ruins after a couple of lumbering steps reaching for Snake.

Once in my taloned fist, he seemed remarkably tiny, even given my increase in size.

"P-Please! Mercy! Spare me."

"Why?" I grumbled low in my throat. The sulfur-flavored word stung my throat as smoke curled from my nostrils.

I felt something warm and wet spreading in my hand and I grimaced in disgust. *Is this creature really the almighty Snake Bartholomew? The man who almost stole two kingdoms?* I'd never been any great thief, and I had still managed not to wet myself the first time a dragon had grabbed me.

"I can pay you, riches beyond your imagining."

"I can imagine quite a lot," I grumbled low. **"And your loot is safely in the Lendowyn treasury now, remember?"**

"I have more . . ."

I shook my head slowly.

"And I'm a prince. Help me regain the Grünwald crown and . . ."

"You think you care about that? You think you have anything to offer me? You think there is *anything* that

can compensate for what you've done?" I raised him up to my face, hesitating only because I couldn't decide what was more appropriate: belching what remained of my fire into his face, biting his head off his body, or just squeezing him like an overripe grape.

From somewhere below us, I heard a slow clapping.

I glanced down and suffered from a sense of vertigo. Not from height this time, but from looking down at a ground that wasn't where the ground should be. The red-tinted mist floated around us, carrying the distant wails of a legion of agonized children.

Snake started blubbering again, "No. Not this. Anything but this."

"Oh shut up."

Below me, the Dark Lord Nâtlac walked into view, still clapping. "Impressive, Frank."

Even in my new form, the Dark Lord's presence still felt incredibly unnerving, like maggots burrowing under my scales, or a thousand tiny *Dracheslayer*s poking into my brain.

"Why are you here?"

I felt Snake vainly trying to kick his way free of my grasp. He screeched, "Lord Nâtlac, save me!"

I briefly wondered why I was still a dragon in the Dark Lord's realm. Then Lord Nâtlac spoke and his gimlet words bore into my ears.

"There is something Prince Bartholomew can grant you. Some compensation for the troubles he has caused you."

"What?"

Snake just shook his head and wept.

"You gave me the queen. Give me the prince."

"No," sobbed Snake.

I shook him and said, **"Shut up."**

"Sacrifice that wretch in my name, and all that is his can be yours."

"He has nothing anymore." *Not even any self-respect.*

"Nothing?" asked the Dark Lord. Watching him smile was akin to watching an open wound give birth to a million spiders. "He has one thing you do not. Something you desperately want."

"What would that be?"

"You know what it is, Frank. It is quivering in your palm."

"I just have . . ."

Oh.

"You see now, don't you?"

"I had his body. With his history it is more trouble than it's worth."

For the first time ever, I saw the Dark Lord Nâtlac nonplussed. It lasted a fraction of a second before the spider smile returned full force. "I have many followers, Frank, many bodies. That confused oaf of a knight of yours is considered handsome, isn't he?"

Sir Forsythe? I shuddered internally.

"Give me this wretch, on this ground, and you can name your price."

Even under assault by the gangrenous itch of the Dark Lord's presence, I instinctively realized something. The Dark Lord Nâtlac was not negotiating from a position of power.

What does he want?

"Why do you hesitate, Frank? You know that he would gladly give you to me."

I looked at Snake, blubbering incoherently in my scaled fist. **"I am sure it is something he would do."**

"You know he deserves it."

"I am certain he does."

"What do you want, Frank? Name it."

"I'm wondering what you want."

"Only his soul."

I laughed. It hurt, as if the air stabbed barbed fishhooks into the base of my teeth, but I couldn't help myself. Even Snake had stopped blubbering enough to stare at me as if I'd gone insane.

"What do you find amusing?" The slight displeasure in the Dark Lord's voice was enough to melt iron, but the dragon's bowels were made of sterner stuff.

"I'm sure you have his soul already. He's part of the Grünwald royal family. That's almost a given. No, you want his blood spilled here, in your name, by a nominal high priestess."

"Meh, you're speaking in technicalities."

Did the Dark Lord Nâtlac just say "Meh?"

"You live by technicalities."

"That is all beside the point. Give me what I want and I can give you what you want."

"But 'here,' on 'this ground' you said. We haven't left Lysea's garden, have we? That's why I'm still a dragon."

"Again, beside the point."

"This is still her garden, isn't it? All it took was one offering and she took it back, and that galls you."

"Enough of this!" The Dark Lord Nâtlac tore free of his nominal human guise and suddenly loomed

over me, the way I loomed over Snake. Everything about the Dark Lord's appearance was wrong in ways that it is impossible for me to articulate. It glared down at us with a face swirling with eyes, teeth, and waving insectile *things*. *"What do you want?"* the Dark Lord demanded.

I couldn't look at it. I averted my gaze and said, **"Your jewel thought me and Snake were alike."**

"Kindred spirits, meant to be thieves and kings," the Dark Lord said, half spoken, and half carved inside my skull with a rusty nail.

"And he would sacrifice me to you."

"You know he would."

"So what do I want?"

"Yes." The word was filled with loathsome desire, like the lust of a bloated corpse.

"I want to be different from him," I said.

"What?" Even not looking at the Dark Lord, I could feel it deflate a bit.

"I don't want to be him, and I don't want to serve you."

And just like that, the presence receded and the mists withdrew. I felt the air go cold again and I was back in Lysea's garden, in front of her temple. A small vortex of red mist and wrongness remained at the base of the stairs to Lysea's temple, and the more human-form Nâtlac stood within it.

"Well played, Frank Blackthorne."

"Uh—" Now *I* was left somewhat nonplussed. I had expected more pushback from an angry deity.

His smile was still full of spiders. "The jewel was not wrong. You can take the same horse down many different paths. Unlike Prince Bartholomew, though, yours seems not to lead toward me."

"No, I don't think so."

"Fair warning, Frank Blackthorne, we are not parting amicably. You have made an enemy."

"I expect so."

"You should consider if the blubbering idiot in your hand was worth it," the Dark Lord said, vanishing in a swirl of red mist and unease.

I looked at Snake, who appeared to have completely withdrawn from the proceedings, shaking, weeping, burying his face into the scales of my fingers.

"No. He isn't."

But it was never about him anyway.

CHAPTER 36

In the end, Dermonica got Snake Bartholomew to do with as they wished and Lendowyn got a peace treaty that removed Dermonica troops from their soil. While Lendowyn had lost the services of most of the Grünwald defectors—aside from a handful like Sir Forsythe—Snake's attempted coup had damaged Grünwald's military to a point where it wouldn't be a threat for years. Lendowyn Castle was a mess. And, after all the foreign forces took their cut of Snake's loot, the treasury sat nearly empty.

But what else was new?

The girls stayed, and Lucille honored my offer to employ them. For some reason she had inherited my sensitivity to having retainers she could trust.

And, yeah, I was still a dragon.

Worse, sometime after I had crashed into the forest, I lost track of the Tear of Nâtlac. So I really *was* stuck. With Snake and Lucille back in their respective bodies, waiting a year and a day wouldn't do anything, and even someone dying wouldn't undo things.

Then again, even if I still had the Tear, what would I do with it? If I wore it, would I switch with Snake again? Snake the dragon wasn't a good idea. And if I

didn't swap with Snake ... was *anyone* else in this lizard skin a good idea?

So I camped out in the dragon's old lair while they
worked to fix the castle. I spent my time healing and
trying to resign myself to my fate. I told myself that I
had adjusted to being a princess, I could adjust to this.

Of course, I *hadn't* adjusted to being a princess,
which was why this had all happened in the first place.

I don't know how long I'd been sulking and licking my
wounds when she came. I just opened my eyes, and
there Lucille was, standing in the mouth of the dragon's cave, backlit by a rosy sunrise.

I groaned.

She walked down from the entrance. "How are you
doing?"

I sighed, and the sound rumbled the ground beneath me.

"That well?"

I rolled on my side and snaked my neck so I could
see her better. **"I think I know how you felt after you
dive-bombed all those Grünwald archers."**

She smiled weakly. "Don't forget Elhared and that
damn sword."

"Yeah."

"You'll heal."

"I know."

"Thank you."

I snorted. It was a half chuckle, half sob. **"For what?
It was my screw up—"**

"Thank you for coming back."

"What else was I going to do?"

"Assume Snake's identity. Find his treasure. Buy a small kingdom." I don't know what it said about me that I'd never thought of that. She paced in front of me, slowly turning around the lair. "This is where we first met."

"I know . . ."

"I remember thinking you were sort of a pathetic hero."

"I guess I am."

"No!" She spun around to face me. "You're not!"

"Come on. Look at the mess I've made of things—"

"Would you please stop with the self-pity?"

I opened my mouth, and closed it as confused wisps of smoke curled out of my nostrils.

"I know you don't like lords and titles and nobility—"

"What does that have to do—"

"Please shut up."

I shut up.

"You might not like it, but you're in that role now. And when you say the lords and nobles aren't any better than anyone else, you're right. We're human. You're human."

"Um—"

"You know what I mean!"

"Yes, ma'am."

"We all make mistakes. The difference is *our* mistakes affect whole kingdoms. The kind of noble you despise, the kind of noble Prince Bartholomew was, simply disregards the consequences of the power they wield. But you don't, even when you try and give it up." She walked up to me and placed her hand on my nose. "You could be a great prince."

"I never wanted to be a prince."

"I didn't choose to be a princess either."

"And I'm still a dragon."

"I know how that feels."

"And I'm sorry."

"I told you to stop with the self-pity."

"No, Lucille. I'm sorry that I've stolen your body. Again."

Her smile froze and she shook her head, patting my nose. "This was never my body, really."

"But Crumley—"

"Never mind that. I'm in my own body now."

"—he said you had grown beyond it."

She wiped her eyes and turned around. "Come on. Yes, I miss it a little. Who wouldn't? You must see why I liked being the dragon now, don't you?"

"Not really."

"What?" She sounded genuinely shocked. "You hated being the princess."

"I found it annoying, but it's much more Frank Blackthorne than a fifty-ton lizard could be." I raised a taloned hand and flexed my fingers. **"I don't see me picking any pockets."**

"You really would prefer being the princess to being the dragon?"

"As if we had a choice." I sighed.

"You're serious." She turned back to face me. "You're really serious."

"Lucille, if I could trade you back, I'd do it in a heartbeat."

"I was sure that once you felt the power. By the gods, the ability to fly—"

"The height makes me nauseous."

"I can't imagine *not* preferring it."

"That's why you make the better dragon."

She looked down and shook her head. Something happened to her smile; it had simultaneously become more genuine, and much slyer. "Daddy is going to be so angry at me," she whispered.

Before I could say anything, she pulled a familiar evil-looking gem from the folds in her chemise and started putting the chain around her neck.

"No, wait! That's a really bad—"

The world exploded around me, spun 180 degrees and I finished saying, "idea," in Lucille's voice before the disorientation dropped me to her knees. My head throbbed and the cavern spun around me, and it was an effort not to puke up a breakfast I hadn't eaten.

I blinked the blur from my eyes and looked up to see a huge dragon's skull lift off the ground, point at the cavern ceiling, and roar, **"Yes!"** while spraying flame across the ceiling.

The single syllable slammed daggers into my throbbing head, so I could only imagine what she felt as she grabbed the sides of her own head and moaned, slamming her nose into the ground in front of me.

"OOOOoooooooooohhhh."

I pushed myself up off the ground and stumbled back and sat down on a rock. "That was a stupid stunt!"

"Ugh. I was excited," she tried to whisper into the ground.

"I'm not talking about yelling."

"I know," she said to the ground while she rubbed her skull.

I rubbed my own temples in sympathy. "That was as bad an idea as it was for me to wear this jewel in the first place."

She raised her head to look at me. The way she tilted her head marked her instantly as Lucille. **"Then we're even."**

"Where in the seven hells did you get it?"

"From that boyish girl, Krys."

"*She* had it?!" My head throbbed at the force of my words.

"She asked me to give it back to you. To tell you, 'You were right.'"

About something, at least. I sighed. "And what made you think that would even work?"

"After the body you were born with . . . It's where the soul feels most comfortable."

I could see the pain in her body language. I remembered all the wounds I'd been feeling and imagined what that must be like after the onslaught of the nasty head trolls that came with the jewel's transfer. Despite all that, I could tell she was genuinely happy.

"And what if this undoes itself in a year and a day?"

She shrugged with a wince. **"You get another chance to be the dragon."**

CHAPTER 37

I left Lucille in the lair to sleep off her injuries, and as I descended the cliff face she began snoring. I had nearly reached the ground when I realized that she had gotten her revenge on me. I was the one left to tell her father what had just happened.

I wondered if there were any new diplomatic missions to faraway lands that needed a royal accompaniment.

Waiting below were six armored figures and seven horses. I walked over to Krys.

"You stole the Tear of Nâtlac?"

"Frank?" she asked.

"What do you think?"

Around me I heard a couple of the other girls giggling. Before I could say anything, Krys turned to them and said, "Stop that!"

"Why?" I asked.

She turned to me, looking sheepish. "You know why."

"But you didn't use it."

"I couldn't in the middle of the fighting. And, after, I had time to think about it. You were right."

"I'm glad my bad example is good for something."

Mary walked over and squeezed Krys's shoulder. "That, and She wouldn't like us using that thing."

"Who wouldn't?" I asked. "Lucille?"

"Come on, Princess Frank," Grace said, "Let's get you back to your castle."

I still felt disoriented from finding myself back in the princess's body, so I passively noticed things about my handmaid's escort without really paying much attention. They had all kept the hairstyle that they'd received at the Temple of Lysea, albeit without the flower garland. In Grace's case, she had replaced the garland with a brass circlet with an engraved floral pattern.

They also, for the first time, wore armor that seemed designed to fit them. The leather seemed of better quality than Lendowyn could typically afford, and was embossed with more of the winding floral motif. And they all seemed to have adopted a badge; every one of them had a red cloth embroidered with a single white rose.

I remember thinking that it wasn't a bad idea for their group to have their own heraldic mark if they were serving in a royal court, but the flower motif seemed at odds with what I knew about them. A dagger cleaving a human skull seemed more their speed.

Lendowyn Castle was in better shape than I had left it. Workers had cleared most of the wreckage of the battle, and people worked on repairing the section of the castle where I had fallen. Apparently more had remained in the treasury than I had thought.

Grace escorted me inside, leaving the others to

take care of the horses. "Your chambers weren't damaged in the battle," she said.

"I guess we should count our blessings," I whispered to myself, my head still spinning, wondering how so much could happen and still leave me in the same place we started.

Grace touched my hand, and said without a trace of irony, "Yes, Your Highness, we should."

I stopped short. "After everything, do we need the 'Highness'? I get enough of that from Sir Forsythe."

"I never thanked you."

"You don't have to."

"Like hell I don't!" she snapped.

I couldn't help smiling. "With that 'Highness' I thought we might have lost you."

"Forgive me for trying to do my job."

"That doesn't have to mean acting like someone else."

She sighed. "What about stealth and a low profile? If your handmaids are on a first-name basis with you in public, that's sort of noticeable."

"You have a point."

"Of course I do." We stopped in front of the door to my chambers. "But I'm serious. Those girls are my family, and I've always been afraid that I'd lose them like the one I was born with—"

I know.

"We wouldn't have lasted the winter. You gave us a home."

"Sorry it was so rough getting here."

"But we got here," she said. "Thank you."

"You're welcome."

She bowed her head in recognition and said, "I'll leave you now, Your Highness. You have a visitor in your chambers."

I reached for the door handle, and then I turned to ask, "Visitor?"

Grace had gone.

What the . . .

Who visits the princess in her private chambers?

I opened the door and my eyes widened.

"Finally! Princess Frank."

Sitting cross-legged on a couch across from the door was the Goddess Lysea. She wore the same sheer gown that she'd worn in my vision, but out of direct sunlight it wasn't nearly as translucent. She wore a garland of flowers that filled the room with scents that didn't belong in the middle of winter.

"You?" I said.

"Me," she said. "Close the door, it's drafty in here."

I did as instructed, a little clumsily since I couldn't take my eyes off of her. Amazingly, the more opaque her gown was, the more it emphasized her figure.

"I'm here to thank you."

"Surprising number of people doing that lately." She laughed, and it was like someone taking a feather and running it up the princess's legs. "You already thanked me for the story."

"Oh." She waved her hand. "Not that."

"What, then?" I asked, almost afraid of the answer.

"Come on, you not only re-consecrate my temple with your amazing offering, but you stood down tall, dark, and gruesome on my behalf."

"That was on *my* behalf."

"That is, as my unpleasant sibling said, a 'technicality.' And that's not all. Thanks to you, I've discovered how fun it is to have a warrior order."

"I'm happy you—wait, what?"

She stood and stretched, and I was briefly thankful I was no longer male, as the sight would have been painful as well as arousing. "Everyone has them, you know. Some group of acolytes that take up the sword on their deity's behalf. That was never my style. I mean an armed poet? Warrior painters? But those girls you brought me? I *love* them! Should have done this aeons ago."

"You're . . . welcome."

"So, Frank Blackthorne, I've brought you a gift in thanks."

Oh crap. I immediately thought of the last gift that some deity had left in my chambers. Whatever it was, I couldn't possibly see it going well. "No, that isn't necessary."

"Oh, Frank, you're not going to refuse me this kindness? I would be soooo disappointed."

The slight shadow that crossed her face was enough to nearly make me wet myself. "No!" I held up my hands. "Not that. I just didn't want you to trouble yourself on my account."

She smiled. "I'm a goddess, Frank, and this was no trouble at all."

"Oh."

"This will be so much fun!" She walked up to me and bent over to kiss me on the lips. I think the contact with her must have made me black out momentarily, because when I opened my eyes, she was gone.

I blinked a couple of times. *Gift? What gift?*
Maybe she forgot?

The hope was short-lived when I heard someone
yawn. I spun around and saw a naked woman in my
bed, half covered in a sheet, stretching. Her eyes met
mine and a smile crossed her lips.

"Mistress. What do you wish of me?"

"E-Evelyn," I stammered. "You're all right."

I'm pretty sure the Goddess's heart was in the right
place, but staring at the intact serving wench from The
Three-Legged Boar filled me less with relief and more
with a gnawing existential panic. Everything had spun
around full circle, and I was seeing a whole host of
roads before me that I didn't want to ride down again.

I backed to the door and opened it again.

"Mistress?"

I held up a hand and said, "Hold that thought."

I called down the corridor, "Grace, get back here!"

"Mistress. What's the matter?" She sat on the edge
of the bed, her seductive smile replaced by confusion.

I saw the fantasy crack behind her eyes and I felt a
wave of guilt, along with the impulse to tell her some
sort of comforting story to reassure her and get her
out of my bedroom. I thanked all the deities I had yet
to anger that I hadn't imbibed any alcohol that would
have encouraged me along any further bad life
choices. Instead of a comforting lie, I steeled myself
and told her the truth.

"I'm sorry, I really am. This was always a bad idea.
I turned to you out of frustration, and it was unfair to
you and my wi—husband."

"But the Goddess . . ."

"I have a bad habit of disappointing major deities lately."

She bit her lower lip and stared at the floor. "I see," she whispered.

"I can't do this."

"Because I'm just a common—"

"No!" I snapped.

She looked up at me with shiny eyes.

"It's not you. It was never you, or where you came from. It's just . . ." I sighed and sat down next to her and hugged her shoulders in what I hoped was a sisterly manner. "I make bad decisions, and they hurt people I care about. I'm trying to stop doing that."

"I was a bad decision?"

Damn it! "Trying a clandestine affair in my situation, my complicated *married* situation, was a bad decision. I just tried to make you an accomplice."

She looked away from me and sniffed.

"You have every right to be angry at me."

"I do," she whispered. She stood up, dragging the bed sheets after her, covering herself. "I am."

"Good."

"What is the matter with you?" She spun around, knocking me stumbling off the bed as the sheets yanked from beneath me. "You drag me across a kingdom so a dragon can call me a whore? You defend me to that monster and disappear? Do you have any idea what I went through after that, after you played seductress, hero, and then abandon me?"

"I'm sorry," I said as I got to my feet.

"I didn't know whether to worship you or burn you in effigy."

"I—"

"And then you send a goddess to fetch me just so you can say 'bad decision'?"

"That wasn't my idea."

"You're damn right this was a bad decision! After everything—"

To my relief the door to my chambers opened and Grace stepped in. "Your Highness?"

Took you long enough. "Grace, this is Evelyn. Evelyn, Grace."

"What?"

"You're still my guest," I said. "You need a room, a meal—"

"And some clothes," Grace added helpfully.

She looked from me to Grace and all the emotion seemed to leak out of her. "Y-yes."

I asked Grace, "How long were you listening?"

"Your Highness? I just arrived." Her grin told another story. At least someone found this all amusing.

"Grace will take care of you." I gave my chief retainer a stern look. "She'll get you everything you need."

Evelyn nodded wordlessly and walked toward the door, providing me a completely unnecessary view of her uncovered backside. As drafty as it was for her, I felt the room become unaccountably warmer.

She looked over her shoulder as Grace took her arm. "Do you love him?"

"Him?" I asked.

"Your dragon."

"Uh—"

Grace had enough mercy on me to lead Evelyn out

of my chambers before I stammered something embarrassing.

Do I love him? Pronoun confusion, the bane of my existence.

Do I love *her?*

I had just kicked a willing lover out of my bed to avoid hurting Lucille. Did that make any objective sense at all? It's not as if my prince was going to warm my bedchambers anytime soon—which was a good thing as that phrase had a wholly different connotation when dragons were involved.

But I didn't want to hurt Lucille any more than I already had.

I threw myself down on my now-sheetless bed.

Do I love her?

"Good question," I whispered.

S. Andrew Swann
The Apotheosis Trilogy

It's been nearly two hundred years since the collapse of the
Confederacy, the last government to claim humanity's col-
onies. So when signals come in revealing lost human colo-
nies that could shift the power balance, the race is on
between the Caliphate ships and a small team of scientists
and mercenaries. But what awaits them all is a threat far
beyond the scope of any human government.

PROPHETS
978-0-7564-0541-0

HERETICS
978-0-7564-0613-4

MESSIAH
978-0-7564-0657-8

To Order Call: 1-800-788-6262
www.dawbooks.com

Seanan McGuire

The InCryptid Novels

"McGuire kicks off a new series with a smart-mouthed, engaging heroine and a city full of fantastical creatures. This may seem like familiar ground to McGuire fans, but she makes New York her own, twisting the city and its residents into curious shapes that will leave you wanting more. Verity's voice is strong and sure as McGuire hints at a deeper history, one that future volumes will hopefully explore."

—*RT Book Reviews*

DISCOUNT ARMAGEDDON
978-0-7564-0713-1

MIDNIGHT BLUE-LIGHT SPECIAL
978-0-7564-0792-6

HALF-OFF RAGNAROK
978-0-7564-0811-4

"The only thing more fun than an October Daye book is an InCryptid book. Swift narrative, charm, great world-building . . . all the McGuire trademarks."

—Charlaine Harris

Jim Hines

The Jig the Goblin series

"Clever satire… Reminiscent of Terry Pratchett and Robert Asprin at their best."
—*Romantic Times*

"If you've always kinda rooted for the little guy, even maybe had a bit of a place in your heart for Gollum, rather than the Boromirs and Gandalfs of the world, pick up Goblin Quest."
—*The SF Site*

"This exciting adult fairy tale is filled with adventure and action, but the keys to the fantasy are Jig and the belief that the mythological creatures are real in the realm of Jim C. Hines."
—*Midwest Book Review*

"A rollicking ride, enjoyable from beginning to end… Jim Hines has just become one of my must-read authors." —Julie E. Czerneda

GOBLIN QUEST   978-07564-0400-0
GOBLIN HERO   978-07564-0442-0
GOBLIN WAR   978-07564-0493-2

To Order Call: 1-800-788-6262
www.dawbooks.com

DAW 100